"Nothing exposes the existential threats we face better than a fast-paced plot like the one in *The Spy from Beijing*, by Joan M. Kop. Not only do you feel the tension between two super powers, but you get to eavesdrop on the lives of the regular people caught up in the front lines of a cyber war, as you experience the real-life drama of the characters as they stand between the biggest threat to our democracy and a global takeover by the Chinese Communist Party. This novel will keep you on the edge of your seat in every chapter."

—Pat Nohrden, author of
The Crystal Monkey and *Min Li's Perfect Place*

"Boasting a twisty tale and a feisty, engaging protagonist, *The Spy from Beijing* is an entertaining and imaginative novel, full of unusual intrigue and sharp, contemporary relevance."

—The Book Review Directory, 5-star review

"If you are looking for a fast-paced espionage thriller laced with a gripping tale of love, heartbreak, deceit, secrets, blackmail, power, espionage, betrayal, loyalty, murder, double agents, traitors, bureaucrats, and operatives, Joan M. Kop's *The Spy from Beijing* is a must-read."

—Readers' Favorite, 5-star review

"*The Spy from Beijing* is a thrilling rollercoaster ride of espionage, intrigue, and moral quandaries, and a must-read for anyone who enjoys a suspenseful tale that explores the blurred lines between loyalty and love."

—Readers' Favorite, 5-star review

"*The Spy from Beijing* is a true thriller, fast-paced and full of action. Joan M. Kop's story will pull you in from page one and grip you to the very end."

—Readers' Favorite, 5-star review

"*The Spy from Beijing* is a riveting read that will appeal to both long-time readers of the spy/thriller genre and newcomers alike. Kop delivers a vibrant narrative that will hold your attention from the beginning and keep it until the final page."

—Literary Titan, 5-star review

"This winding espionage story makes for a page-turner."

—Prairies Book Review, 5-star review

"If you like spy novels with unique and relevant storylines, you will love this plot and these characters."

—Reader Views, 5-star review

THE SPY FROM BEIJING

AN ESPIONAGE THRILLER

JOAN M KOP

Apple Tree Press
Books Books Books

The Spy from Beijing

Copyright © 2025 by Joan M. Kopczynski

All rights reserved. No part of this book may be reproduced in any form or by any electronic or mechanical means including information storage and retrieval systems without the permission in writing from the publisher.

ISBN: 979-8-89145-589-4 (Paperback)
      979-8-89766-755-0 (Hardback)
      979-8-89184-040-9 (eBook)

Library of Congress Control Number: 2025902372
Published in Spokane, Washington

Book cover and interior design by TeaBerryCreative.com
Author photo taken by Sri Maiava, www.mybellalunastudios.com

*For Dave Kamakaris,
a hell raiser and a helluva good friend*

March 2020
CHAPTER 1

A passenger in an aisle seat pushed the emergency call button in the first leg of a twelve-hour United flight from San Francisco to Beijing. Jen Hae Chu, or "Jenny," as the other flight attendants called her, reached a forty-five-year-old man in distress after a fast walk down the aisle. Jenny's training in the art of dealing with irate passengers came in handy.

"I'm not wearing this!" the blond-haired, unruly man said, as he took off his black face mask and threw it on the floor.

"I'm sorry, but you'll need to keep your face mask on," Jenny said, picking it up off the floor and handing it to the wiry man. She noticed an empty liquor bottle on the passenger's lap.

The passenger stood. "You goddamn Chink! This is a communist plot from *your* country."

Horrified, Jenny responded in a calm voice, as she had been trained. "I'm American. Please sit down."

The hostile man pushed Jenny away and punched her in the face, knocking out a tooth. Jenny froze temporarily. She could feel her face getting hot, as blood gushed from her mouth.

She touched her hand to her mouth and felt the loose tooth. *Mom said there'd be days like this when the job wouldn't be much fun. This guy's only testing me. I'll show him who's boss.*

In a split-second Jenny's gym training in her off hours kicked in. She had learned not only kick boxing, but also a wrestling technique called the Canadian Paralyzer. As the man turned around, Jenny came up behind him in a flash, hooked her left arm with the passenger's left, wrapped her right arm underneath the man's chin, and clasped her hands above his left shoulder, squeezing hard enough to render him almost powerless.

"Fuck you!" the man shouted. "You goddamn bitch!"

As the man continued to yell obscenities, another man who sat several rows down, rushed up to the front to help Jenny subdue him until the man no longer resisted.

Jenny noticed another flight attendant who raced to the cockpit in her navy-blue uniform to inform the pilots. She overheard her say, "There's a man in Seat 12C who just assaulted one of us. He knocked out one of Jenny's teeth."

"My God!" she heard the captain say. Jenny later learned he radioed his United dispatcher and explained the incident, and after discussing its severity and options, he made the call to return to San Francisco. The pilot also later explained to Jenny that he had radioed the air traffic controller and assured him this was not a hijacking or terrorist threat while declaring it an emergency and requesting police and medical help. Then the controller gave the captain authorization to make the descent.

Over the loudspeaker, Jenny heard the captain announce to the passengers, "We are returning to San Francisco because of an onboard medical emergency."

One of the flight attendants asked if there was a medical doctor on board, but Jenny didn't wait for an answer. She rushed into the restroom to wipe the blood off her face and uniform while the man who'd helped her—Dave, as he'd introduced himself—restrained the disruptive man until the plane landed.

Jenny watched as Dave handed over the belligerent man to the police.

Standing by the police car after she made a statement to them, minutes later, Dave touched Jenny on the shoulder. He flashed his FBI badge at her—Dave Kamakaris. "Are you all right?"

Jenny, still in shock, could barely speak. "My mouth hurts, but I'm ok."

"You sure?"

She looked at his badge and locked eyes with him. *FBI? I've wanted to be an agent since I was a kid. Those warm eyes of his. Nice to feel someone cares.* "Although I never imagined this would happen to me, I guess it comes with the job."

"Maybe," he said. "But you didn't deserve it. I'm sure United will put our guy on the Do Not Fly List."

Jenny breathed a sigh of relief. "Will he face criminal prosecution?"

"Definitely. He may have to pay a hefty FAA fine. Out of curiosity, have you been accosted before because of your ethnicity?"

"This was the first time. But now everyone knows where Wuhan, China is and that the virus came from there. They blame anyone who looks Asian."

"You handled the situation well."

"Thank you." She thought it was nice he was so concerned, plus he was good-looking, especially his warm eyes and friendly smile. They walked side by side up the ramp to the airport.

"Do you live in San Francisco?" Dave said.

Jenny watched a medical services vehicle turn in the distance and accelerate their approach.

"No," she answered. "I'm originally from California, but now I live in Seattle."

"I'm based in San Francisco, but I've put in for a transfer to Seattle. Housing prices here have skyrocketed. It's difficult to afford a decent house in San Francisco on a government salary."

Although Jenny was in pain and would rather not have a conversation right now, she was too polite to cut the conversation short. Besides, they were the only ones walking up the ramp.

"I hear you, but Seattle is also getting crowded. Luckily, I bought at the right time."

"I could use some advice about the Seattle housing market. Maybe we could get together sometime, maybe for coffee."

It sounded innocent enough, but Jenny had been burned once by a man who betrayed her. She wasn't about to let that happen again.

"I'm not looking for a relationship, if that's what you're after."

"No. No. I'm not either. Although I'm divorced, I consider my marriage a jail sentence. Marty Stuart's 'Jailhouse' song fits me perfectly. Some people aren't meant to be caged. Not likely to make the same mistake again."

Her eyes widened. She wanted to laugh but thought it was better to remain polite and keep listening.

He looked her straight in the eye. "It's just you seem like an intelligent, nice person and I want to make sure you're all right."

He seemed harmless. "Okay," she said. She gave him her phone number. "Give me a week or so to get my tooth fixed."

"You've got it."

After a week and half, Dave went to Seattle to discuss his transfer with higherups. As the meeting didn't start until 10:30, he had plenty of time for coffee at a local Starbucks. It was a short, brisk walk from the FBI's main building on Third. The sun glinted off windows of the nearby shops, brightening his day and lifting his spirits.

He arrived at Starbucks in no time. Wearing jeans, a tan sports jacket and a white shirt, he entered the restaurant and got in line behind several others. The smell of Starbucks' signature roast coffee wafted in the air.

He buzzed Jenny's cell phone. "Jenny, this is Dave from San Francisco.

I'm in town on business. I'm at Starbucks near the Seattle Central Library on Fourth Avenue. Could you possibly meet me for coffee this morning?"

"You're in luck. I just got my tooth fixed yesterday, so, yes, I'd be happy to."

He gave her the address. "I'll order you a coffee. What's your favorite?"

"Vanilla latte."

"How long will it take you to get here?"

"Twenty minutes. I'm on my way."

While he waited, Dave smoothed his brown hair and stood in line, towering over most people with his six-foot frame. His beard itched. He wore a black face mask, and when he finally got to the counter, he ordered a vanilla latte and a black coffee, then sat down at a nearby table and studied a copy of *The Seattle Times* while sipping his drink.

Minutes later, Jenny arrived. She was petite, half his size. Her shoulder-length, black hair was pulled back in a ponytail and she wore jeans, a red sweater and a red face mask.

When he saw her, he started to rise from his chair.

She smiled. "Don't get up." He saw her glance at the newspaper. "What's in the news?" she said. "I haven't had time to read the paper yet."

"Big story about BGI Group trying to collect Americans' DNA data."

"What is BGI Group?"

Dave folded the newspaper and put it aside. "It's a Chinese biotech firm. It was formerly known as Beijing Genomics Institute."

"I assume it's based in Beijing."

"No, but it's close. It's south of there in Shenzhen. It offered Governor Isaacs COVID-19 testing support, as well as five other states, including New York and California. It seemed like an offer the state couldn't refuse, but Isaacs nixed it."

Jenny took a sip of her latte. "Why?"

"He warned hospitals, associations and clinics to beware of foreign governments trying to collect, store and exploit biometric information from Covid tests. The reason is with Chinese testing labs, China could mine patient data in order to manipulate Americans."

"That's pretty scary! Good for Isaacs turning them down. I really hate this whole coronavirus thing. The president's rhetoric only makes it worse."

"I hear ya. I'm sure it's given more people cause to hate Asian-Americans."

"Hating China is like hating my ancestors."

Dave nodded. "I always thought patriotism was more important than family, but after a failed marriage, I'm not so sure anymore."

Her piercing dark eyes studied him in silence.

Dave moved to a new topic. "What was it like for you growing up?"

"My father was a math professor who taught calculus at the local college and my mother was an accomplished violinist turned teacher. I grew up speaking Mandarin, the only language spoken in my household."

"Were you an only child?"

"Yes. I would've given anything to have a playmate, but my parents lived in a neighborhood full of retirees. The elders doted on me. I got lots of attention."

"What motivated you to become a flight attendant?"

"Traveling is in my blood. My parents lived in a modest home, preferring to use their discretionary income on travel instead of putting the money into fixing up their house or buying up each year. I got used to visiting exotic countries and meeting a variety of people from different cultures."

It had been a long time since he'd done this—sat at a table sharing coffee with someone in a non-business setting. Especially with a woman.

Dave sipped his black coffee and tried hard to keep his nervous leg from bouncing underneath the table. "Wow! What an education. I envy you."

"By the time I was nine years old, I had seen big game while on an

African safari, lived in a yurt for a month in northern China, ridden an elephant in Laos, and enjoyed a gondola ride in Venice."

"Makes me wish I had traveled more."

The table they were seated next to was filled with loud college students, so Jenny had to occasionally lean in so Dave could hear her.

"Since then, I've seen the famous *Mousetrap* play in London, visited an ashram in India for two months, and saw a glimmer of wealth in Dubai in the Middle East."

This time it was Dave who leaned in. "I'm definitely not as cultured. The Bureau could use someone like you, especially someone who handles themselves so well in a crisis."

After taking another sip of her latte, she wiped her lips with a napkin, then said, "What do you *do* for fun?"

"I'm a beach bum and a runner. I take my dog with me. He's a Chesapeake Bay retriever."

"Oh, a retriever. I know people who have golden retrievers. Are Chesapeakes anything like them?"

Dave's eyes lit up at the chance to educate her.

He laughed. "Well, both breeds have retriever in their names and both love the water, but the similarities end there. Chesapeake retrievers are all business, have obnoxious attitudes and are tough enough to back them up. A lot of chessie owners say you can train a Golden, distract a Labrador, but you negotiate with a Chesapeake."

Jenny laughed.

Dave smiled. *So glad she likes my sense of humor.* "My dog's name is Pax. He's not the fastest runner, but he can outswim any other dog. I also take him duck hunting in Oregon."

"Sounds like you enjoy the outdoors."

"What I really like is to go somewhere off the grid where there's no running water, cell phones, or internet connection. I visit a place in Vermont for a couple weeks every year."

He expected a negative reaction from her but didn't get it.

She returned to the topic of pets.

"By the way, I have cat. She's a spunky, independent calico. Her name is Daisy."

Dave was a dog lover, not cat lover, so he didn't say anything.

After an awkward silence, she smiled, then changed the subject. "Why did *you* join the Bureau? Patriotism?"

"My dad was in law enforcement and my mother worked in administration. I do love this country of ours, and I'd hate to see our democracy wither, but I have to admit my patriotism stems from Dad instilling values in me at an early age, like keeping America safe from terrorists, violent criminals, drug pushers and political corruption."

"I'd say you're *very* patriotic."

He smiled and drained his cup. "I guess I am. Most agents are. What about you?"

Did Jenny just squirm? She probably hates being put on the spot like this.

"I think most people would say I'm patriotic. My travels around the world convinced me America is one of the greatest countries, if not *the* greatest on Earth."

"Maybe you should think about joining the Bureau."

From the look on her face, he wondered if he had zeroed in on a secret desire of hers to join the FBI. Maybe something she'd always wanted to do. *If so, I doubt she wanted to reveal that to someone she just met. Dave, don't push your luck!*

She glanced momentarily at the baristas serving customers, then back at Dave.

"*Me?*" she said, raising her eyebrows, as if his suggestion was shocking.

"Yes."

"Why?"

"If what I saw of you on the plane handling that volatile passenger is any indication of your capabilities, the Bureau would do well to hire you. Plus, they're hard up for Mandarin speakers right now. With your language skills, you'd be a shoo-in. You'd have to pass a physical fitness test, though."

Her eyes beamed at his compliment. "Involving what?"

"There're four main events—no more than five minutes of rest between each. You have to do a maximum number of sit-ups in one minute, a timed 300-meter sprint, a maximum number of continuous pushups, and a timed 1.5-mile run."

"Sounds difficult."

He shook his head. "Not if you train for it ahead of time. You look like you're in great shape. I don't think you'd have a problem."

"What about the pay?"

"I have no idea what salary you make as a flight attendant, but my guess is you'd earn more as an agent, plus you'd have a higher goal. You could really make a difference; help preserve democracy as we know it."

"Hmmm."

"Don't say 'no' right now."

"Okay, I'll think about it."

March 2020

CHAPTER 2

On a cold rainy day in Beijing, Yìchén and his father, Bohai, sat inside Yìchén's warm apartment in Qian Men, playing China's most revered board game, *Weiqi*, better known as the Japanese game Go, which dates back to 475-221 BCE—China's Warring States period.

Yìchén selected the 180 white stones in the dish while Bohai selected the 181 black stones. Because Bohai selected black, he was considered the weaker player and went first. They received points by either capturing opponent stones, called prisoners, or controlling empty territory on the board.

While amateurs hold a stone between their thumb and forefinger, Yìchén and Bohai did it the correct way, holding a stone between the tips of their index and middle fingers and placing it gently on a point on the board. Both were silent as they placed the first stones on the board. Bohai placed his stone in the top left corner. Yìchén placed his next to Bohai's, hoping to encircle his dad's stones and fill in the vast number of empty spaces in order to control the territory.

A tall man with thick glasses, Bohai worked for the Ministry of State Security (MSS), China's intelligence service, but was a private man of few words and almost never spoke about his work with his son. Yìchén, his only child, followed in his father's footsteps and also worked for the MSS, though both worked in different divisions.

Yìchén loved his no-nonsense business-like father even though he was always a little distant. Today, Bohai was more talkative than usual. Yìchén wondered why. Perhaps it was to hide his true intentions and keep his son off balance in the game, hoping to deceive him into feeling satisfied so his son used up his turns. Yìchén quickly dismissed such unbecoming thoughts of his father.

"Watch the Warriors' game last night?" Bohai said, talking about basketball.

"I did," Yìchén said, coughing. "The big three were hot. Steph Curry had the most three-pointers, assists and steals. Draymond and Klay weren't far behind him."

"They had quite the challenger in LeBron James."

"I'll bet the Warriors win the NBA championship this year though—not the Lakers. Steph will probably get the MVP award again."

"Oh?"

"One year he won by a unanimous vote. I wish Beijing's team did better."

"The Ducks are progressing nicely." He took a black stone from his dish and placed it on the board.

"I mean, yes, but they're tied with the Liaoning Leopards and are ranked third or fourth behind the Xinjiang Flying Tigers and the Guangdong Southern Tigers. American teams are more competitive."

"They've been at the game longer. I might remind you when the Houston Rockets drafted Yao Ming."

"You make it sound like it was yesterday. That was twenty years ago, Father." Yìchén placed a white stone near the center. "I'd like to go to America sometime, but I don't think I'd like to live there permanently. Authoritarian regimes outlast democracies."

Bohai frowned. "What makes you think *that*?"

"Just look at Zimbabwe. Mugabe has proven he can keep more control over the country. We've already supplied him with arms, but now he needs internet surveillance hardware and other technology to maintain his grip on the country. Crucial to control the Zimbabwean people."

They had never had such a conversation. Usually, Bohai was so busy with work, Yìchén felt he neglected to get to know him well. As they talked, Yìchén initiated new positions on the board while Bohai deceptively encircled his white stones with black. Yìchén unaware of his father's true strategy.

"You've been brainwashed," Bohai said. "Sounds like you've learned deceit well. Too well, maybe."

He coughed. "No, I haven't. No disrespect, sir, but your thinking is outdated."

"I don't think I need to remind you what happened at Tiananmen."

"You've told me a thousand times."

"I don't think it sunk in. Do you really believe everything the Chinese government tells the Americans? That we have no strategy at all? Certainly, no Chinese believe that."

Yìchén was silent. *Why does Dad have to be so disagreeable?*

"Or how about that we've been muddling through the past three decades with hopeless backwardness and are just rising out of poverty? I swear, what we tell them is just a ruse to get them to help us."

"This is a new generation, Father. Biotech is the upcoming revolution on the planet, the last one being digital—the computer and internet. America won that one, but if we play our cards right, China will be the leader in biotech. We'll have a good chance at mining patient data."

Bohai raised an eyebrow. "Where have I failed you, son?"

During the conversation, Bohai managed to encircle Yìchén's white stones, capturing two and taking the prisoners off the board. Yet, his son kept talking.

"Think of it. China will one day control the lives of every American citizen."

"And you think that's good?"

"Yes. With unprecedented power like that, China will take its rightful place in the world order. American democracy will die a natural death."

Shocked, Bohai stared at his son, but remained silent. Yìchén misread his reaction and took that as a sign his father agreed with him.

While most Westerners were ignorant of China's long history, Yìchén was indoctrinated in school at an early age and was proud of his heritage. In five centuries of wars and rivalries, seven major states—the Chu, Han, Qi, Qin, Wei, Yan and Zhao—with vertical and horizontal alliances, vied for control of China. The Qin dynasty won in 221 BCE, culminating in the unification of China. Dynasties and rulers have come and gone, and, in Yìchén's way of thinking, they would come and go for millennia to come.

In contrast, most Westerners had no concept of life dating that far back. In Yìchén's eyes, most Americans, with their blurred short-term memories, couldn't tell you which side won the Civil War or even who ran in the last elections. *What fools!*

Father and son were now in the middle game of *Weiqi* with less than 150 spaces left to fill on the board. While the son spoke, the father continued to encircle white stones with black while Yìchén continued to initiate new positions on the board.

"I might also mention, at one time, China provided more loans than the World Bank to governments in developing countries. Imagine the clout that gives us by spending two trillion dollars on unconditional lending. By comparison, the Americans have donated millions for vaccines, a small pittance compared to China's trillions. The West has no chance of catching up."

"I wouldn't be so sure."

Yìchén winced. His tone of voice was confident, if not downright arrogant. "The SCO can counter NATO."

He was talking about the Shanghai Cooperation Organization, whose members included China, Russia, Kazakhstan, Kyrgyzstan, Tajikistan and Uzbekistan.

"I'm well aware," Bohai said. "It'll take more than that group, however, for China to become the dominant superpower. Don't forget about Russia."

Yìchén scoffed. "With our assurances that China will support freer trade, stop intellectual property theft, end currency manipulation, we'll convince the West that we are on the long road toward democracy."

"All lies. I don't want any part of that. Maybe it's because you've never tasted freedom. Myself, I crave it."

Bohai kept encircling his son's white stones. They were fast approaching the end game, and Bohai, the weakest player, had already encircled more of Yìchén's white stones. With patience and deceit, he was sure to win.

Yìchén coughed again. From his studies at Tsinghua University, Yìchén learned people in the West were mostly concerned about short-term profits for shareholders, whereas China's strategy was for the long term. The Chinese are patient, and even if it took several generations to accomplish their goal, Yìchén was sure they would eventually win. The West would be defeated.

He kept up his tirade about the glories of Communist China for twenty minutes more with Bohai looking like he was ready to vomit after hearing his son's words. Finally, Yìchén said, "My real goal is to settle in the West where there is fresh air. This cough is slowly killing me."

"So, you're saying the West isn't all that bad after all?"

"I give America that. Besides, that's where the real action is right now." *As an MSS agent, I'll be a prize the Americans won't be able to resist.*

He wondered if Bohai had the same kind of dreams when he was his age. *The difference, as I see it, is that I'm obviously a risk-taker, whereas my father isn't. Dad stayed stuck in the same job, married to the same woman for over thirty years, and lived in the same country where he grew up.*

Like many millennials, Yìchén was not afraid to move somewhere else in the global world he inherited. His father never said much, for whatever reason, which cemented in Yìchén's mind a feeling of righteousness about his own ambitions and aspirations.

"You talk as if it's a reality. I hope you do settle in the West," Bohai said. "Your mother and I want nothing more than happiness for you. Don't ever forget that!"

"I won't."

Bohai smiled at his son and resigned the game. He counted the stones on the board. "Look," he said, pointing to the board. "I've beaten you."

Astonishment, followed by anger, flashed on Yìchén's face.

Bohai arched an eyebrow. "Never take your eyes off the goal of encircling your enemy. Don't let your opponent keep you off balance like I have done. You were too self-absorbed to notice. You acted foolish."

Although he was seething inside, Yìchén adored his father and was not about to disrespect him by being rude. "Yes, sir," he said.

"I hope this game isn't any indication of your future."

"It won't be, Father. I can promise you that."

March 2020
CHAPTER 3

Jenny lived with her calico cat in a small two-bedroom Roosevelt Cottage built in the forties on Forty-Eighth Avenue in West Seattle. The square, one-story structure was covered by a hipped roof with minimal eave overhangs.

After she put food and water in Daisy's bowls, she logged into Facebook. In early January, she received a friend request from Rick, a former coworker, and pressed the CONFIRM button. Today, she received an instant message from him.

The message was about a grant he received from FPWA. Jenny had never heard of this organization, so she researched it and found it stands for Federation of Protestant Welfare Agencies and is actually a charity. This piqued her curiosity further.

Rick said he had gotten $60,000 from them and to text them to see if she was on the list. This sounded too good to be true, but she was curious, so she texted the number.

The man on the other end said he was Agent Michael R. McGowan and he asked for Jenny's full name.

Jen Hae Chu.

The next morning, Agent McGowan told Jenny she was on the list of people who were eligible for a grant. They texted back and forth.

Do you need to pay back the grant?
No.
Who provides the grant?
The federal government.
The U.S. government?
Yes.
Is it taxable?
Yes.
What city are you located in?
New York City.

Then he told her she would need to fill out an application and include name, address, sex, date of birth, email, phone/text number and previous occupation.

She would also need to answer the following questions:

Do you have credit card?
Do you own house or rent?
Do you want cash or check?
Did you have cash app or PayPal?

Possible red flag, she thought.

Then Jenny asked,
Is there an application on the website?
No, you fill it out via text.

Still suspicious, Jenny did more research. She checked the area code of the number she had texted. It was an area code in Chicago, not New York City. There was also information on the internet about this being a possible scam. She instant messaged Rick.

This is a scam. FPWA does not make grants directly to individuals. It works with its member agency partners and reputable community-based organizations to direct support to families and individuals in New York communities.

Rick wrote back, *It's not a scam. I got my money yesterday. It was delivered to my house. Meet me for coffee this afternoon and we'll talk it about it further.*

Okay, how about our usual Starbucks?
I'd rather meet you at the Starbucks near Pike's Place Market.
It's a deal. I'll be there in a half hour.
I'll be wearing a black face mask with white lettering that says 'Got milk?' on it. My wife made it for me out of one of her black bras.
Too funny! See you soon.

They weren't close friends. But he was also Chinese American, and she had known Rick for over five years and trusted him, yet her gut told her something wasn't right. She wondered why he had messaged her on Facebook instead of sending her an email. She was used to sending Rick emails because they often exchanged email jokes or political stuff.

What to do in the meantime? Should she go to Starbucks?

Yes, she decided. She was probably being overly cautious. Besides, she didn't want to disappoint Rick.

She was out the door in a flash.

She parked her SUV in a parking lot near Pike's Place Market and strolled over to Starbucks' entrance. Near the front door, a man was standing with the 'Got milk?' face mask on. He whisked her to a seat in front of a small round table with two cups of coffee sitting on it. A faint bitter-almond odor wafted in the air.

Something was off. He had the same hair color as Rick but she hadn't seen him in years and his eyes looked more slanted than she remembered. Most of his face was covered with the black face mask.

She didn't have time to react or object before he motioned for her to sit, then offered one of the cups of coffee before taking a sip of his own.

Then, just like that, he gasped for breath, had difficulty speaking, then vomited and toppled over before his body convulsed in a seizure.

Her seat toppled backward as she stood. Confusion already seemed to be spreading to the surrounding tables. Several people gasped. Others screamed.

What's happening here?

She dropped to the floor and checked his pulse. There was none.

A man approached from behind her and asked if she wanted him to perform CPR. Her hand numbly found the side of her neck as she stood and nodded without really knowing if CPR was okay during a pandemic. The face mask was suddenly torn away, and that's when she realized.

This man was not Rick.

Then who…? She steadied herself against the window as chest compressions began. Her vision blurred at the edges, and she forced her eyes shut.

The police showed up as well as an ambulance. The guy was pronounced dead at the scene and transported to the morgue.

Jenny was left with a lot of questions to answer. She spent a couple of hours with the police explaining what had happened and that the guy wasn't Rick, the friend whom she thought she was meeting. She didn't know his identity, but the police did. He was a member of a Chinese gang.

Later that afternoon, she received a call from the FBI.

It was Dave who had been assigned to the case. His transfer must've have gone through quickly or maybe he had been working on it for a long time, she wasn't sure.

"The autopsy showed the guy had prussic acid in his blood."

"What is it?"

"It's a form of cyanide that causes internal asphyxia. A lethal amount is enough to kill someone in less than five minutes. It made headlines in 1983 when several people in Chicago died when they took cyanide-laced capsules of Extra Strength Tylenol."

"Oh yeah. I remember my dad telling me the Nazis used hydrogen cyanide in their gas chambers. But why would anyone poison this guy?"

"Did you see him drink anything?"

"There were two Starbucks coffee cups on the table when I got there. He took a sip from one of them."

"Do you think he drank from the wrong cup? Maybe the poison was meant for you."

"Oh my God! That never crossed my mind till now."

"How did you know him?"

"I didn't. I thought I was meeting my friend Rick, who I've known for about five years."

"This guy was a gang member. The Chinese Triads. Do you have any affiliation with them?"

"Of course not. I thought the guy was Rick. He instant messaged me on Facebook telling me about what I considered a scam. He said he'd explain it all when we met for coffee."

"Any reason a Chinese gang member might be after you?"

"This is beginning to scare me."

"So, you said you talked to the guy you thought was Rick on the phone?"

"We texted briefly."

"That means your cell phone number is connected to the case."

"Oh my God! This nightmare won't go away!"

"Do you know if your Facebook site was hacked?"

"I don't know."

"Could you check it now for me?"

Jenny did and found she had received another instant message, this time from a girlfriend who said she had received a friend request from Jenny, but that the profile had a different photo, and she thought Jenny's account had been hacked.

Then she heard from another friend who had also received a bogus friend request.

"Dave, you were right. I've been hacked. What do I do?"

"Report it to Facebook and immediately change your password. Criminals are getting way more sophisticated. We've been getting a lot of these cases lately."

"Any notion of who might be doing it?" Jenny said.

"We don't have definite proof yet, but we think it might be a hacker called Zazbo."

"Is it a U.S. group?"

"No, it operates out of China."

"With the government's approval?"

"Possibly. Not sure yet. Do me another favor. Call your friend Rick for me."

"I don't have a phone number for him. He changed his number, but I do have an email address. I'll send him an email and ask him whether he sent me any messages on Instant Messenger."

"Great. Give him your phone number and tell him to call you immediately."

Rick called right away.

"I never sent you any messages on Instant Messenger," he said. "My Facebook account must've been hacked or someone created a duplicate account."

"Oh my God! That's what I was afraid of. Whoever it was met me at Starbucks with a black face mask on with white letters that said 'Got milk?'" But as I was sitting down, he keeled over. Dead on the spot."

"My word! That's ghastly."

"This has been a total nightmare. My Facebook account was hacked, too. I received a friend request from you in January, not realizing you were already a Facebook friend. I'm going to unfriend both accounts now, just to be sure I'm not still friends with the hacker."

A further reason to dislike her ancestors' autocratic government. She was more than frustrated now. She was grit-your-teeth angry.

Throughout her travels as an airline stewardess, she had become aware that if someone got off a plane in Beijing, even if that person had never visited the country before, the MSS could use their voluminous facial recognition data bank to access that person's real name and background information by the time he or she got to the immigration booth, a data bank they probably obtained through computer hacking. But why the Chinese might be after her, she didn't know.

She remembered hearing something on TV by the famous Israeli historian, Professor Daniel Noah Uri, author of *Life Lessons for Today's Global World.* He suggested that in an open society like America, it was easy for businesses as well as an autocratic, secretive government like China to gather data about your heart rate, how much you exercise, what your habits are, your likes, your dislikes, and then exploit them.

"Google and social media know what we click on, Amazon knows our buying preferences, streaming services know which movies we like to watch, and Apple knows who we talk to." Professor Uri alluded to a future with biometrics and gene editing which might enable a country, such as China, to "know us better than we know ourselves" in order for them to manipulate unsuspecting, freedom-loving Americans.

The thought gives me nightmares.

All Jenny really wanted, besides a sibling, was a simple, quiet life where she enjoyed peace and prosperity. She was glad she lived in America under a democratic form of government, but maybe she needed to help protect the freedoms she enjoyed. She thought about Dave's suggestion that she should apply for a job with the FBI. That would be a drastic career move and a life-changing event. Her stomach growled with tension. Anxious thoughts kept ricocheting in her head. *Could I make the career switch? Should I? Would they even accept me? What will I be giving up? What will I get in return?*

She put water in Daisy's bowl. Daisy brushed up against her leg.

She reached down and petted her. "Thanks for giving me permission, Daisy." *Unconditional love is so freeing.* She needed it now more than ever. It would be a huge change for both of them.

"I need to think this through and be logical about this," she said out loud, for Daisy's benefit. She crossed the room to her desk and took out a piece of paper and pen to write down the pros and cons. She identified seven pros, including being able to make a difference in the world, enjoying more adventure and exciting work, and having intelligent, responsible, trustworthy, patriotic coworkers. Then she thought about the drawbacks: dangerous work, long hours and bureaucratic red tape.

She sighed. She wanted to discuss this with her mother. She and her mother were close and her mother was good about giving her career advice. Unfortunately, her mother was visiting her sister, Jenny's aunt, in the small town of Leavenworth and wouldn't be back for a few weeks.

Her father lived in a nearby retirement home. He wasn't much use as an advisor, as he suffered from dementia. If only she had a sibling. She thought about calling one of her flight-attendant friends, but she wasn't really close with any of them. She had a million casual friends, but hardly any close ones. Besides, she didn't want anyone to give away her secret until she actually quit.

What about Dad's professor friend? Then she remembered he was on sabbatical and was going big game hunting in Africa for a month. *Who else can I trust?*

Finally, she got up the nerve to call Dave back.

"I assume you're calling to give me a detail you'd forgotten about the investigation," he said.

"That's not why I'm calling you."

"Then to what do I owe this pleasure?"

She liked the sound of his nasal voice and his upstate New York accent. "This isn't about the crap I face because of the Chinese gang member who was poisoned."

"What then?"

"It's about your recommendation to join the Bureau. I think I've decided to apply, but I'm not one hundred percent sure yet."

There was surprise in his voice. "Why?"

"I've actually wanted to become an FBI agent since I was a kid and decided maybe I need to help protect the freedoms we enjoy, but I'm having doubts about such a drastic career move. I came up with seven positives, but it's the negatives I can't get over."

"Like what?"

"Like it might be dangerous work and I'd probably need to work long hours. Then there's all the documentation and bureaucratic red tape."

"It's dangerous to be a flight attendant these days. You'd be better prepared with training."

"Good point."

"Plus, the way it is now, you have to suffer through jet lag and sometimes crazy schedules, right?"

"Yes."

"You'll get used to all the paperwork after a while and you'll come to realize how important and necessary it is."

"But I'm afraid I won't be able to travel as much as I'm used to."

"You might travel more. Who knows? Besides, don't you get tired living out of a suitcase, especially the older you get?"

"You're right. It sometimes gets a little old."

"Now that we've taken care of that, what's stopping you?"

"I just fell for an online scam. Wouldn't the Bureau question my judgment because of that?"

"It could've happened to anyone. They won't care."

"What about the fact that I'm involved in an open investigation?"

"You're not guilty, are you?"

"No."
"Then there's no problem. Anything else?"
"I guess nothing. Thanks for your reassurance."
"Anytime. Hey, whaddya say we go for a run together sometime?"
"I'm game. You're on!"

April 2020
CHAPTER 4

Two guards wearing face masks escorted Yìchén in handcuffs to a secret room inside a building at the large, governmental MSS compound in Xiyuan in the Dongchen district. Yìchén didn't know why he was being taken there, what he'd see or how long he would have to stay. He also didn't know what crime he had committed. As far as he knew, he had obeyed all the rules. Never told anyone about sources or methods of the secretive MSS.

He asked why he was being detained, but no one would give him an answer. They hadn't even given him time to call a lawyer or his parents. His mother would be worried sick about him if she knew. He had been a "mama's boy" since he was born.

He thought back to the *Weiqi* game he played with his father. No, his father couldn't possibly have betrayed him, no matter what differences they had. His father loved him, and he, in turn, loved his dad.

The guards opened the door to the room. He wasn't prepared for the revulsion and pure terror he was about to witness. Yìchén was looking down at his feet when he noticed a trail of red from the door to the center of the room atop a tarp someone had laid on the floor. Then he saw and heard an older man in the center, who was kneeling before the guards. The man was screaming out in pain, blood dripping from his cut-off hands.

The man's black hair with tufts of gray at the temples looked familiar. His dark eyes, white complexion and nose similar to Yìchén's, however, his face was bloodied and bruised beyond recognition. The guard next to him had a mean look on his scarred face and a zhanmajian—a single-edged saber with a long, broad blade and extended handle—in his hands.

Yìchén inched closer. *No, it can't be. Yes, it is. It's Bohai.*

"Dad?"

"Tell your son what you did to deserve this," the guard said in his booming voice. "Tell him, or I'll cut off your head with this sword."

Bohai was silent.

"Tell him how you've been giving away MSS secrets to the Americans for the past thirty years," the guard shouted.

Bohai stared hard at his son, a look of pleading in his eyes.

"How could *you*, Dad?" His tone was accusatory.

Bohai didn't say a word, only closed his eyes.

"Off with it!" the other guard shouted. *"Now!"*

"No...no...no!" Yìchén screamed and watched in horror as blood dripped down Bohai's shirt when the guard severed his head.

After it was all over, the guards took Yìchén away, tears streaming down his cheeks. *He's dead. Really dead. Gone.* His lungs struggled to take in the stale air. The guards brought him to a room next door where Chen Pao, his boss, was waiting.

"The same goes for you if we ever catch you spying. You'll do as I say or I'll see to it your mother gets the same treatment."

A sudden, gruesome image smeared across his mind and sent a flood of numbness through his limbs. "What do you want from me?" Yìchén asked, crying.

"We want you to become a walk-in at the U.S. Embassy here in Beijing."

Besides his father's traitorous acts, Yìchén was correct to assume there were other reasons for China's current revenge, such as the damage done by the trade wars, which resulted in rising tensions between the U.S. and China, as well as the failed attempt to gather DNA data. He was a mere pawn in the conflict.

"A double?"

"Yes. With your father's history with them, you're likely to be a high prize."

"And if I say no?"

"We'll see to it that you'll never see your mother again. Or, if you do, it will only be to witness her decapitation like your father's."

Yìchén stared back at Chen, holding his anger in check. He'd do as he was told.

The MSS, China's civilian intelligence, security and secret police agency and one of the most secretive intelligence organizations in the world, knew who came and went at the U.S. Embassy, and that fact was not lost on the Americans, so it didn't matter what time of day he would choose. He just knew that he couldn't stay long, so as not to arouse suspicion.

He chose early Thursday morning, fighting blustery winds and dense traffic in his Wuling Hongguang, a popular compact car. Beijing citizens were only allowed to drive on certain days because of the air pollution, and Thursday happened to be such a day. Without heavy traffic, it would only be an hour drive. However, today was not his lucky day. It took him two hours to get to the U.S. Embassy, which was located northeast of Beijing on An Jia Lou Road in the Chaoyang District. He arrived there around ten o'clock.

Situated on ten acres, the embassy consisted of six separate modern buildings, including an eight-story main chancery, a three-story atrium office building, and a consular building, which are protected by a perimeter wall. However, the wall in front of the consular section has thick, blast-proof, transparent glass, allowing a view inside the compound.

The main building was covered from ground to rooftop in square lattice windows; four evenly spaced poles jutted out at the front entrance and the embassy seal (in English and Chinese) was prominently displayed to the right on a stone wall. Yìchén couldn't see the full city skyline because of the smog, but he could hear water quietly rippling in the pool near the embassy.

Like others, Yìchén did not stay long outside if he could help it because the air quality index (AQI) hovered near 50-100, an AQI which the Chinese government said was "light," but the World Health Organization (WHO) labeled as "moderate" because the AQI was still well above WHO guidelines. It was a far cry from November 2010, when Beijing's AQI was in the 562 range, being so "hazardous," it was off the charts.

Yìchén knew all too well that Beijing's pollution was due largely to a domino effect—factories fueled by coal helped bring on an economic boom, which in turn brought on a surge in motorized vehicles. Two very costly environmental outcomes which led to poor health and wellbeing for Beijing's over twenty-one million citizens.

He also found out PM2.5 are the most dangerous type of air pollutants—invisible particles, much smaller than the diameter of a human hair—which are small enough to enter the lungs and bloodstream, where they can cause serious heart and lung issues.

By 2013, China began setting policies to decrease the smog, but Yìchén had lived in Beijing for most of his adult life, and the damage to his lungs had been done. Like his parents and others, he often had shortness of breath, coughing, wheezing, asthma episodes and chest pain.

When Yìchén walked through the embassy door, wearing a black face mask, he was met by a Marine guard in the foyer who also wore a face mask. The Marines were used to walk-ins. Often, they included a frantic Chinese bride pleading for a U.S. visa to marry her American fiancé or a deranged person whose paranoid eyes darted back and forth. Some people were legitimate—a scientist, a diplomat or an intelligence officer—and wanted to pass on information for money, or to switch sides out of revenge, or because of ideological differences with a boss or a system he or she no longer believed in.

The Marine guard looked at his watch, noted the time, checked Yìchén for weapons and/or packages and then took him to a windowless walk-in room on the ground floor, filled with audio equipment, video cameras and secure digital equipment.

Since Yìchén identified himself as a member of the MSS who had information to share, the guard alerted the ambassador's office, who within minutes brought it to the attention of the CIA Chief of Station (COS). The short, stout man with white hair, who liked to smoke a good Cuban cigar, buzzed Virginia Langford and told her to come to the front office immediately.

Virginia was a seasoned veteran, having worked in the Operations Directorate for the past twenty years. She was tall with red hair and had a forgettable face and the personality of a soft old shoe. She was able to elicit information from people easily without undue stress.

"There's a walk-in downstairs," the COS said, puffing on his cigar. "Might be a free recruitment if we play our cards right. Could be worth his weight in gold. Do the usual: grill him, make a quick assessment, attempt to flip him, and arrange recontact as soon as possible. Get on it right away. He needs to be out the door in thirty minutes or less to avoid suspicion of counterintelligence watchdogs."

"Got it, sir."

She adjusted her face mask and hurried down to the ground floor, nodded to the Marine and said, "I'll take it from here."

Upon entering the room, she saw a short, thin Chinese man, about millennial age, wearing black-rimmed glasses and a navy business suit and tie. He sat at a small desk.

After they exchanged pleasantries, she introduced herself as Mary and kept the conversation simple, asking him point-blank questions, "Who are you? Do you have any identification documents?"

Yìchén handed her his passport and government ID.

Zhang Yìchén. She knew the Chinese listed their last names first, out of reverence for their ancestors. He was born August 8, 1990 in Shenzhen, China. He was thirty years old. Yep, a millennial.

She thought he was about as bland-looking as you could get. There were millions like him in China. He wouldn't stick out in a crowd. All the better if he wanted to be a spy. The ID card photo showed him dressed in a dark navy blue MSS official uniform with a State Security badge on the right arm.

"I see you're dressed in uniform. Very nice photo." She smiled. "I assume you work for the Ministry of State Security."

She was fully aware that the MSS was China's intelligence service.

He nodded.

This was huge. She kept calm, even though she realized the magnitude of this. She was curious, yet patient. "Which location?"

"In the Dongchen District, near Tiananmen Square."

"Which Bureau?"

"Three."

"The Political and Economic Division?"

She knew this division was responsible for gathering political, economic and scientific intelligence from multiple countries around the world.

He nodded.

While he was talking, Virginia went to the corner of the room, unlocked the doors to a small cabinet and copied Yìchén's passport and government ID after firing up the digital equipment. Then she texted her office upstairs to start traces, knowing they were listening in on the audio portion of this meeting. The images of the passport and ID would be encrypted and sent to her counterpart at Langley headquarters within fifteen seconds.

Virginia was good at reading people as well as eliciting necessary information from potential recruits without intimidating them. "Are you a scientist?" she asked Yìchén.

"No."

"You seem very intelligent. Where did you go to school?"

"Tsinghua University."

"What did you study?"

"Information Science and Technology." Actually, he had an undergraduate degree in biometrics and gene editing from a different university, but he didn't tell her that. A little omission lie.

She handed back his passport. "What can we do for you?"

"I want to live in the U.S."

"So, you want help with a visa?"

"It's more complicated. My government will never allow me to leave because of who I work for. I should be a lot further along in my career, but it's my boss who holds me back. He doesn't appreciate all the hard work I've done. I've also developed health problems from living here." He coughed.

Virginia didn't say anything, just kept listening.

"That's why I cough. My government doesn't care. They would just as soon kill their people like they're doing to the Uighurs. Yet they hide this from the Chinese people."

"So, you'd like to teach your boss that he has made a grave mistake overlooking your talents and you'd like to live somewhere where there is clean air, is that it?"

"Yes. Exactly."

He had the proper motivation, but Virginia knew cases like this that appeared to be a slam dunk needed further investigation. Headquarters would check him out. In the meantime, she wanted to know more. *I'm not totally convinced yet.*

He kept talking.

"I'm an honest person. Too honest, maybe. I have made some mistakes. My father was almost killed during the Tiananmen uprising." Tears welled up in his eyes.

Virginia noticed. *Are they genuine or is he playing me for a fool?* She didn't know, but she wanted to believe him. This recruitment would definitely help her career.

"He was never arrested, however, and even though he had his doubts, afterward he professed his loyalty to the Chinese leaders. He has paid for that patriotism with his family's health. I want to live somewhere where the air is clean and the government respects the rights of their citizens. I heard there are blue skies in America." He coughed again. *Is he trying to impress me by coughing?*

Virginia *was* impressed but remained calm and kept listening until there was a long pause.

"I can supply you with information about my government in exchange for my freedom in your country."

After a long silence, she asked, "Are you married?"

"No."

"Any children?"

He shook his head.

"What about siblings?"

"I am an only child. You know, the one-child policy?"

"Yes. I know. What are your parents' names?"

"My father is Bohai Zhang. My mother's name is Mei."

Virginia kept a blank look on her face, but inside fireworks were going off.

"Where do your parents work?"

"My father worked for the MSS, in a different division than me, but he was recently killed in an accident. My mother stays at home."

It was as Virginia suspected. Bohai was known as SPARKPLUG. He was one of the CIA's highest spies in China. He had been working for the U.S. government for over thirty years.

"I'm sorry your father was killed. What type of accident was it?"

"Work-related."

She arched an eyebrow. "Does your mother know your wish to live in the United States?"

"I haven't talked to her about it, but like most parents, she just wants me to be happy and, of course, live a long life. She also has health problems due to Beijing's air quality. She and my father both hoped for a better future for me. I won't last long if I stay here."

"We'll need a test of your commitment."

"I don't think I've given you a reason not to trust me, but I fully understand."

"Yìchén, I know you're honest, as you say. I think that's evident. But can you get us some documents to prove you are legitimate and that you're willing to help the United States?"

"Like what?"

"I don't know. Maybe about China's missile or submarine technology." She smiled.

"That might be difficult." He coughed again. She wondered if his coughs were to buy time.

"So, what kind of intel could you offer us?"

"Political and economic information China has collected about different countries in order to exploit them."

"Countries such as the U.S.?"

"Yes, as well as some in the developing world."

"I suppose that will have to do for a start if that's the best you can offer."

"I can provide you with photos of the documents using my phone."

"Too risky. Put them on a thumb drive." She went to the corner cabinet again and took out several new 32GB thumb drives and handed them to him. Rather than give him some sophisticated equipment that might be compromised if he was caught with it, she provided him with items anyone could purchase at a local store in Beijing. If he lost or misplaced them, no one could trace them back to the CIA. She'd supply him with more sophisticated equipment once he was tested and proved he was reliable. "You'll need more than one."

"How long will I have to do this before I am allowed to move to the U.S.?"

She smiled and shook her head. He'd need to pass on classified documents as well as other verifiable information to the CIA from the get-go to establish his bona fides. They would try to keep him in place for as long as they possibly could until such time when it aroused suspicion. "I can't tell you that. It will depend, but I can tell you we are most concerned for your safety…and your health."

"Where and when should I drop it off?"

"Is there a park near where you live?"

"Yes. Beihai. Do you know it?"

Virginia knew the public park he mentioned. It was built in the eleventh century, covered 175 acres, was among the largest Chinese gardens and featured a massive lake.

"Yes, I know it. It's in the Xicheng District on Wenjin Street. Do you have a dog?"

He coughed. "Yes, why? What does that have to do with it?"

"I'll tell you in a minute. What breed?"

"He's a golden retriever."

"They're great dogs, aren't they? Make nice pets. I had one once."

"So, why the dog?"

"He'll help you with a dead drop. Feed him a healthy serving of dog food that morning before you go to the park. When you pick up your dog poop, put it in a plastic baggy along with the thumb drive hidden in it and throw it into a trash can in the park near the entrance to the boat launch on the lake. We'll have a garbage collector retrieve it from the drop site. Make sure you watch out for any signs of surveillance. I assume you're familiar with basic surveillance methods and all the meticulous planning that goes into it since you work for the MSS."

"Yes."

She raised an eyebrow. "Are you certain you're aware of surveillance methods? We don't want any slip-ups."

"Yes, I'm sure. What day and time?"

"Monday morning when the park opens at 6:30 a.m. Here's some *yaun* to cover the entrance fee. There shouldn't be too many people in the park then. How can we contact you again if we need to?"

"I have a burner phone." He gave her the number.

"If the drop goes well," she said, "Cousin Guang will leave a message referring to the '*delicious*' San Xian noodles he enjoyed eating at a local restaurant. If the drop went badly, he'll say the '*lousy*' San Xian noodles he enjoyed eating. Got it?"

"Yes."

"If by any chance you or I decide we need to meet again, here's how to contact me." She handed him a slip of paper with instructions on it. "Okay, now, what will you say if someone asks you why you came to the U.S. Embassy today?"

"I was checking on a visa for my mother who wants to travel to America."

"Good." She looked at her watch. "You've been here for thirty minutes already, so you need to leave. We don't want any unwanted attention drawn to you. Perhaps your coworkers might notice if you are gone from work too long."

He coughed. "I don't think there will be any problem."

Yìchén smiled after leaving the embassy and getting into his car, as if he had found out how easy it was to fool the Americans. He had no idea of the trouble to come.

April 2020
CHAPTER 5

Jenny got groceries at Costco, but the store was totally out of bathroom tissue, so she went to the nearest grocery store to get some. Nope! They were out, too. That night, she heard on the evening news that people were buying up toilet paper and hoarding it. *For God's sake!*

Luckily, Jenny had two rolls left, but that wouldn't last long. She looked on the internet and was surprised to find that even Amazon had low supplies. She ordered some just in case, but it wouldn't arrive until next week, so she texted her mother that night to please bring some if she could as she was planning to see her tomorrow morning.

The next day, she put water and cat food in Daisy's bowls. She expected her mother to arrive any minute now. They had tickets to attend the Broadway show *Hamilton* at the Paramount Theatre in Seattle in the evening and planned to have lunch around noon.

Her mother, whom she also called Peggy besides Mom, was vacationing with her sister in Leavenworth, a Bavarian-styled village in the Cascade Mountains east of Seattle in central Washington. Leavenworth had Alpine-style buildings and restaurants that served German beer and food and was a two-hour drive east from Seattle.

After waiting a half hour, Jenny texted her mother at 12:30 but did not receive a reply. This was so unlike her reliable mother. She waited another half hour, texted her again, only to receive the same result.

Jenny checked the weather. Clear skies in Seattle with light rain, but near Leavenworth, it was cloudy and overcast with fog. She phoned her aunt, who planned to stay a week longer in Leavenworth.

"Where's Mom?"

"I don't know. She left over an hour ago. She was headed out Highway 97."

"That two-lane road going to the freeway?"

"Yes."

Jenny's eyes widened. Panic and fear shot through her veins. "This is so unlike her. I'm calling the Washington State Patrol."

At 2:15 p.m. Jenny's aunt called her back just as two State Patrol officers appeared on Jenny's doorstep. She opened the door and noticed that one officer wore a badge on that said, "Chaplain." Fearing the worst, she burst into tears.

"No! No! No!" she screamed. "This can't be happening!"

"I'm so sorry," the patrol officer said, trying to console her.

Jenny blinked back tears and took a breath. "What happened?"

"Your mother was traveling in dense fog heading south on Highway 97 towards I-90, when an eighty-one-year-old man in a van tried to pass a semi-truck going seventy miles per hour. He hit her head on."

"Tell me she didn't suffer. Please, tell me she didn't suffer."

"She died on impact, suffering a broken neck."

"Oh God, no. This can't be!" Tears streamed from her face. The chaplain offered her a handkerchief. She took it and wiped her swollen eyes.

"What about the man? What happened to him?"

"He walked away with a few injuries. I'm so sorry."

After they left, she closed the door and wept. Her mother meant everything to her. She talked to her by phone every day, sometimes twice a day, often chatting for over an hour each time. They discussed her dad's heath, his care, their diets, exercise, food, nature walks and hiking trails, books, politics, the latest news, and all of her boyfriends and reminisced about her childhood. She also had frequent in-person contact with her mother. They got together for lunch at least once a week.

Her death left a large hole not only in her life but also in her heart.

She missed her so much already.

After crying for over two hours, she phoned Dave, and told him, through tears, what had happened.

"My mother was my best friend," she sobbed. "She's all I had left, since Dad has Alzheimer's. I feel so alone. So terribly *alone*!"

"You're not alone, Jenny. You'll never be alone. The Bureau will become your family, like it has for me."

"No one can ever replace her."

"I don't know how to comfort you, other than by saying it will get better with time. You'll see."

She wiped her tears. "You promise?"

"Yes, I promise."

"By the way, Dave…this is rather embarrassing, but I'm almost out of toilet paper. I'm sure you've heard on the news about the shortage. You wouldn't have any to spare, would you?"

"I was able to buy a stash at Costco before they ran out. I'd be happy to share."

"Thank you. You're a lifesaver in more ways than one."

"My pleasure."

April 2020

CHAPTER 6

It was early Monday morning two weeks later. Decked out in a white tank top and blue running shorts, Jenny heard horns tooting, looked out Elliot Bay beach and saw ferry boats lit up like Christmas trees as the fog began to lift. Ferries to Bremerton and Bainbridge Island came and went every fifty minutes. The Seattle skyline was ablaze with bright downtown lights—the Space Needle on the left and the thirty-eight-story century-old Smith Tower skyscraper on the right. At sunrise, the blue sky burst into shades of pink and yellow, eliciting a smile and a sigh from Jenny.

"You're breathing better today," Dave said as he and Jenny and Pax ran along Alki Avenue in Alki Beach Park, near where Jenny lived in West Seattle. After Dave moved to Seattle, he and Jenny mapped out a route along the five-mile trail between Alki Point and Duwamish Head.

"Slow down a bit, please. I can't keep up."

"Yes, you can." He sped up. It forced her to speed up, too, which both irritated and amused her.

Since she had already applied, Jenny now focused her mind on acing the timed 1.5-mile run, as well as the timed 300-meter sprint, necessary to qualify for the physical fitness portion of the FBI's test. Last week she was running nine-minute miles and breathing hard. Today she was down to less than seven, although she preferred to run at a slower pace.

With Dave at her side, this became virtually impossible. He was constantly pushing her to exceed her goal.

"Dave, please slow down so I can catch my breath and we can talk."

He slowed and she finally managed to keep abreast of him.

"So, what's on your mind?"

"I've been thinking how much I love this place—the sand, the saltwater, the lighthouse, the kayaks, not to mention the bungalows and great local restaurants. We're way more fortunate than people in India, China or Africa."

"I wouldn't have thought of that. Shows how much you've traveled. I just think it's a great place to people-watch and hang out. Plus, you can build campfires. Did I ever mention I'm great at building campfires?"

"No."

"I'll build one for you sometime."

They ran hard and fast, kicking up sand as they went. They met several young athletes as well as an older jogger with his yellow lab along the route.

Pax, in attack mode, pulled on his leash, but Dave restrained him. "Pax would give that yellow lab a run for his money if I let him. But whenever he meets other dogs, he tries to hump them. I call him Red Ruffansore."

Jenny was surprised at his crude sense of humor, but laughed anyway. Apparently, Dave was known by his friends as a hell-raiser. "That definitely would have slowed us down. We don't lack for much here, that's for sure."

"Except maybe warm water in the Puget Sound so we could swim. These waters are *way* too cold."

"You can swim in Green Lake."

Dave had no trouble talking while he ran. "I heard there are an amazing number and variety of fish in that lake...Are you still breathing?"

Jenny smiled. "Yes, silly, I have great lungs."

"I'll say. That's not the only thing great about you!" He winked at her.

"Oh, Dave!" She blushed.

He grinned. "I've been doing a lot of thinking lately, too. I wish I knew more about my paternal grandfather."

"I don't know *anything* about my grandparents. It was not something my mother or father ever talked about."

"Too bad."

Jenny nodded. "I know."

"My ancestors were Greek," Dave said. "After Grandpa returned to his home on the volcanic Greek island of Milos from the Balkan War, he found out his dad and his friend Nicholas arranged a marriage between his son—my grandpa—and Nicholas's daughter. Well, that girl must have really been something to look at because instead of marrying her, Grandpa ran away and joined the French Foreign Legion."

Dave's choice of words made Jenny laugh.

"The selection process for the Legion is brutal—only one in nine candidates will ever wear the Legion's characteristic white cap called the Kepi. But I think I would rather have a root canal with *no* Novocain than enlist in that outfit."

Jenny laughed again.

"You sign up for a five-year hitch. He was stationed somewhere in northern Africa, probably Algeria, but went AWOL during his third year. Grandpa's lucky he got away because the Foreign Legion chases deserters like bloodhounds and have killed them in the past. Grandpa managed to stow away on a steamer to the United States, and somehow ended up working in the coal mines in West Virginia."

"Why did he leave the Foreign Legion?"

"I don't know."

"Fascinating," Jenny said. "Wonder what *my* ancestors did."

"There's more. Apparently, Grandpa had a bootlegging business on the side and was doing quite well with it. This was during the Prohibition.

Once it became clear to him that the Feds were closing in, he sold his still, bought a car, packed up Dad, my aunt and Grandma and headed to Alfred, New York, where he ran a restaurant called The Collegiate that still exists today. He passed away when I was six years old. I remember what he looked and sounded like—very heavy Greek accent—and grip that could bend steel."

"Wow! You seem to know a lot about your relatives."

"Grandpa told the most fantastic ghost stories that I wish I could remember. They even scared Dad, and I didn't think anything could scare him. I'm doing a DNA test on LineageFinder.com to find out more. You should do one."

"What?" Jenny said.

"A DNA test."

"I dunno," she said, frowning. "I'm kind of leery about stuff like that. Seems like another way to invade your privacy, if you ask me. Is it expensive?"

"Not very. They usually run specials around the holidays." Dave sped up. "Race you the next three hundred meters!"

"You're on!"

Jenny managed to sprint several feet ahead of Dave because Pax stopped suddenly to poop, or, in Dave's words, Pax had just dropped a bomb. While Dave spent five or ten minutes picking up the poop from Pax's latest bombing mission, Jenny raced ahead and was attacked by a short, blonde-haired guy with pimples, wearing a red ballcap. She started kick boxing him.

Jenny's ponytail swished as she whipped her body around and kicked the backside of her right foot to the attacker's head with such force that his red ballcap accelerated off his head with warp speed, immediately followed by another right-foot kick to his head. After the blond-haired punk lunged at her, she spun around and kicked her right foot to his head again, followed by an immediate right-foot kick to his stomach.

The little pimply-faced blond punk groaned in pain, but Jenny wasn't finished with him yet. She flipped around in a split second and kicked his head again with the back of her right foot and repeated it. Then a second later, she kicked his stomach with both feet in succession.

She doubled down with a right-foot kick, a left-foot kick, then two feet in succession twice. The little punk reeled back, then gained his equilibrium and headed toward Jenny, growling and hissing. Jenny stepped back, then ran toward him, throwing herself on him at the waist, and put her legs backward over his head to topple him to the ground.

Thirty seconds later, after Jenny applied more brutal force to the punk's ribs and a final right foot kick to his head, Dave walked toward them, surveyed the carnage and found the little punk lying unconscious on the ground with what appeared to be multiple broken bones and a serious concussion.

Pax went over to Jenny's assailant and put his mark on his pimpled face.

Dave stared at Jenny for a moment. "Whoa! That was amazing, Jenny! Let's call an ambulance for this guy and get the hell out of here. It's true what they say..."

Jenny leaned forward and placed her hands on her knees as she fought for breath. The adrenaline brought everything into focus and filled her body with nervous energy that now had nowhere to go. Dave was saying something, but she shook her head at him, head still down, letting him know she needed a minute longer.

She caught the last words he spoke, "It's true what they say, *though she may be but little, she is fierce!*"

"One of my favorite lines from Shakespeare's *A Midsummer Night's Dream*."

"After that little number on the trail, there's no doubt in my mind you'll pass the Bureau's fitness test. They have no idea who they are getting. Come on, Pax, let's go!"

Jenny aced the tests with flying colors—she was first out of a class of six hundred—and on Sunday, after a five-hour, non-stop flight from Seattle to Washington, DC, Jenny gathered her bags, rented a car, and headed south on I-95 to the Marine Corps Base at Quantico, Virginia for New Agent Training.

She had mixed feelings about this new career change. She was super excited at the prospect of doing something new, yet she was sad that she couldn't share her joy and happiness with her mother. *I wonder what mom would say about my new career choice. Would she be happy for me? Hopefully this new focus will help me box away the grief for the moment.*

She was also worried that her time in training at the Academy would put distance between her and Dave. *Do long distance relationships ever work? I hope so. I really hope so.*

After exiting the freeway, she passed through a checkpoint, and continued driving on a long and winding two-lane road until she came to a sign that said, "FBI Academy." After another half mile, she was greeted by an efficient guard who checked her driver's license against the names on his list of the lucky six hundred FBI applicants out of twelve thousand who applied that year.

The possibility of her being in the ten to twenty percent who fail the four-and-a-half-month FBI agent training course was out of the question. It was not how she was raised. Her educator parents expected good grades. She had never failed a course in her life and was always in the top percentile of her class.

She had managed to complete a degree in psychology in her spare time from the University of Washington in Seattle. She also achieved high marks in her eight-week flight attendant training course at United, where she mastered the often-grueling courses in CPR and first aid, using fire extinguishers and oxygen masks, de-escalation techniques for aggressive passengers, passenger personality assessments, defensive tactics, and learning basic foreign language phrases.

As she passed through open fields surrounded by acres and acres of rolling Virginia woodlands, ponds and streams, anxiety of the unknown twisted in her stomach. On her right was a series of sniper ranges. On her left stood an intimidating military compound known as "the FBI Academy."

She pulled into a parking lot in front of an eight-story building full of dorm rooms. Each small room had a closet, two single beds, and two desks. Elevators were forbidden, so she climbed five flights of stairs with her face mask on.

When she got to her room on the fifth floor, her roommate, Francine Edwards, was waiting, unmasked. Francine was a tall, wiry redhead from Tennessee with the aggressiveness of an angry bee.

Jenny extended her hand. "Hi, I'm Jenny."

"We go by last names here. Mine is Edwards, what's y'all's?"

"Chu."

"Surprised to see what a stunner this place is. The National Guard didn't have any training facilities like this. Where're y'all from?"

"Seattle. Uh…I hate to ask, but are you planning to get vaccinated if a vaccine becomes available?"

She shook her head. "I don't worry about it. God will protect me."

Holy crap! An anti-vaxxer! Just my luck! I hope I'm not going to be sorry rooming with her. "Which state did you say you're from?"

"Tennessee. Home of the *real* America."

Jenny scoffed. *Oh, Jeezus!*

"What kind of work did y'all do?"

"Flight attendant for United. You?"

"Accountant for one of the Big Four. I've also been with the National Guard for the past several years. Y'all could say discipline, rule-following and bureaucracy are in my blood."

The way she said it implied her superiority over people like Jenny. Jenny disliked bean counters like her and felt the need to brag about her own accomplishments.

"I may not have that kind of experience, but I've traveled a lot."

"Like where?"

"China four times, the Middle East and India twice, Europe several times as well as South Africa and South America. And every year I do a yoga retreat in Mexico. I love the diversity of foreign cultures, don't you?"

"I haven't traveled much outside the States. I don't seem to have much free time, but when I do, I like to go caving. Ruby Falls in Tennessee, of course. I like the deep, dark and sometimes cramped spaces you find underground."

"Sounds awesome."

Jenny yawned. She was exhausted from her trip and wanted to get to bed, but she was polite enough to keep the conversation going.

But she couldn't stop yawning.

"Listen," Francine said, "y'all look exhausted and I'm keeping you up. We'll talk more tomorrow."

The next day, Jenny and Francine ate lunch in the cafeteria and were seated across the table from one another. They chit-chatted about how the FBI's training was like boot camp, law school, and grad school combined.

"Getting through this grueling training takes a lot of guts," Francine said, "but it's not just men who are up to the task."

She smiled.

Jenny returned her smile.

After an awkward silence, Francine looked Jenny straight in the eye and said, "I didn't know someone like y'all could be interested in someone like me." She held her gaze too long for Jenny's comfort.

From the way Francine had said it, Jenny felt there were sexual overtones. *Oh Dave... Hmm...What should I do now about rooming with her? As if I don't have enough stress already! I need to be direct with her.*

"Just to be clear, I'm not *into* women."

There was an uncomfortable silence.

That night, Jenny, feeling awkward, put on her pajamas in the bathroom, crawled underneath the covers, and fidgeted until she heard Francine snoring. She woke up when the alarm went off. She showered, dressed in a hurry and was out the door in a flash. She marveled at the sun coming up as she strolled to another building to take her first class.

After the morning orientation class, Jenny heard Francine tell the instructor she wasn't feeling well. She said she had a fever, and had lost her sense of smell and also had body aches and shortness of breath. He advised Francine to get a COVID test.

Later that day, Francine drove herself to the emergency room at Sentara Northern Virginia Medical Center in Woodbridge, Virginia, where she got a COVID test. It came back positive. Luckily, they had an empty bed and because of her status as an FBI recruit, Francine was able to stay overnight for observation.

When Jenny heard the news from a fellow classmate, she shook her head in disbelief at the irony of the situation. After her classes were over for the day, Jenny hiked up the five flights of stairs in her dormitory and wiped down her room with disinfectant wipes. She had survived one hurdle.

She picked up her textbook for tomorrow's class on personality assessment and wondered what else would be thrown at her.

Because of her new relationship with Dave, Jenny had done a lot of soul-searching in the past couple of weeks, trying to identify exactly why she had a trust problem. She had a nagging feeling that whoever she loved would end up abandoning her. Was it because she had just lost her mother, her best friend? Or was it because she was an only child with no family left once her parents died? Or was it because her last boyfriend ran off with another woman? Was she ever going to overcome this feeling, or would it follow her the rest of her life?

Two weeks into her training at the FBI Academy, Jenny attended a lecture in a personality assessment class taught by Joe Navarro, a Cuban-born, retired FBI Special Agent and internationally acclaimed expert on body language and nonverbal communication. *Hopefully, now with this class, I'll know who to trust.*

All 200 seats in the auditorium were filled. Someone must've turned on the air conditioning, even though it was still spring. Jenny shivered in her seat and put on her hooded gray and purple Washington Huskies sweatshirt. She exchanged pleasantries with a Chicago attorney who sat next to her, until the lecture began.

Jenny leaned forward, listening to Navarro's every word. He identified the four most common dangerous personalities. One of the most lethal included the narcissistic/paranoid personality combination.

"Joseph Stalin," he said, "had this type of personality. He narcissistically craved power and adoration but also had a darker side driven by paranoia. He did not trust minorities, nor his military advisors. After World War I, he gave the order to kill one-quarter of his top military staff, including ninety percent of his generals, because he didn't trust them, which hampered Russia in World War II when those military skills were desperately needed. By conservative estimates, he ended up massacring thirty million people."

There was a low murmur in the crowd.

The Chicago attorney fidgeted in his seat. Jenny shook her head in disbelief. Her knowledge of history, like many Americans, barely touched the surface of world history, and she was stunned by this revelation.

Her Chinese American parents made sure she knew about China's history, but she didn't know much about the history of other countries. Her father talked about unspeakable brutalities under Mao's rule, blind worship, a dark period of paranoia and reckless pursuit of the Cultural

Revolution no matter the human cost. Her parents said Mao's Great Leap Forward, which included the famine, was responsible for the deaths of over forty-five million Chinese people.

Was Mao a paranoid narcissist, too? It gave her nightmares. She wondered why Navarro never mentioned him.

Jenny took a deep breath and exhaled.

Navarro continued with the lecture. "Adolf Hitler, who was responsible for killing more than six million Jews, was also narcissistic—he had a grandiose ego as well as an outsized sense of what belonged to him—and was paranoid about the minority Jewish population. Add to that the number of German soldiers killed on the battlefield in World War II, which is estimated to be between five hundred thousand to six million, although the number is still disputed today."

Jenny raised her hand. "I hate to say this, but that seems like ancient history to us millennials. What about something more recent?"

"Okay," Navarro said. "How about Slobodan Milosević in the 1990s and his xenophobic view of ethnic minorities, especially Muslims and Croats? Or Ratko Mladić, also called the Butcher of Bosnia, accused by the International Criminal Court for the former Yugoslavia in the ethnic killing of more than seven thousand five hundred Bosnian Muslim men and boys in Srebrenica in 1995? Each of these leaders had narcissistic personalities and because of their extreme grandiosity believed that only they had the answers. Their solution was to exterminate millions."

The Chicago attorney raised his hand. "I get it," he said. "But I'm not sure what that has to do with new FBI recruits like us."

"You will more than likely come across people like this in your careers. They could be government leaders or people on the street or someone you might know more intimately. Take, for example, Timothy McVeigh, who planned the bombing of the Alfred P. Murrah Federal Building in Oklahoma City. Prior to the incident, he isolated himself in Arizona and focused on his hatred for the federal government, stemming from the fact he had been turned down for the Green Berets.

"What all of these individuals' personalities have in common," Navarro said, "is that they were people who sought grand, violent solutions to problems and they saw enemies everywhere."

Jenny continued taking notes. She straightened up in her chair and paid close attention when Navarro explained how to identify such people and handed out behavior-based checklists to follow. "The checklists," he said, "were derived from twenty-five years of field work, in the modern jungle." Each checklist contained 130 statements to determine if someone had the features for each of the dangerous personalities.

She looked down at the first sheet for the narcissistic personality and read the first two statements. "Projects self-importance beyond position, experience, or what has been duly earned or deserved. Has a grandiose idea of who he is and what he can achieve."

Her eyes returned to Navarro who was still speaking. "The checklist for the narcissistic personality will also indicate where that person falls on the spectrum: from arrogant and obnoxious to indifferent and callous, and finally to abusive and dangerous. Now, take a moment and look at the Paranoid Personality Checklist."

As Navarro spoke, Jenny read some of them. The first: "Believes that others seek to exploit or harm him in some way." The second: "Is preoccupied with unjustified doubts about the loyalty of others."

"Fascinating," the Chicago attorney said.

"Totally agree," Jenny said.

After class was over, she put her notebook and papers in her satchel and shook Navarro's hand on the way out of the auditorium.

"Thank you so much," she said to Navarro. "I don't know if I'll run into people like you described, but at least now I feel better prepared."

"You'll run into them," he said. "I assure you."

As she walked back to her dorm, the sun was shining and she could feel a new sense of confidence in her stride. She looked forward to her next hurdle tomorrow on the firearms range because she had never shot a gun before.

———◆———

The firing range, for Jenny, was like visiting a foreign country without knowing the local language. She had never even held a gun before, much less shoot one. The learning curve was steep, but she would not be deterred. She was not going to fail.

Jenny was dressed in gray sweats, her hair pulled back in a red baseball cap, and wore hearing protection. Francine, who now tested negative for COVID, was dressed in camouflage gear and ear-muff-style hearing protection, and had much more experience in shooting guns. She stood to Jenny's right.

The indoor shooting range for new recruits like them was twenty-five yards long with shorter distances available using a pulley system that placed the target at various ranges. For beginners like Jenny, the starting range was fifteen feet. The odor of gunpowder wafted in the air.

Jenny took the Glock 19 9mm semi-automatic pistol with a fifteen-round magazine capacity she was given, the cold barrel stinging her hand.

The instructor barked out commands: "Memorize the four universal rules for firearm safety: Treat every firearm as though it is loaded and *always* know the condition of *your* firearm. Never point your firearm at anything that you are not willing to *destroy*. Keep your finger *off* of the trigger until your sights are aligned and the decision to fire has been made. And always *be aware* of what is behind, to the left of and to the right of your target."

How will I ever remember all of that?

"Then clear your gun to ensure it's not loaded."

Jenny raised her hand. "How do you clear a gun?"

"Pick it up. Make sure your fingers are outside the trigger guard.

Don't put your finger on the trigger until you're ready to fire. Press the magazine release button and drop the magazine from the gun."

"Got it," Jenny said.

"I'm not finished yet," the instructor said. "Push the slide to the rear to open the breech. This is called racking the slide. If there is a round chambered, it will eject from the gun. Do it twice to double-check."

"Got it," Jenny said.

"Then lock the slide to the rear and, finally, visually and physically inspect the chamber to see that it's empty. Then you're good to go."

This seems easy enough. She took a deep breath and let out a sigh, her mind filled with worry about making a deadly mistake.

Jenny picked up the gun and racked the slide. The instructor hovered over her like a mother hen with her young chick and noticed Jenny making what could have been a fatal mistake.

"*Chu!*" the instructor screamed at Jenny. "You're gonna get someone killed if you don't pay attention."

"What did I do wrong?" Jenny said, frowning.

"You forgot to drop the magazine."

"Oh, shit!"

"Let's hope you don't do it again."

Jenny had butterflies doing somersaults inside her stomach and could not stop worrying about when the round would discharge. She clasped the Glock firmly, lined up the front sight pin with the notch in the rear sight, and aimed the gun center mass, directly at the 7x9-inch oval heart in the human silhouette, and pulled hard on the trigger.

Even though she wore hearing protection, she heard a thundering bang and was surprised at the mild, but noticeable, recoil. She fired off two more rounds and looked to see where they hit. They were randomly distributed throughout the whole target.

Even though she missed center mass, she felt somewhat good about her attempts until Francine said, "That was pathetic, Chu. You're jerking the trigger. For Chrissakes, you need to do better than that!"

Jenny was seething inside. She hated being singled out by Francine, yet it motivated her to try harder. Jenny gritted her teeth with a fierce determination to succeed.

"What should I do instead?"

"Squeeze the trigger gently with the tip of your index finger," the instructor said, "letting it surprise you when the gun fires."

Jenny fired three more rounds. Then three more. Same random distribution of her first three shots.

She heard Edwards laughing at her.

Even though she didn't like being the brunt of laughter, she wasn't about to give up. After fifteen rounds, she finally hit the target, putting a bullet hole in the silhouette center mass.

The instructor gave her the thumbs up.

"It's about time, Chu," Francine said. "Let's just see if you can do that again!"

Jenny tried to ignore Francine's smart-ass comments, but they kept reverberating in her mind. She was not about to let this National Guard bean-counter flunky get the better of her.

Jenny focused on concentrating her sights on the target. A hit, and then another, until she managed to hit center mass almost three times in five shots.

Now it was Jenny who smiled.

"I dare you to do that again, Greenhorn!" Francine shouted.

"You're on! I'm on a roll."

"I wouldn't be so sure about that if I were you," Francine sneered. "Many, if not all, men shoot close to 50,000 rounds of ammo before they're considered good. You don't come anywhere close to that with so little practice."

I wonder if Francine is being hateful toward me ever since I rejected her flirting or whether she is just being aggressively playful.

"Maybe not, but with more practice I intend to get better."

Bang, bang, bang. Three more hits to center mass.

"That's enough for this session," the instructor said. "Tomorrow, those who qualify will practice on the sniper range."

New recruits, like Jenny, didn't fall into that category.

On weekends, agent trainees had time to themselves, and most spent time relaxing, like going on nature walks on the grounds at Quantico. Jenny was a high-energy person who took full advantage of an opportunity when it presented itself. She had heard that the legendary Israeli historian, Professor Daniel Noah Uri, who wrote the book, *Mankind Through the Millennia*, was giving a talk Saturday afternoon at the Smithsonian in Washington, DC, about his other bestseller, *Life Lessons for Today's Global World*.

The guest appearance was sponsored by LineageFinder.com, a genealogy company headquartered in Seattle, whose main competitors were Ancestry.com, based in Lehi, Utah and MyHeritage.com, headquartered in Israel.

Professor Uri was one person Jenny had on her bucket list to meet. She couldn't believe she'd actually get to hear him speak and did not want to miss this event. She ordered a ticket online.

Now all she had to do was find transportation. Should she take Amtrack or the other commuter train nearby? No, she decided, she'd still need a ride to and from the station. Maybe Uber, although that might be pricey as Quantico was thirty-seven miles from Washington, DC. What about borrowing her roommate's car? After all, Francine had driven to Quantico from Tennessee. Maybe it wasn't so bad rooming with her after all. Jenny got up the nerve to ask her.

"Hey, Edwards, mind if I borrow your car Saturday?"

Francine shot Jenny a bewildered look. "For what?"

"I want to go to DC to catch a talk by an Israeli historian at the Smithsonian."

"Smithsonian?"

"Have you ever been there?"

"No."

"Really? You must see it. Especially the Air and Space Museum. It's to die for. You could visit the museum while I listen to the talk."

"Deal. I'll drive you."

I never thought she'd be that easy.

They left early Saturday morning, driving on I-95 in light traffic. As there was no parking facility on the National Mall, they parked in a garage near the Natural History Museum on Tenth Street between Pennsylvania and E Streets. After they parked, Jenny headed to the Smithsonian building and Francine to the Air and Space Museum on Independence Avenue.

Inside the Smithsonian, Jenny chose a seat near the stage in the lecture hall. She didn't have to wait long until Professor Uri appeared.

He was a thin man, with dark eyebrows, and a shaved, balding head and wore large wire-rimmed glasses. His credentials were impeccable: a PhD in history from Oxford University and a frequent lecturer at Georgetown University, specializing in world history.

When he began speaking, Jenny straightened up in her chair and sat in rapt attention, taking notes, as he spoke about his book.

"DNA knowledge multiplied by algorithms equals ability to hack humans."

Jenny's eyes widened at the thought that something or someone might be able to hack humans. *The next thing you know, we'll all be robots.* She leaned forward in order not to miss a word Professor Uri said.

"There is potential for humans to be manipulated, especially by autocratic forms of government like China. It's well known that China was after Americans' DNA when BGI Group from Shenzhen offered five states, including New York, California and Washington State, COVID-19 testing support."

Several people in the audience nodded their heads and booed.

"When I mentioned algorithms, I meant the step-by-step process for calculations that companies like Google, Netflix, Apple and Facebook rank billions of posted content by an individual user's 'likes' or 'dislikes.' The algorithms make future predictions of behavior based on past reactions to the content so that the company, or say a government like China, can build a profile of the individual."

Jenny took a sip of water from a bottle she had brought, then scribbled down notes with a fury.

Professor Uri spoke in an even tone of voice. "For example, if you clicked 'like' to a post that showed the storming of the Capitol in Washington, DC, more than likely, you will be profiled as a supporter of Donald Trump and you might get targeted for future fundraising efforts by the Republican Party. If you clicked 'like' on a post showing cats or dogs, you will be profiled as someone who likes pets and you might see an ad for you to purchase a product for a dog or cat. Similarly, if you clicked on a nostalgic post showing an item mostly baby boomers would remember, you will be categorized as someone in that age group and you might be targeted by a company that sells Medicare products."

"And Americans don't realize they're being targeted," whispered the woman seated next to Jenny.

Jenny didn't want any distractions. She put her finger to her mouth and the woman got the message.

Professor Uri paused for effect, then continued. "It has become the norm rather than the exception to reflexively click 'like' or 'dislike,' and these choices are often made without giving much thought to a company or government building a profile on you that they can later manipulate for their own benefit. And although many of us are aware it is happening, we often feel powerless to do anything about it."

Jenny thought this book was very different from Professor Uri's book *Mankind Through the Millennia*. It was almost a guidebook and included observations she hadn't thought of until now. She scribbled more notes in her notebook, faster now, as if she couldn't risk not getting it all down on paper so she could remember every word Professor Uri said.

"Of particular concern," Professor Uri said, "is the new biometric sensor. Worn on or inside bodies, it converts biological processes such as heart rate or pulse rate into electronic information that can be stored and analyzed. In effect, it will result in companies or an autocratic government such as China being able to hack all your desires, decisions and opinions."

The crowd booed.

"With enough mined data, an autocratic government like China may be able to make unwanted decisions for you—select your career, your lovers, your mate, your lifestyle, your diet, and how many babies you can have. And most people won't even know they've been manipulated."

There were more murmurs from the crowd who responded with boos and hisses.

Professor Uri adjusted his glasses. "Let me go back to why it is important for scientists to study DNA. The ability to extract DNA is important in studying the genetic causes of disease and for the development of diagnostics and drugs."

Jenny scribbled more notes.

"If you study the genetic causes of disease, a company or government could help prevent the disease, or in the case of an autocratic government like China, it might help cause the disease or a life-threatening virus. It is also important for scientists to study DNA because it is essential for detecting bacteria and viruses, determining paternity, carrying out forensic science, and sequencing genomes."

Jenny raised her hand.

Professor Uri nodded. "Go ahead."

"What does sequencing genomes mean?"

"Good question. A genome is an organism's complete set of DNA and genome sequencing is a laboratory method that is used to determine the entire genetic makeup of a specific organism, like a human being, or a cell type. As you can see, this information is crucial and might be deadly if it gets into the wrong hands."

There were nods in the audience.

Jenny's blood pressure inched up a notch. *That's all we need—for autocratic governments to have information about our genetic makeup!*

Momentarily lost in thought, she remembered her conversation with Dave about China wanting access to Americans' DNA so they could exploit Americans. She remembered him saying, "We all know the Chinese model—a country with extreme secretiveness where its laws are used by the state as an instrument for social control, a country which clearly loves the benefits of capitalism and free enterprise and trade, but also a country that refuses to entertain the idea of free elections."

As she took another sip of water, she couldn't help but think of what else he had said.

"We know China limits which websites the Chinese can access and what type of news they get. China is also the biggest pirate of intellectual property. With Americans' DNA, Beijing might be able to determine who lives and who dies by either providing medical help to those who need it, like cancer patients, or denying care to others. Too bad for the unlucky ones."

Jenny's mind returned to Professor Uri's talk. "The challenge posed to mankind in this century by biotech is a greater disruption than the disruption which occurred in the previous century by steam engines, railroads and electricity."

He paused. "And given the potential destructive power which might result this time around from genetically engineered monstrosities, mankind as we know it might disappear altogether. We cannot afford to let that happen. We need to do better."

The audience burst into applause.

"So, what do we do to counter this?" Professor Uri said. "First, we start with educating the public as to what is happening with their data—scare the bejesus out of them. Next, build firewalls and encrypt the information so that it can't be accessed or stolen. And, pass laws to regulate the information that is collected."

Jenny had ten pages of notes. After Professor Uri's speech was over, the audience gave him a standing ovation. People lined up to buy a copy of his book and have him autograph it. While Jenny waited in line, she texted Francine to meet her at the parking garage.

The lady ahead of her in line, turned around.

"Where're you from?"

"I'm actually in training at Quantico."

"Marines?"

Jenny's stomach gurgled. "No, FBI Academy."

"Will you be working in Washington, DC?"

She had learned to be cautious from her academy training. "I'm not one hundred percent sure, but my guess is I'll be going to the Pacific Northwest."

She really wanted to work undercover with Dave in counterintelligence and hoped that's where her assignment would be, but she could just as easily be assigned to criminal investigation or administration. Only a couple more weeks of training before she'd find that out. It was time now to go meet Francine.

April 2020
CHAPTER 7

The day after he visited the American Embassy, Yìchén left his apartment in Qian Men, where many of the MSS staff and their families lived, and hustled to work early, arriving at the large governmental MSS compound in Xiyuan, on eastern Chiang'an Avenue in the Dongchen district. He marveled at the mild Spring weather, the temperature inching higher each day, much warmer and more pleasant than March, though he still needed a jacket. The plum and cherry blossoms were in bloom and the poplar trees were gradually turning green.

He pushed the elevator button for the fourth floor, and, when the elevator stopped, stepped out, walked down the long hall to his office and found his boss, Chen Pao, waiting.

Chen was a senior Chinese hawk whose reverence for Mao was unrivaled, even though Mao had killed more people than Stalin and Hitler combined. His black hair had tufts of gray near his temples and ears. He had the appearance of an authoritarian strongman with his large, muscular hands, ample belly and broad shoulders. And like a strongman, he demanded incessant loyalty from his underlings, Yìchén included.

Yìchén sat in a chair in front of his boss's desk and told him what had happened at the American Embassy. He showed him the thumb drives the CIA officer had given him to record secret MSS documents and dead drop them to his American handler.

Chen came around the desk and patted Yìchén on the back. "Well done. I am remembering the words of Napoleon Bonaparte: 'Never stop your enemy when he is making a mistake.' The Americans are on their way to further decline. Just like a game of *Weiqi*, all we need to do is pace ourselves, encircle them and be patient. They'll be caught off guard and won't realize what is happening. They'll end up sinking their own ship."

Yìchén nodded, unsmiling. "What documents should I give them?"

Chen's eyebrows were knit together, as if he were concentrating, and he began pacing back and forth. "A few strategic planning documents. High-level stuff at first in order for them to get hooked. Later on, maybe proprietary information, cyberspace plans, perhaps, or political information—but only a teaser, nothing major. Most should be fabrications but realistic enough, so they don't know they've been duped. I'm sure they'll verify the documents using other Chinese spies they have. Those traitors. If they ask for more, we can give them bogus, yet realistic, documents about our activities in Zimbabwe, Syria, Iran, Sudan and Venezuela."

"What about something they'd consider the crown jewels—American spies?"

Chen stopped pacing and stood in front of Yìchén. "Save those for the clincher, if you need them. We'll give you a list. A few high-profile types but most low-level. Use them as you see fit."

Yìchén glanced up at him. "What about surveillance in Beihai Park?"

Chen nodded. "We used to put as many as twenty MSS officers in teams to follow one suspected American spy, but not anymore since we have facial recognition cameras and hidden microphones everywhere—in taxis, elevators, buses, the subway, on traffic lights and even in the sky on drones. Now our officers can follow them in the comfort of our operation centers. As backup, we'll have Poh Pohs in the park watching you as well as other officers dressed as tourists or dog walkers. This will also help us uncover the Chinese who are spying for the Americans. Perhaps they'll also give you new technology in order to contact them. It'll be a bonanza for us to see how they operate."

"How will I make contact when I'm relocated in America?"

"Transmission bursts on shortwave radio to let us know your location and that you have information to drop off. We'll provide you with training before you leave Beijing. Be careful about purchasing a short-wave radio set so that it can't be traced back to you."

"What about dead drop sites?"

Chen sat down in his executive chair. "Too much surveillance by the FBI to try for a location in America, I'm afraid. We've had more success using a tour group as cover in other countries like South America, Africa or in Europe. Let us know the location ahead of time via code on the short-wave transmission burst."

Yìchén had conflicting thoughts about this new adventure. Although his grandparents had been peasants, his family was able to achieve a better life after his father joined the MSS. Yìchén had never suffered adversity or hardship in his life until the MSS beheaded his father. He had always taken his privileged life for granted. Now he was consumed by thoughts of his mother's grief and his task of encircling the enemy so that China could dominate the world order.

"I have no further questions," Yìchén said.

Chen arched an eyebrow. "Not so fast. Most likely the Americans will require you to undergo a polygraph test to verify your honesty. They'll hook you up with sensors, and the machine will buzz if it detects a lie. Both the Cubans and Czechs have found ways to get around it. I'll see to it that you get training soon so that you can practice evading their questions and pass."

"Anything else?"

"We're counting on you to get us intel on the biotech industry, especially 23andMe, Ancestry, MyHeritage and LineageFinder. Even COVID-testing sites. We want background information on all the major players, possible recruitment targets, research and development strategies, manufacturing and marketing plans and customer lists."

"Won't it depend where they relocate me?"

Chen drummed his fingers on the desk. "If they give you a choice, try for Utah first—around the Salt Lake City area or small towns like Lehi where Ancestry's headquarters is located. A subsidiary of MyHeritage is located there as well. Your second choice should be Northern California, near 23andMe's headquarters. If not there, maybe Seattle, where LineageFinder is headquartered."

Yìchén sat glued to his seat.

"Come up with a plausible reason for wanting those areas, like Utah's climate or its mountains, twisting canyons, sandy desert or towering red rocks. Tell them you'd like to ski at Snowbird, Deer Valley or Park City or that you're interested in the Sundance Independent Film Festival in Park City."

Yìchén nodded. "Okay, got it."

After Chen authorized the documents for Yìchén to copy, Yìchén had them uploaded to the thumb drive in no time and was able to get it past security at the entrance when he left work. He drove home, wondering what life would be like in America.

Virginia, wearing a face mask, walked into the Chief of Station's office late Friday afternoon to go over the final details of the operation on Monday morning. As usual, she found him chomping on a cigar.

"You need to double-check that all of the Six were not included in the OPM breach," he said.

He was talking about China's hack of records at the Office of Personnel Management in November 2013. Included in the breach were photos and sensitive data needed for background checks on civilians in order for them to obtain top-secret security clearances as well as their fingerprints.

"I'm way ahead of you, boss," Virginia said. "I've double-checked and triple-checked the Six and no, none of their records were included in the breach."

"The MSS would have an easier time identifying them with all the goddamn cameras they have everywhere."

"Don't forget they'll be wearing face masks."

"I haven't forgotten, but their systems are probably advanced enough to still identify people by their eyes and body shapes. The Six will have their work cut out for them."

The "Six" she and the COS referred to was short for "the Surveillance Six." They consisted of a pair of identical twins, named Lily and Lana; a retired Navy Seal and his wife—John and Maggie—who lived in Beijing; a tall, lanky man in his 40s, named Chet who played basketball for Duke University and, last but not least, a millennial named Rachel who ran track in college for Claremont McKenna.

"Good," he said. "Okay. I assume you've also set up starburst."

"Yes, similar-looking agents, besides the Six, will be out on the streets of Beijing, going in different directions. Let's hope it works to confuse the MSS."

"Let er rip, then. You have my blessing."

Virginia contacted the Six with the go-ahead signal, telling them to begin watching Yìchén early Monday morning when he'd leave his residence in Qian Men and ride the subway to the thousand-year-old Beihai Park in the Xicheng District with his golden retriever to the drop site.

Located near the Ming Dynasty Zhengyagmen Tower, on the southern edge of Tiananmen Square, Yìchén's apartment was not far from Qianmen Street, a famous pedestrian street full of shops, restaurants, culture and entertainment in the central part of Beijing. American shops such as Starbucks, Kentucky Fried Chicken and McDonald's, were landmarks mixed in with the Tongrentang drugstore, Ruifuxiang silk shop, Neiliansheng shoes store and Zhangyiyuan tea shop, which had been operating for over a century.

It was daylight already at 6:05 a.m. when Yìchén and Gǒu, his retriever, left his apartment and walked to the nearby Qianmen subway stop with the Six trailing him to smoke out any surveillance. To avoid being detected by the cameras on street corners and in the subway, many of the Six wore disguises as they followed him. Lily walked on the opposite side of the empty street and watched Yìchén from a distance. She did not detect anything unusual.

Standing at the Qianmen stop entrance, she heard Chet say, "I got your six," over the radio. The phrase originated in WWI, when fighter pilots referenced a pilot's rear as "the six o'clock position." Back then, it meant "I've got you covered so the enemy can't come up behind your back and kill you." To the Six, it meant unquestioned loyalty: "I got your back."

Lily adjusted the ear buds connected to her radio. "Copy," she said into the mic.

She wore thin-striped navy polyester pants with a white V-neck t-shirt and over-sized black frame glasses. Like her twin, Lana, her medium-sized head was not in proportion to her petite frame. She melded into the crowd with her black page-boy wig topped off with a white gardening hat.

Yìchén put on his face mask and ran down the steel-plated steps, then stopped to purchase a ticket. Afterwards, he headed for the train going to Hepingmen on the Blue Line 2 platform, while Chet, close on his heels, put his ticket in the turnstile and hurried after him, keeping a comfortable distance between them.

"Your direction, Lily," Chet said. He wore a black face mask and a pair of black running shorts and bent down to tie his gray sneaker.

"Copy. Heading to train." As she ran toward the train at a steady pace, she bumped into Yìchén and Gǒu on the platform but didn't make eye contact. Instead, she started humming to music as if she were in la-la land, listening to the latest iTunes hit, and pushed her way behind them to get onto the train.

Yìchén took his time getting on with Gǒu and had to stand, holding onto the pole. Chet headed to the rear of the car, while Lily sat down next to a young businessman, who slid off his face mask and broke Chinese custom by smiling at her. She looked away and didn't say anything, knowing the Chinese do not smile at strangers, foreign or not, so her gut told her this man's behavior was indeed suspicious.

Instead, she concentrated on the train car, careful not to make eye contact while observing the space around Yìchén, looking for any subtle movements of anyone—any signaling, any communication, or even just proximity in conjunction with Yìchén's movements and location.

"What music are you listening to?" the man in the business suit asked in perfect Mandarin.

"'Drivers License' by Olivia Rodrigo," Lily answered in Mandarin.

"Are you an American?"

"No, I just like American music." A little white lie.

"Would you like to have tea sometime?"

Yìchén's ears perked up. Then Gǒu softly whined, so Yìchén reached in his pocket, pulled out a treat and gave it to the dog.

Lily grumbled at the businessman. "With *you*?"

"Yes, who else?"

"I'm afraid I'm taken." Another lie. She moved to a different seat.

The man followed her. Lily watched Yìchén's eyes follow him.

"I'm sorry if I disturbed you," he said. "Please accept my apology. It's just that I rarely meet such an attractive woman like yourself. I would like to be friends. What's your name?"

Lily had a black belt in karate and could easily have taken any man down who was bothering her—like this man in the business suit—but she held her frustration in check. Much better to use her other weapon—her mouth.

"Gun kai!" She told him to "Get lost" in her best authoritative voice, scowling at him.

The man's eyes bulged out at the insult. He got up, glared at her and then moved back to his original seat.

Yìchén had a puzzled look on his face.

The train stopped at the next station—Gung'anmennei. Yìchén and his dog got off. So did Lily and Chet, with a reasonable distance between them. They followed the crowd to catch the next train on the Daxing Line, Line 4.

"Stranger danger," Lily said into the mic.

"Copy," Chet said. "Possible rival?"

"Perhaps. Will see if he follows target."

"I'll take it from here," Chet said. They reversed roles in order to remain undetected. "Changing to Line 6 at Ping'anli," he said. "Next stop is Beihai."

———— ❖ ————

After Yìchén and his dog boarded the train, Chet sprinted and was the last one on board. The businessman did not follow. Chet hung onto the pole this time, taking up Lily's position, while Yìchén took a seat with Gǒu at his feet. The dog was quiet.

Yìchén shared a joke with a middle-aged Chinese man. Was he just a casual acquaintance, or were they old friends? In countersurveillance, every nod, every smile, every glance, and every word that is or isn't spoken is taken into consideration. One couldn't be too careful.

Does that person's face look familiar? Have I seen him before?

Why did he just nod or smile? Could it be a signal?

Does it mean something that he is the only one on the escalator or in the train car or deserted subway platform or on the deserted street? Could he be following me?

Usually, surveillance or countersurveillance lasted ten or twelve hours and often more—even twenty or more—hours were needed. The Six were professionals, and every Surveillance Detection Route (SDR) was important no matter the status of the target.

Chet was within earshot but did not make eye contact with either man. Instead, he yawned to feign disinterest. He took off his face mask to take a sip of water from a bottle he had in his backpack and stared at the newspaper he had brought with him. The watching always created butterflies in Chet's stomach, but he never let on. He scanned the faces around him everywhere he went.

He signaled to Lily. "Blue shorts."

"Copy," Lily said into the mic. "Looks like he's getting off at this stop."

The conductor announced, "Ping'anli."

A young Chinese woman wearing workout gear, a lot of makeup and heavy perfume hopped aboard and took the middle-aged man's seat next to Yìchén. There was no conversation between the two. However, Yìchén did put his finger up to his nose after sniffing the air. Was that a subtle signal?

Chet noticed that Yìchén yawned. He watched him doze off and then jerk awake. *Perhaps he's afraid he might miss his stop.*

When the train approached the Beihai station, Yìchén got up from his seat and stood near the door with his dog in tow. They rushed out the door when the train stopped.

"Leaving," Chet said into his ear bud radio, huffing from jostling the crowds. "Joked with a middle-aged man on the train, maybe five-five with a paunch, blue tank top and running shorts, who nodded when he got off at Ping'anli. Might not be anything, but better not to assume."

"Copy," said the four Six members stationed around the park.

———————— ✦ ————————

When the park opened at 6:30 a.m., the sun was already shining. Yìchén paid the entrance fee with the yuan the CIA officer had given him and strolled around the walkway near the massive Taiye Lake. The boats on the lake were various sizes to accommodate however many people wanted to ride and were similar to flat-bottomed jon boats with small outboard motors and awnings large enough to cover most of the seating space on the boats.

The morning temperature was cool and a soft breeze whipping across the lake did its best to burn off the morning mist. In the distance, Yìchén could see the exquisite Daning Palace on Qionghua Island as he and Gǒu meandered along the path, sniffing the crisp morning air.

The park was quiet at that hour, save for the occasional encounter with a jogger, a tourist, or an elderly couple seated on a park bench, or when he bumped into another dog walker. Yìchén did not detect anyone following him or even looking at him with suspicion. *Good.*

He saw a millennial girl wearing a track suit run past him and an older couple sitting on a park bench along the foot path near the boat launch entrance, but dismissed them as tourists because they seemed disinterred in what he and his dog were doing.

While strolling on the foot path, Yìchén and his retriever came across a Peking willow tree, where Gǒu lifted up his hind leg and put his mark on the tree trunk. Yìchén held the plastic bag he had brought with him in the palm of his hand, with the thumb drive inside, ready just in case. He had inserted the thumb drive into the plastic bag so that when he stooped to pick up his dog's poop, he didn't have to fumble with the thumb drive and it wouldn't take more time than necessary.

While Gǒu crouched to poop, a young Japanese tourist walking a fluffy white Bichon Frise came near them. Gǒu, spraying saliva, growled and barked so hard and loud at the dog that the sound hurt Yìchén's ears. He pulled on Gǒu's leash to keep him from tearing into the other dog.

"Easy, boy," Yìchén whispered as the plastic bag with the thumb drive dropped from his hands. "Oops!" He stooped to pick it up.

"I can get that for you," the young man said.

"Not necessary," Yìchén said. "I've got it." He snatched the bag and hoped the young man and his dog would move on. Instead, the young man lingered, wanting to chat.

"Nice day, isn't it?"

"Yes, it is." Yìchén gritted his teeth.

"What's your dog's name?"

"Gǒu."

"Mine's Aika. It means 'love song.' I've seen you before. Do you come here often?"

Yìchén thought about the plastic bag he held in his hand and wondered how to pick up the poop with this young man watching. *Is he a spy? And, if so, is it the Americans keeping tabs on me or is it the MSS?*

Yìchén acted as if he didn't hear the question, hoping the man would move on, but the Japanese tourist continued asking questions.

"How long have you had your dog? How old is he?"

"Going on eight years."

"Where did you get him?"

Yìchén let out a long sigh. This casual talk was annoying. Plus, it was keeping him from accomplishing the task.

"From a local breeder."

"Very nice-looking dog. If you don't mind me asking, what did you pay for it?"

"A reasonable price."

"Does your wife like the dog?"

"I'm not married."

"Do you work somewhere or mostly spend your days here in the park?"

Isn't he a curious twit? Asks a lot of personal questions. How can I get rid of him?

"It's none of your business," Yìchén said, frowning.

"Sorry, man. Didn't mean to pry. Have a good day." With that, the young man nodded, and he and his dog left.

Yìchén looked around. No one was near them, so he stooped to pick up the poop, put it inside the plastic bag with the thumb drive and carried it, passing the elderly couple on the bench while guiding Gǒu back to the boat launch entrance.

When he reached the trash can, he looked in the opposite direction while he was dropping the plastic bag into the trash container.

The elderly couple looked in the same direction, following his gaze.

Yìchén and his dog walked past them and left the park.

Rènwù wánchéng. Mission accomplished.

Later, the Six focused on the possible suspects to determine their true identities and reported their findings back to Virginia via secure phone at the American Embassy.

"Three were definitely part of an MSS surveillance team," the Six agreed.

"Why do you say that?" Virginia asked.

"The Chinese businessman was a little too inquisitive with me," Lily said. "Definitely a trademark of an intelligence operator. Plus, it's odd for a Chinese to smile or interact with someone they just met."

"Go on," Virginia said. "What else?"

"The elderly man who shared a joke with Yìchén on the subway ended up giving him a klutzy nod when he got off at Ping'anli," Chet said. "An obvious signal."

"Yes," John and Maggie chimed in. "And there was no way in hell the Japanese tourist would have been working for Kōanchōsa-Chō, Japan's intelligence service, because of the legendary enmity between Japan and China. He had to have been working for the MSS."

"Well, then," Virginia said. "I know what my message will be to Yìchén."

That night Yìchén received a voicemail on his phone that said *Cousin Guang* did not enjoy the *'lousy'* San Xian noodles he ate at a local restaurant.

He wondered what went wrong.

May 2020

CHAPTER 8

After her training at Quantico, Jenny returned to Seattle and was elated to find out she was instructed to work undercover with Dave in counterintelligence. He had been assigned to the Liu case.

Charles Liu, a Boeing engineer, and his wife, Elizabeth, who had emigrated from Hong Kong in the sixties, were suspected of passing on secrets about Boeing's new, highly classified laser technology to Beijing.

Although new hires, like Jenny, were rarely assigned to the better cases, like this one, Jenny had an excellent background and exceeded all test scores, which greatly appealed to higher-ups. She was fluent in Mandarin, thanks to her parents, graduated first out of 600 in her training class, proved to have extraordinary technical skills and excelled in her personality assessment and psychology courses at Quantico.

Jenny and Dave moved to a four-bedroom house next door to the Lius in Federal Way in order to keep tabs on them. Jenny was fine with the arrangement since they did not have to share a bedroom.

Dave took on the persona of a wealthy businessman from Hawaii and grew a beard and mustache to enhance his cover. The owner of Seattle Realty was a retired undercover FBI agent who backstopped Dave. Jenny assumed the role of a homemaker and had her head shaved to portray that she was undergoing chemo. She looked in the mirror and gasped. *Never realized what women who have cancer go through.* Yet, she was excited to take on this new persona, new identity and new assignment.

They knocked on the Lius' door to introduce themselves.

Charles Liu answered the door.

"Hi, I'm Bret Hartgren," Dave said. He held out his hand to shake. "And this is my wife, Charlotte." He nodded to Jenny.

Charles acted as if they were intruding. Although Mr. Liu was known to be friendly and helpful at Boeing, they pretty much kept to themselves in their neighborhood. He stared at Jenny.

"My hair isn't usually like this," Jenny said. "I'm undergoing chemo treatments for breast cancer."

"Oh. Sorry." After a pause, he held out his hand. "I'm Charles Liu. My wife is busy right now or I'd introduce her."

Dave shook his hand. "What type of work do you do?" he asked.

"I'm an engineer."

"For what company?"

"Boeing."

"Really? Say, I've been a realtor for the past ten years. The market is hot right now. I don't suppose you know anyone who wants to buy or sell a house?"

Mr. Liu didn't invite them in. "No, I don't," he said. He started to close the door.

"Do you have any kids?" Jenny asked.

"No."

"Neither do we," Dave said, "but I hope you like dogs. I've got a Chesapeake Bay retriever."

By the look on Mr. Liu's face, it was clear he was not fond of animals.

"I don't mean to be rude, but I have some work to do. If you'll excuse me…"

"Sure," Dave said. "No problem. Good to meet you. Have a nice day!"

Jenny's first assignment, after moving in and making friends with the Lius, was to bug the Lius' house. She did not have to worry about tapping the phone lines because with modern digital equipment the function is already built into the apparatus. Relevant commands would be entered by the phone company at the console after receiving prior authorization from FBI Headquarters.

In the Liu case, because they were suspected of passing on secrets about Boeing's laser technology to Beijing, the FBI had the needed justification to obtain a warrant and asked the telecom operator to enter the relevant commands. Everything was now in place. The phone conversations would be recorded by switching equipment without connecting anything to the phone line. It was up to Jenny to plant other bugs in the Lius' house.

On Monday, a week after they had moved in, as soon as Jenny heard the Lius' garage door shut and them backing out of the driveway, Jenny crept out to the back door of their garage, picked the lock and easily got in. Once inside, she took a moment to scan the garage.

All of a sudden, she heard a car drive up and the garage door opening again. She panicked. Her heart started pounding. A drop of sweat ran down her forehead to her nose. She thought the intruders must be the Lius, but why were they returning and where should she go now to cover herself?

She was over on the far side of the garage, and it would take a minute or two to get out through the kitchen door. It only took six seconds for the garage door to open completely. She made a split-second decision to just hide somewhere in the garage, figuring she was petite enough not to have them notice. But where?

Four tires were piled up on top of each other in one corner, a large trash bin sat nearby and two ten-speed bicycles stood over by the wall. She chose the tires, ducked behind them and waited, hoping not to wet her pants.

The Lius pulled up in the garage and Mrs. Liu went to the kitchen door where she stopped suddenly and paused a moment reflectively. Jenny held her breath and tried to think of some plausible reason she could give for hiding in their garage. Her thoughts were racing like wildfire as she began to pray. She heard footsteps coming toward her. Mrs. Liu had turned around and was walking toward where Jenny was hiding. She wanted to die. She could hardly breathe. She wondered if hell was any hotter than she felt right now.

Suddenly, however, Mrs. Liu seemed to remember what she had forgotten and went to search her purse in the front seat. After she had found whatever it was that was lost, Mr. Liu started the car again and pulled out of the garage and the driveway, and drove off.

When the garage door closed, Jenny unlocked her knees and quickly ran to the bedroom, taking her gym bag and a kitchen chair to stand on. Hoping to God that the Lius wouldn't return soon, she took a piece of plastic from her bag and spread it on the floor beneath the door.

She took out a hand-held cordless drill with a half-inch drill in it. She stood on the chair, found the center of the door and drilled a half-inch hole in the top of the door. Next, she took a nylon pantyhose from the bag and cut one leg off. Jenny stuffed one leg with a battery pack, which consisted of three batteries connected to a microphone and transmitter and then three larger batteries. She lowered this into the hole, hanging onto the nylon at the top.

Jenny filled the stocking at the top with Styrofoam pellets and jiggled the door to make sure there was no noise. Once full, she dropped the rest of the nylon into the hole, making sure the nylon was flush with the door. Then she took a cork and forced it down into the hole in the door.

She ran her hand across the top to make sure it was flush. Then she cleaned up, grabbing the pellets and the drill, and folded up the plastic. She put clothes back in the top of her bag to cover up her tools.

Then she went to the living room. She quickly installed a listening device behind what she thought was a fake Picasso on the wall, until she noticed the signature on the painting, which proved it was authentic. No time to think about that now.

The installation took only two seconds. One side of a miniature microphone and transmitter was gummed with sticky adhesive. She installed it in the indentation in the back of the painting where no one would notice. This listening device wouldn't last as long as the one in the bedroom, which had a five-mile range and would last anywhere from six to nine months.

She took her gym bag and left the house. Except for the rocky start, everything went as planned.

While Dave was responsible for monitoring the daily wiretap as well as the comings and goings of the Lius, Jenny was assigned to trash duty. Each week the Lius' garbage was intercepted before it was dropped off at the dump. Every week, Jenny sorted and closely examined it in an empty garage in King County. What she found gave the FBI a clearer picture of the Lius.

Today, Jenny put on her cargo pants, boots, and a long-sleeved plaid work shirt and drove to the garage where she sorted the trash, wearing a face mask. With puncture-proof gloves, she opened the Lius' garbage bags and dumped them on a canvas tarp spread out on the floor. It was like a game of hide-and-seek or a treasure hunt. She didn't look for specific items so that she could discover what she didn't expect.

Next to a toilet paper roll, she found grocery receipts, one from Hong Kong Market, another from Costco. She found a gas receipt from Costco and next to it a bill from Lakehaven Water & Sewer. Nothing from department stores, like Macy's or Nordstrom. No receipts for new clothes.

There were several bundles of wrapped newspaper. She opened one bundle. Inside were the remains of a meal the Lius had eaten, including some chicken bones. Fish remnants were in another. In others, she found Chinese noodles, tofu, rice, and stir-fry vegetables. No desserts.

Jenny wondered why they ate on newspaper because sixty-four-year-old Charles Liu earned a decent salary at Boeing and was able to purchase a nice home in Federal Way, so why were they living as if they were subsisting on dimes and pennies?

The next item Jenny found, piqued her interest. A to-do list Mr. Liu had written and torn into shreds. All handwritten or printed notes, especially in Chinese, were of particular interest. It looked as if Mr. Liu had ripped up this paper, so Jenny pulled out the small squares and laid them out on a table. She pieced the paper back together and translated it: a shopping list for hardware items.

Were they planning to purchase them from Home Depot? Why did he tear up the list when they were common household items?

Dave, who had nearly a decade of working undercover for the Bureau, inconspicuously trailed Charles and Elizabeth to LA Fitness, a gym located on Baker Boulevard in Tukwila, not far from Boeing's facility. He drove a "clean" Mercedes he had gotten from a different retired undercover agent who owned a used car dealership.

Dave kept his distance from the Lius, remaining far enough back in traffic so as not to be detected.

After arriving at the gym and while checking out its facilities, "Bret" ran into an old college buddy who knew him as Dave.

"Hey, Dave, long time no see!" his buddy said, slapping him on the back near the entrance, in full view and earshot of one of the trainers.

Dave shook his head. "I'm sorry. You must have me confused with someone else. My name is Bret."

"Sure, it is! Don't you remember me? We were in the same fraternity together at USC."

"I assure you I don't know you. I never went to USC. I graduated from the University of Hawaii."

"Right! And the Pope is Jewish. Come on, Dave. Why don't we go have a drink and remember the good times we've had?" He put his arm around Dave.

"Get your hands off me! I told you, I don't know you. And, what's more, I don't want to know you, so leave me *alone*!"

"Okay, man. If you say so. No harm, no foul."

Since Dave's cover had almost been blown, he decided to leave the gym. He returned home, determined to follow the Lius the next day, along with a surveillance team. Tomorrow was Saturday and he'd find out what they did on the weekends when they weren't at work.

Saturday, the Lius went to Home Depot on 352nd Street in Federal Way. They took their time as they strolled down the kitchen aisle, then the carpet aisle, then the gardening aisle, never handling anything, until they got to the lumber aisle, where they each got a free cup of coffee and then left the store.

Dave and his surveillance team did not detect them making a drop or passing on information—only taking advantage of the free coffee.

———•✦•———

That night, after dinner, when Jenny and Dave were seated in the living room, sharing a glass of wine, she told Dave what she had found.

"Good work," he said, congratulating her.

"Thanks. How was *your* day?"

He told her about his college buddy almost blowing his cover and the Lius taking advantage of the free coffee offered in the lumber aisle at Home Depot.

"I'd say we both had quite a day! To us!" she said, lifting her wine glass in a toast.

"Cheers!" he said, doing the same.

This house arrangement was working out well for them as they were able to keep it professional. They worked well together, complemented each other. They always worked as a team now and even ate all their meals together, which drew them closer and closer to each other.

Dave was easy to talk to, and although he was a little clumsy at times and even wore some loud Hawaiian shirts, she wasn't embarrassed by him or them.

He accepted her as she was, too. Even her flaws didn't seem to matter to him. He was never critical of her. He never asked or insinuated that she should act or be any differently than who she was, and he seemed genuinely interested in her life goals and aspirations to the point where he was actively trying to help her achieve those goals. If she made a mistake, he was forgiving right away and never held grudges.

He was so easy to be around. The unconditional love he offered was so hypnotizing that Jenny wondered about his previous marriage. Why on earth had it failed? Tonight, she got brave enough to ask.

"My ex-wife always tried to change me. She wanted the perfect husband. I often came up short. The clothes I selected were never good enough for her. Neither were my friends. We were exact opposites. She was extremely religious; I'm a hell-raiser. I felt like a caged animal when I lived with her."

"That must have been hard."

"She also had a habit of making people's lives miserable if hers wasn't going well, and she had a deep-seated need to disguise her true motives." He paused. Maybe he felt he had said too much. "Enough about me. What about you? Why aren't *you* married?"

Jenny took a sip of her wine. She didn't like discussing her private life, but because Dave was so honest about his, she opened up to him about hers.

"You could say I was a fool and fell in love with Mr. Creep."

"I think we've all been there. If you don't mind me asking, what happened?"

"Mark and I both liked to travel. We also liked to cook exotic meals. We planned to celebrate the anniversary of our six months together. I prepared our special dish, set the table with candles, bought an expensive bottle of champagne to celebrate, but he didn't show."

"Well, I've been guilty of that myself a time or two." He smiled.

Dave's smile was like a dopamine rush to Jenny. He could have said he was guilty of murder and it wouldn't have mattered with that smile. It made her heart melt and took her breath away. She knew she could trust him with her story.

"I wondered if I missed signs that our relationship might be over, like he had to get off the phone in a hurry the day before and said he needed to spend more time with his kids…but he had promised me he would celebrate our anniversary, and I believed him. I wondered why his sudden change of heart. I wasn't willing to face the truth at the moment, so I waited a week to call him.

When I called his house, his roommate said Mark was having an affair with a married woman. What a fool I was! He must have slept with me one night and her the next."

"You're not a fool. It's happened to the best of us. I'm so sorry you had to go through that, Jenny. Did you ever confront him about it?"

"I called Mark the next day at work and asked him to meet me for lunch. We met at a fast-food restaurant, made small talk, and then I went in for the kill. As I spoke, I saw guilt choking him. I've had a bit of a trust problem since."

"Understandable. It takes time to get over something like that. You seem pretty strong now though. I never would have guessed."

"Thanks."

There was an awkward silence that accompanied a feeling of being too vulnerable. She wondered if it was a mistake to let her guard down. *Here is that trust problem again.*

"Hey," Dave said. "How `bout I play a song on the guitar?"

"I'd love that."

He fetched his Gibson J-150 from his bedroom.

"This is a song by Jimmy Hill. I think you'll like it. It's in the key of C."

Only a professional would know that. "How do you know it's in that key?"

"I'm blessed with perfect pitch."

She looked at him in awe.

He strummed the guitar. "Here goes:

You're my little buttercup, my sweet pea

And I want to take care of you.

You'll have less stress and love to spare,

If I take care of you."

Jenny squirmed in her chair, slightly uncomfortable. Dave continued singing.

I'm your rock of strength when you're weak,

I'll always take care of you.

Show you good times when life gets bad,

I'll always take care of you.

Is this his idea of romance? Dave must be old school. He is going to think I'm a live hand grenade, the pin has been pulled and the fuse is burning, but I can't stand to listen to this.

"Stop!" Jenny said. "I don't want to hear any more. You obviously are singing it to the wrong girl. I don't want *anyone* to take care of me. I can take care of *myself*."

Dave had a surprised and hurt look on his face.

"Uh oh. I've wounded mama grizzly." He shrugged. "I'll back off. So sorry."

Now I feel bad. He's such a nice guy. He didn't mean any harm.

She bit her lip. "I'm sorry, too."

He drained his glass. "If you don't mind, I think we should call it a night and hit the hay. I need to get up early tomorrow."

"I'm with you," she said, rising from the chair.

They nodded to each other as they went to their separate bedrooms.

May 2020

CHAPTER 9

Yìchén strutted into his boss's office and found Chen Pao sitting behind his large governmental desk in his gun-metal gray executive chair, wearing a face mask. He acted civil to his boss even though now he now hated him after Bohai's execution. It was all an act.

"Have you drunk tea?" Yìchén said. The question, a popular greeting with Guangzhou residents who lived nearby Shenzhen, where Yìchén grew up, was an old habit he had acquired from childhood.

"I was about to pour myself a cup."

"I'll get it." Yìchén went over to the tea service. "Green or oolong?"

"Oolong." He cleared his throat. "We need to go over a few things. I have a hunch the Americans may think you're lying to them and will ask you to undergo a polygraph test soon. You need to be prepared."

Yìchén brought the tea and took a seat in front of Chen's desk. "Nothing like hot tea to warm us on a cold day, huh?"

Chen nodded and took a sip of the bitter tea.

"About the polygraph…can you give me a short lesson?"

"Of course. First of all, you need to understand a polygraph only captures a person's physiological changes in the body, like fast pulse, sweating, unusual breathing and high blood pressure. If a person lies, their heart races, they start to pant, their blood pressure skyrockets and they sweat like crazy."

"All detected by a machine? I find that hard to believe." He took two gulps of his tea.

"The examiner puts a wire or monitor on your index finger and ring finger of your left hand and also on the middle finger of your right hand as well as wires on your chest and above your stomach. If you get a real qualified professional as an examiner, the accuracy is up to ninety-eight percent."

"Slim chance of me passing." He rolled his eyes.

"Well, interpreting a polygraph is an art, not a science. It can be very subjective. Let's hope the Americans don't have such a person in their arsenal at the embassy."

The hair on Yìchén's arms bristled. "There must be a way I can beat it. How did you say the Cubans and Czechs overcame it?" He took another swallow of tea.

"No need to ask the Cubans or the Czechs. The internet is full of information. Now you can find YouTube videos that tell you how to pass such a test and prepare for it."

Chen wasn't telling Yìchén that he needed to seek training on the internet only that that's one place it's available.

"Do the videos tell you the tricks?"

"They suggest not to use any of the old tricks. People used to put a tack in their shoe and step on it every time they needed to get the right reaction. Another one was to bite their tongue or tense up their muscles."

"Sounds like good ideas."

"Experienced experts are wise to such tricks. An examiner might ask you to remove your shoes since they're all too familiar with such schemes. A lie detector test can distinguish a deceptive reaction due to physical pain. If you get caught, the examiner might evaluate your results more strictly, taking into account the tricks you tried to pull. So, don't try any tricks."

"What other advice did they give?" He drained his cup.

"Plenty."

"More tea?" Yìchén rose to get another cup.

"No, I'm fine. They also recommend letting yourself be nervous because it can help you pass the test."

"What? How can that be?"

"The examiner will ask you two types of questions. You need to know the difference between the two. A general question might be: 'Have you ever lied?' However, a more relevant question might be: 'Have you ever lied to your employer?' See the difference?"

Yìchén took the cup of tea and returned to his seat. "Yes, but why is that important?"

"If you are nervous or anxious when you answer general questions, you'll react in the same manner to the relevant questions and the examiner will interpret your answers to the relevant questions as truthful."

"Got it."

"It's important that you stay calm when you answer. But if you want to show a different reaction, like being anxious, think of something scary or unpleasant or something that embarrassed you a great deal."

Yìchén swilled the tea in his cup. "What else?"

"Don't lie about small details and don't give away more information than is absolutely necessary. I've heard of some examiners who use dirty tricks to make you admit you're lying. Don't fall for it…and don't confess anything."

Yìchén finished the last of his tea and set the cup on Chen's desk. "I assure you that will never happen."

"Keep your answers concise and simple and take your time answering the questions. Pause and figure out what type of question the examiner is asking. Is it a general question or a relevant question? The best answer to either question is always a yes or no."

After a moment of silence, Yìchén said, "Are we through here? I still have some work I need to do."

"One last thing. If you realize you need to lie, imagine you don't have a care in the world or something pleasant to keep you calm. It's much easier to be nervous than it is to think of something happy, but it will show in your body if you do."

Yìchén got up to leave. Chen walked him to the door, his arm around his shoulder.

"This might just be the hardest thing I've ever had to do. My neck is already hurting from the added pressure."

"You must pass it. The MSS is counting on it."

Back at the American Embassy, the short white-haired CIA Chief of Station asked his secretary to buzz Virginia Langford, Yìchén's handler, and demand she come to the front office secure conference room at once.

He puffed his cigar smoke at her when she appeared at the door. "What the hell went wrong yesterday?" he asked.

"That fucking nightmare told me he knew surveillance methods, but he wasn't 'black' when he made the drop at the park. The Six determined some MSS goons were following him. They spent more than five hours in preparation, covering the perimeter of the park in the Xicheng District around the lake as well as main thoroughfares like Wenjin Street and Jingshan West Street, not to mention following him on the subway and crossing paths with him at the park."

"You mentioned they found surveillance. Did they identify any suspects or find anything out of the ordinary or what seemed ordinary but wasn't?"

She told him about the elderly man who shared a joke with Yìchén as well as the Japanese tourist.

"What's the plan now?"

"Meet him at the Haidian safehouse and grill him as well as give him a polygraph. I hope that turd doesn't skunk us by not showing."

"I assume you'll get the Six to do surveillance again."

"It's on my to-do list. First, I need to make contact with Yìchén to tell him where we'll meet."

Yìchén listened to the voicemail message from Cousin Guang again on his burner phone. Besides not enjoying the "lousy" San Xian noodles he ate, Guang suggested they meet again, and he'd let him know where and when.

The next day, he reported all this to Chen Pao, his boss and a senior Chinese hawk. Yìchén pulled up his face mask over his nose.

Chen arched an eyebrow. "You should have anticipated trouble. This game isn't over yet. What did your father teach you about *Weiqi*?"

The mere mention of Bohai brought chills to Yìchén's spine; however, he answered the question as if nothing had ever happened to his father.

"Never take your eyes off the goal of encircling your enemy. Don't let your opponent keep you off balance."

"Exactly. Perhaps they'll have you meet at the safehouse we know the Americans have near the Daxing airport. We've managed to encircle their operations by watching that safehouse for over a year now to see who comes and goes. It has been more important to see which CIA people frequent the place than to arrest anyone just yet. If Cousin Guang suggests another safehouse, it will be even better, as we'll put surveillance on that safehouse as well."

"Which team will do the surveillance?"

"This time the Poh Pohs—mostly retired State Security members. Grandmothers pushing baby strollers with a grandchild in it. A grandfather walking with a cane alongside his grandchild. Not a chance the Americans will suspect them. Don't make eye contact with anyone."

Yìchén's burner phone buzzed. He stepped outside the office in the long empty hall where it was quiet.

The caller's voice sounded as if it was Cousin Guang. "I will contact you at the Wudaokou subway stop tonight at eight o'clock. Can you make it?"

"Yes," Yìchén said.

"I'll reveal the address where we'll meet five minutes after you arrive at Wudaokou. Don't be late!"

He hung up, then walked back into Chen's office and told him what he had just learned, since it was expected of him.

"I'll alert the surveillance team to get on it right away," Chen said. "What fools the Americans are."

"I know. I'm smarter by far."

"The credit is not yours to take."

Yìchén stared at Chen, unbelieving. *How dare he treat me like this!* One day he'd get back at him. He hoped that day would come soon. For now, he decided a lie and bit of humility was needed, appealing to what he knew most MSS officers believed, even though he no longer did. "Only one thing is certain," he said. "There isn't a better intelligence service than the MSS in the whole world."

―――・✦・―――

It was dark outside when Yìchén left his apartment and headed to the subway stop at Qianmen. Virginia had again instigated an organized starburst of all available embassy personnel, spread out in all directions, hoping to confuse the MSS.

Following at a distance from Yìchén was a member of the Six: Rachel, who had chestnut hair and wore a black face mask, gray sweats and white Nikes. Chet saw her jog past an older couple but she didn't speak to them or make eye contact. Neither did Yìchén.

Yìchén ran down the steel-plated steps and put on his face mask and inserted his all-day ticket into the turnstile, then headed for the Blue Line 2 platform to catch the train going to Changchunjie. Rachel followed, wearing a face mask, but stopped to purchase a ticket.

"I'll follow from here," Chet said over the radio. He was dressed in a dark business suit and tie and wore yellow tinted glasses and a white face mask.

"Copy," Rachel said into the mic. "Heading to back of train car. Got your six."

Yìchén boarded the subway train and sat down in a seat near the door. Chet followed and took a seat on the opposite side of the car in close proximity, where he could observe him for any slight movements or signals without making eye contact.

A heavy-set woman dressed in olive green canvas pants, a light-blue face mask and a black sweatshirt hoodie, which covered her hair, began speaking out loud in Mandarin. This roaring Godzilla woman's tonal language sounded like shouting to a Caucasian like Chet, but most Chinese speakers sounded like that. What was worse, her cheap perfume wafted in the air, causing Chet to sneeze when she sat down next to him.

"By nature," she said loudly, "men are nearly alike; it is by custom and habit that they are set apart."

Yìchén's ears perked up. He stared at her quizzically.

The woman continued her rant, oblivious that no one was listening. "Yes, and everything has beauty, but not everyone sees it. Grandmother told me that. She was wise beyond her years. What a smart grandmother I have!"

Yìchén looked annoyed. "No, you're confused. It was Confucius who said that."

Chet sat in silence, feigning uninterest by searching for something in his newspaper while observing them both behind his yellow-tinted glasses.

The roaring Godzilla woman stared straight ahead. "Don't be obnoxious, young man. It was my grandmother. My grandfather said, 'What the superior man seeks is in himself; what the small man seeks is in others.'"

"Lady, my grandfather said the same thing, but he was quoting Confucius."

She ignored his comment and kept on talking. "In a country well governed, poverty is something to be ashamed of. My grandfather also said that. We should be ashamed of President Xi. He has not done enough for us."

Chet noticed Yìchén was hesitant to reply and wondered if it was because he knew there were cameras and listening devices on the subway. He was amazed when Yìchén finally said, "Old woman, shut the *fuck* up!"

Yìchén soon changed trains at Xizhiman to Line 4 Daxing Line and rode till the next stop to get on the Yellow Line 13, which would take him all the way to Wudaokou.

One stop further on the Daxing Line and he would've ended up at the Beijing Zoo where Chet figured Yìchén believed the roaring Godzilla belonged.

"*Zou Kai!*" the woman said when Yìchén got off at Xizhiman. She told him to "piss off."

Rachel reversed roles with Chet on the Yellow Line 13 to Wudaokou, sitting several passengers away from Yìchén. Chet radioed her and the rest of the Six and let them know about the dispute Yìchén had with the heavy-set woman and cautioned Rachel to watch for any further altercations.

Yìchén kept to himself and didn't interact with anyone the rest of the way. Good, he was "black." When he got off at the Wudaokou subway stop, he charged up the stairs from the platform and waited outside near the entrance for five minutes for the call from Cousin Guang.

Lana, Lily's twin, hovered near the entrance but she did not make contact with Yìchén and he did not notice her.

She whispered "It's on. He's black," into her mic, so Yìchén couldn't hear.

At exactly 8:00 p.m. Yìchén received a call on his burner phone. The caller did not identify himself, but it was the same voice as the other calls from Cousin Guang. He gave him directions to the safehouse where they were to meet.

The safehouse was located on Chengfu Road, not far from where China University of Geosciences and Beijing Language and Culture University could be found in the Haidian District.

The Haidian District is about the size of the borough of Queens in New York City and is the location of the majority of the top Chinese and international high-tech companies, as well as many wholesale electronics and computer parts companies. Lots of Chinese millennials frequented the area, as well as some young and some middle-aged foreigners. A Caucasian who occasionally wandered through would not feel out of place.

Several large student dormitories were on Chengfu Road. The safehouse was in a courtyard with six other apartments, surrounded by other courtyards exactly the same. The place was quiet and the street had a modest amount of traffic. The location was saturated with nearby apartment buildings, and a five-minute walk led to a shopping area with small clothing stores, a news stand, a drugstore called An Jian Xing, two supermarkets—Xueyou and Chaoshifa—and a few restaurants like Haoshi Spicy Hot Pot or Hangzhou Snack as well as a hardware store called Xinglong. Beyond that was the Wudaokou subway stop, where Yìchén was now walking from.

Yìchén strolled in to the safehouse and saw a familiar face and also a man he didn't know.

"Nice to see you again, Mary," Yìchén said to Virginia. His eyes smiled at her behind his face mask, knowing full well he planned to play hardball with her because she probably planned to play hardball with him. "And who are you?" he said, giving the man standing next to her a nod.

"You can call me Tom," Melvin said. "I'm here to help Mary."

"Are you a case officer?"

"I wouldn't say that, but I work closely with them."

"I see." He coughed.

"Did you bring the thumb drive?" Virginia said.

He shook his head. "No, I put it in the plastic bag along with the dog poop like you asked and dumped it in the trash can."

"You were followed. We never received it. You weren't 'black.'"

Yìchén could feel Virginia staring at him. *Probably to see my reaction.* He gave her a defiant stare and coughed again.

"How do you know?"

She ignored his response and answered him with another question. "Who was the elderly man you shared a joke with on the subway who gave you a nod when he got off at Ping'anli?"

"I swear I don't know him. I had never met him before."

"And the Japanese tourist? You didn't know him either?"

He coughed. "I have no idea who you're talking about."

"Is that so? Maybe a little lie detector test will refresh your memory."

Yìchén felt his heart rate spike. He needed to gain control of his mental state. Now. "Be my guest. I'm clean."

Melvin unlocked the suitcase he brought and put the machine on the table. He asked Yìchén to take a nearby seat.

Deep breath. Release the tension. He eased himself into the chair.

"It'll only take a few minutes to get you hooked up. Hold out your hands."

When Yìchén did, Melvin put a monitor on his index finger and ring finger of his left hand and also on the middle finger of his right hand as well as wires on his chest and above his stomach.

Yìchén watched the process as though it were happening to someone else. Someone else's hands were now connected to this machine. He could separate himself from this moment if he focused—answered the questions as though he were someone else completely.

"First, I'll ask you some general questions to get you acclimated to the machine," Melvin said.

Yìchén nodded. Chen had prepared him for this.

"What is your name and date of birth?"

"Yìchén Zhang. August 8, 1990."

"In what city were you born?"

"Shenzhen."

"Are you a communist?"

"Yes."

"Who do you work for?"

"The Ministry of State Security."

"Have you ever lied?"

Yìchén paused after each question to decide if the question was general or relevant. *This is a general question. He'll ask me something more specific later on. I should appear nervous now so he'll believe that I told the truth later.* He fidgeted in his seat.

"Yes, of course, I've lied." He could hear the scratch of the machine as he answered.

"Have you ever lied to your employer?"

"No." Again the buzz of the machine.

"Do you know the man you shared a joke with on the subway who got off at Ping'anli?"

Yìchén went to his happy place, thinking about something pleasant or positive, because he knew he needed to lie.

"No." The machine scratched again.

"Did you or do you know the Japanese tourist who talked to you at Beihai Park?"

"No." The machine buzzed like crazy.

"Are you lying now?"

"No." The machine reacted again.

"Are you a double agent?"

"No." Yìchén heard scratching again. He coughed. "Take this damn thing off me. I swear I am telling the truth. Your questions are ridiculous. Why would anyone jeopardize his family, his country, and his health when he is treated as if he is the lowest scum on earth? I don't deserve this. I refuse to give you any more information unless I get a visa and plane ticket to America."

"I'm afraid that's not possible," "Mary" said. "We need proof of your commitment."

"You'll get all you want in due time. If I stay here, you get nothing."

"That wasn't the deal we made and you know it."

He coughed again. "I drive a hard bargain, but I assure you I am worth it."

"Mary" appeared to keep her temper under control even though Yìchén was sure it made her furious. She glanced at Melvin.

She probably hopes I failed the polygraph.

He saw "Tom" nod to her. *It's probably a signal between them that I passed.*

She looked dumbfounded but quickly recovered.

"Okay," she said to Yìchén. "I promise you'll get them."

"Now you're talking," Yìchén said. "When?"

"I don't know when," she said.

He'd have to report this to Chen Pao. Yìchén stood his ground. "I need them now."

"Why?" she said.

"Because of my health condition."

"Tom is also a medical doctor. He can examine you today—take a blood test, check your weight and get a urine sample."

"How convenient. You people think of everything."

"We try to."

If they do a medical test, they might find out my illness isn't as bad as I portray it.

"And if I refuse the test?"

"No visa. No ticket."

"Sounds like blackmail."

"Call it what you want. We're not about to let you go unless you pass both tests. Do you understand?"

Yìchén gritted his teeth. He hoped Chen Pao would believe him when he reported this. He also hoped his mother would not be harmed.

May 2020

CHAPTER 10

Jenny continued to sort and closely examine the Lius trash each day in an empty garage in King County. There hadn't been anything unusual for some time now. Today, however, she came across a brochure for the San Juan Islands. She reported her "find" to Dave that evening, over glasses of Chardonnay they shared in the living room.

"Do you suppose they are planning a vacation?" Dave said, taking a sip of the wine.

"Considering how frugal they are, I would be surprised. Didn't you say your surveillance team decided they go to Home Depot every week for the free cup of coffee?"

"I did, but why in the world would a Boeing engineer do something like that? It just doesn't make sense."

"I never imagined how invasive going through someone's trash could be. I know more about the Lius than I know about myself."

"Speaking of knowing about yourself, I received my DNA test results today."

"And?"

"They surprised me. I'm only eight percent Greek."

"What? You're kidding, right? With a name like Kamakaris, how could that be?"

"I know. I'm thirty percent German, twenty-seven percent English and tiny bits of everything else."

"Asian, too?"

"No, not Asian. A minestrone mix of mostly Europe, including a micro smattering of Eastern Europe and Russia."

"Fascinating. I wonder what my test will show."

"I didn't know you decided to do one."

Jenny sipped her wine. "I sent my sample in about a week or two ago. I should get the results back soon. After hearing about yours, I can't wait to see what mine are."

"New topic," Dave said. "How 'bout we go over to Alki Beach tomorrow night. We could go for a run along the trail and then I could make a campfire for us. It'd be a nice way to end the week. Whaddya say?"

"Sounds like a great idea. I'll bring a bottle of Beaulieu Vineyards Cabernet and some French Basque Ossau-Iraty cheese along with whole wheat crackers for us to eat."

"And I'll bring Pax and my guitar. On second thought, maybe I'll also bring my boat. I've got an eighteen-foot Adirondack Guideboat, I made myself that we could use to navigate around Elliot Bay."

The boat he talked about looks similar to a canoe but was propelled by oars rather than by paddling, and was made out of western red cedar with chevrons made out of alternating pieces of ash and walnut running the length of the boat. The paintings on the oars depicted scenes from the North Woods and were hand-painted by Julie Hewitt, an artist from Virginia Beach.

Although I don't want a man to take care of me, there's nothing wrong in wanting to spend time with him.

"I'd love that. Sounds fun."

"It's a date then. I'm heading off to bed. See you in the morning."

"You too," she said as she got up from her chair, put her wine glass on the kitchen counter, and headed to her separate bedroom.

Friday came, and after Jenny put in another grueling day going through the Lius' trash and coming up empty, she changed into blue running shorts and a slim-fitting white t-shirt. She checked her email and saw a reply from LineageFinder.com, clicked on it and could not believe the results of her DNA test. They must've made some mistake. She was sure of it. Right now, she needed to hurry and meet Dave at Alki Beach. She made sure Daisy had enough water and food, then gathered the bottle of cabernet as well as the cheese and crackers and wine glasses into a canvas tote bag and raced out the door.

Dave, dressed in an olive-green t-shirt and gray sweat running shorts, was waiting in his car in the parking lot with Pax and the Adirondack Guideboat when she arrived.

"Hi, Jen. Let's go for a run before we take the boat out," Dave said, smiling, as he got out of his car to greet her. "Come on, Pax!"

"Great idea!"

He put the leash on the dog. "Let's go, Pax! Atta boy!"

"Race you the first three hundred meters," Jenny said.

"Oh, yeah?" Dave said. "You'll be kicking up my dust."

"Nuh uh. You'll see."

They both took off running, with Pax at Dave's side. Dave managed to get ahead of Jenny, but she soon caught up and overpowered him.

"Okay," he said. "Stop. Stop. You got me. Let's slow down so we can talk. Oh shit! I just got a text. What the hell does *she* want?"

He stopped to read the text.

"Who's it *from*?" Jenny said as she slowed to a leisurely pace.

"The old ball and chain—my ex-wife. I'll deal with it later. Right now, my focus is on you. Let's talk."

Jenny smiled. "So, tell me how your day went."

"The surveillance team and I followed the Lius to the gym again this morning. They play racquetball and pretty much keep to themselves. Didn't see them interact with anyone except the trainer. How was *your* day?"

"Uneventful as far as the Lius' trash is concerned, but I got my DNA results today from LineageFinder. It was very upsetting."

"How so?"

"It shows I have different biological parents. My mother's name is Mei, not Peggy. My father's name is Bo, not Edward." Her voice was low. "I must have been adopted. I love my adoptive parents but I feel sort of betrayed by them." She sighed.

"Oh my God! That's hard to believe."

"I know. Is LineageFinder ever wrong?"

"I dunno. Never heard that they were ever wrong. I'd suggest asking your parents."

He probably forgot what I said about them. No use making a big deal of it.

"I think I told you Mom is dead. I still miss her and wish she were alive so I could ask her. Dad is in a memory care facility. I doubt he'd remember who I was, much less be able to tell me he was not my real father. Plus, I don't know if I want to trouble him with the news if he's managed to keep it from me all these years."

"Well, he might die, and then you'll never know the truth."

"I just can't believe my parents would lie to me for thirty years."

"I'm so sorry, Jen."

There was a comfortable silence until Pax barked at a passing dog.

"Let's talk about something more pleasant," Dave said, reigning in Pax on his leash.

"You always seem to have a happy outlook on life," Jenny said, smiling.

"I've lived a decent life so far. Besides, it's a hellava lot more fun enjoying life rather than brooding about the bad times."

"Agreed. Whaddya say we head back and take that boat ride you promised me?"

"Deal. Let's go before the sun goes down."

When they got back to Dave's car, the sun was beginning to set over Elliot Bay. The Seattle coastline shimmered in the waning light. Dave unhitched the boat from the trailer, then installed a temporary center thwart before flipping the boat over and putting it on his shoulders to carry it.

"Hey," Jenny said, "do you want some help? It must be heavy."

"Nah, it's only about ninety pounds. Piece of cake! I'll let you carry the oars, though."

He put it in the water, and Jenny and Pax climbed aboard. Jenny and Dave sat on either end, ten feet apart, facing each other, with Pax on the floor of the boat between them.

While Jenny sat in her seat enjoying the show, Dave used the oars to row the boat out from the shoreline, using the back-stroke. Since he couldn't see where he was rowing, he relied on Jenny to tell him which way to steer.

"To your left. I can see your muscles are going to ache after this," Jenny said, while Pax stood on all fours and barked at the ferry-boat passing by further out.

"I've always said, you're as young as you act. I'm fourteen, by the way."

"Mentally fourteen, maybe, but keep rowing, Hercules!"

"I resemble that remark."

Jenny grinned. "In your dreams, Davy Crockett!"

"You're being about as subtle as a ton of dynamite in a hot tub full of habanero chili."

"And you're being about as pleasant to be around as a skunk on steroids."

"Touché. Girl after my own heart." Dave blew a kiss in her direction.

Dave rowed for another twenty minutes, and then they enjoyed the peacefulness of floating aimlessly in the water, with only the sounds of the lapping waves against the boat and the slight creak of the oars.

"This reminds me of the song I heard on the radio on the way out here," Dave said.

"That jazzy one you told me about yesterday?"

"Yeah. Peter White. 'Here We Go.' That song reminded me of the dream I had of hiking in the Sierras without a care in the world. I'm absolutely loving the wonderful, love-filled, carefree image."

She smiled. "Me too."

"There's an alto saxophone in the song. There's also a killer bassline that I would love to play, but I'd need a five-string bass to play it. My bass only has four strings. Speaking of guitars, don't let me forget to get mine out of the car."

I can't believe how much fun and entertaining Dave is. He's also one of the most kind and thoughtful men I've ever met. She felt she had been wise to drop her guard around him. In a matter of weeks, her trust problem seemed all but gone. *But why do I still have that gut feeling that comes from being abandoned? Will I ever get over it?*

Right now, she relished being the object of Dave's affection. Besides, her clock was ticking. She was thirty years old and had always wanted a family. If she didn't start now, it might never happen. It was too soon to see if this relationship would ever go anywhere. Dave had told her he never wanted to be married again. He said it was a jail sentence. *What would it take to change his mind?*

It was dusk when they headed back to shore. Dave hitched up the boat to the trailer while Jenny retrieved the canvas tote bag from the trunk of her car, which contained the wine, cheese, crackers and wine glasses in it. She also took a blanket for them to sit on.

Dave had brought along some good-sized western hemlock branches to start a campfire with, which he unloaded at Alki Beach. Beach fires were only allowed in designated fire rings and were available on a first-come, first-served basis. Dave lucked out, finding a perfect spot. Fires needed to be completely doused by 9:30 p.m. but that wouldn't be a problem for Jenny and Dave.

Pax followed closely on Dave's heels, sniffing the fire ring and putting his mark on it before Dave began building the fire. Dave pulled the smallest twigs off the branches and squashed them into a ball for tinder. He took slightly larger twigs, breaking them into pieces, then placed them over the tinder in the shape of a tent. He used a moderate amount of kindling at first so air could get to the tinder.

"Back when I was in Boy Scouts, you couldn't pass Tenderfoot unless you could get a fire started using no more than two matches."

"I have a question. Why don't you simply use a lighter?"

Dave's chin fell. He stared incredulously at Jen, then looked up to the sky and said, "Lord Jesus. Please watch out for this poor woman." He cleared his throat. "Can't always rely on a lighter. It may not work. If you can't rely on one, you need to go back to a more traditional method of starting a fire."

"Well, if tradition is all that important to you, why don't you rub two sticks together?"

An amused Dave rolled his eyes and sighed. "That will be your next assignment if I am besmirched any further."

Jenny immediately regretted her impulsive words. Tonight was not about competition or one-upmanship. If she didn't watch it, she would end up spoiling what promised to be a very romantic evening.

"I'm sorry. I didn't mean that. My adoptive mother—God rest her soul—would hate me for saying this, but I probably sound like her."

Dave nodded. "Apology accepted."

She spread out the blanket near the fire ring. "I think I'll open the bottle of wine and pour us a glass. Did I tell you it's a 2013 Georges Latour?"

"You speak my language. Good year for Beaulieu Vineyards."

There was now a bed of glowing embers at the base of the fire, so Dave started putting on larger pieces of wood. He sat down on the blanket by Jenny and shared a glass of cabernet. The wine had an uninhibiting effect on them, even made them both a little woozy, a little drunk with love. Dave went back to his car and got his guitar. Pax followed him.

Jenny felt a touch of angst. *Oh no. I hope he doesn't sing another song like the last one he sang, 'I Wanna Take Care of You.' What a way to ruin a perfect evening! Be kind, Jenny. This too shall pass.*

When Dave came back with the guitar and Pax, Jenny said, with dread in her voice, "What's it going to be this time? Another Jimmy Hill song?"

"The same song, but I rewrote the lyrics…just for you. I hope you like it." He started strumming his guitar and sang along.

You're like a little buttercup, a sweet pea

And I want to be there with you.

You'll have less stress and love to spare,

If I am there with you.

I can be your rock of strength when you're weak,

I'll always be there with you.

Show you good times when life gets bad,

I'll always be there with you.

Jenny's heart raced. She knew that music came from Dave's heart and it was meant for her and her alone. She couldn't remember when she had felt so loved as her heart was bursting with tender feelings for Dave. Not only did he light the campfire, but it was also as if he had suddenly lit a fire within her, a burning passion so fierce it would take an iceberg to put it out. She wondered what it would be like to kiss him.

He stopped playing, forgetting the wine and cheese for a moment, and moved within inches of her face. He took her head in his hands, and gently touched his lips to hers. It sent sparks through her. She could now see each star in the universe with clarity.

Then he kissed her harder, with more passion. She returned his kisses just as hard. It was as if they were afraid to stop, afraid the passion might die.

"Maybe we should continue this party at home," Dave said, breathless.

"Yes," Jenny said, breathing just as hard. "Let's do that."

In twenty minutes, Dave and Jenny were at the Bureau safehouse next to the Lius. Once inside, Dave took Jenny's hand and led her into his bedroom. She felt lightheaded, savoring the buzz from drinking the wine as well as being intoxicated with love.

The wine also made Jenny giddy. "What would you do if I claimed sexual harassment, Boss Man?" she said, giggling and kissing Dave, while he began undressing her.

"I'm not your boss. Besides, a pretty girl like you would never do such a thing," he said, kissing her back, as he unsnapped her bra and slipped off her panties. "God, you're gorgeous!"

"You're not so bad yourself," she said, as she slid off his t-shirt, sweatpants and underwear.

Dave looked up at the ceiling. "Good Lord! Please watch over this poor woman if she thinks that."

Jenny laughed. *He's so entertaining.*

The night couldn't have been more perfect. A full moon shone through his bedroom window. He pulled the shade down and then threw back the sheets and blankets on his bed and they laid upon it, sharing his pillow.

"I love this, do you?" he said, caressing her breasts and kissing her neck. It was obvious to Jenny the sight of her pale breasts sent flare flashes through him. His breathing became ragged.

She moaned softly and caught her breath, stirring emotions in her she had never felt with another man. She looked at him and could not see any flaws. He was so damned attractive—the looks, the personality, the humor. Even so, she was surprised by the overwhelming longing inside her for him. It was not as if she could turn it off like you turned off a faucet. There was no stopping her passion now. All she wanted to do was devour his mouth, devour his love.

"Yes, I do," she said, breathless. Her face touched his and she moaned again, kissing him from his chin to his ears.

He rolled on top of her, fondling her.

"I love you," he whispered in her ear. "I never thought I'd say that again to another woman, but I can't hide my feelings for you."

It felt so right. He was like a big cuddly teddy bear and the best friend she had always wanted. She laid her bald "chemo-head" down on one side of his pillow.

"I love you, too, Dave," she whispered back, breathing hard. Her mind raced with thoughts of their hot, sweaty sex.

He cupped her face with his hands and kissed her hard with a passion so hot it almost frightened her. She gasped for breath as she gave in to him. Then several minutes later, after what felt like an eternity, their lovemaking was over. She couldn't remember when she had felt so utterly satisfied.

They continued to hold each other, cuddling, not moving, realizing the gravity of what had just transpired between them. Their relationship was forever changed.

In the middle of this tender moment, which Jenny later attributed to Dave wading into one of his loony spells because of a full moon, and just when Jenny drifted away on lovely dreams, Dave said, "Wanna hear my favorite poem?"

She sighed, leaned back on his shoulder, and closed her eyes. "Go ahead."

Then he cackled the poem:
The big gray wolf howls at the sky.
He wonders what, then wonders why.
Should I laugh, or should I cry?
I think I'll just unzip my fly.

Jenny sat straight up in bed. "That does it!" she said. "After that shoddy little ditty, I *am* going to claim sexual harassment!"

Dave glanced at her, stunned, but when Jenny smiled, he burst out laughing.

May 2020
CHAPTER 11

Amanda Casey, a CIA case officer from headquarters, who spoke fluent Mandarin, was designated to pick Yìchén up at SeaTac, the largest airport in the Pacific Northwest, and debrief him since she had years of experience in debriefing Chinese nationals. However, at the last minute, Amanda came down with Covid, so the CIA scrambled to find a quick substitute. Information in their data base pointed to Fred Ainsley as a likely candidate since he also spoke Mandarin and was based in Seattle.

Fred was a veteran case officer with weather-beaten skin, deep lines on his face and the body of a seasoned football player. He waited for face-masked Yìchén outside the gate. He had no trouble spotting Yìchén as he looked exactly like the profile picture in his file.

Fred introduced himself as Mort, exchanged pleasantries through face masks, and headed out of the baggage area. Fred placed a wad of Skoal wintergreen snuff tobacco in his mouth between his cheek and gum as he and Yìchén ducked into a black SUV, trying to get out of the rain.

While hardly a day went by without Seattle residents being reminded of the rain's presence, it became so commonplace that almost no one ever took notice and most didn't even use an umbrella or wear a raincoat. They knew it would soon pass. Life went on as usual. Just a minor inconvenience Fred told Yìchén he would need to get used to.

As Fred, aka Mort, drove north on I-5 towards Vancouver, BC, Yìchén cracked open a window.

"Ahh, fresh air. It feels moist. What is that scent I smell?"

"Evergreens," Fred said, "and fresh cut grass. You'll notice on each side of the road there is lush greenery, including many different kinds of deciduous trees, as well as moss which gathered on the popular wooden siding of Seattle homes."

"Nice," Yìchén said. "I think I'll like it here."

When they reached the city of Burlington, they caught State Route 20, heading west to Anacortes, where they drove through the town and followed ferry signs that said the San Juans.

"How many islands are there?" Yìchén said.

"One hundred and seventy-two," Fred said. "The four largest are Lopez, Shaw, Orcas and San Juan."

Fred had instructions to keep Yìchén awake and debrief him immediately, depriving him of much needed sleep, in order to squeeze as much information out of him as possible. The Agency had long ago learned that when you're tired you make mistakes and sometimes say something you shouldn't.

He tried his best to keep Yìchén stimulated by pointing out interesting facts. "Some of the smaller islands are inhabited by only one person or less," he said dryly. "There are private homes on those islands which can only be reached by a private plane or a boat. Others house wildlife sanctuaries or university-run studies."

"What's the population?" Yìchén said, yawning.

"Shaw's got a population of one hundred sixty-five; the others have between two thousand to seven thousand residents. We're headed to Orcas, which has a population of four thousand, five hundred—the last stop on the ferry ride."

Yìchén yawned again. He suffered from jet lag and looked like he wanted to lie down and go to sleep, but Fred kept him awake with his nonstop chatter.

After paying the toll at Anacortes, a ferry attendant directed Fred to line up his SUV behind others in Lane 3, one of twelve long rows. To their left were large department store delivery trucks, a U-Haul truck, several large vans and a cement mixer truck waiting to be loaded onto the ferry. To their right were heavily forested evergreens interspersed with a variety of leafy green trees on the island in the distance.

Less than five minutes later, Fred and Yìchén heard the loudspeaker announce that the ferry going to Lopez, Shaw and Orcas islands was now boarding. Fred followed the line of cars onto the second floor of the white-painted steel ferry-boat called Kaleetan.

The ferry chugged its way first to Lopez Island. Yìchén and Fred got out of the car and stood by the side taking pictures, but the only thing they saw was water and a forest-covered island.

"Bill Gates owns a home on Shaw—the next island," Fred pointed out. "However, it became known as 'the nuns' island,' because Franciscans lived there till 2004, and it still has Benedictines as well as a small contingent of the Sisters of Mercy."

"What is a nun?" Yìchén said, yawning again.

"Oh, I guess you wouldn't know, would you? Well…they are celibate single women in a religious order. I just named three religious orders: Franciscans, Benedictines and Sisters of Mercy."

After what seemed like an interminably long ferry ride to Yìchén, they finally arrived at Orcas. Yìchén's eyelids heavy, he seemed beyond tired, yet remained polite enough.

Fred drove the SUV off the ferry and up the hill where he turned left onto a winding and hilly road that crossed farm pastures with goats, sheep and/or cattle and certain areas with tall evergreens and a leafy variety that arched the road.

He continued on this road, following the string of cars that came from the ferry for about twenty minutes, driving through the town of Eastsound, where there were a couple restaurants, gift shops, a few banks, and some gas stations. They followed Main Street, going past a gas station, then turned right at the stop sign, making another right into the Rosario Resort.

"The resort was originally built by a wealthy Seattle shipbuilder and later Mayor of Seattle named Robert Moran," Fred said as if he was a tour guide. "He purchased over seven thousand acres of land on Orcas Island in the early 1900s to build his retirement home, which he called Rosario. It's spread out over thirty waterfront acres and was turned over to the public in 1960."

Yìchén let go another yawn. "How many rooms?"

"Almost ninety."

"What do they rent for?"

"Anywhere from two hundred to four hundred dollars a night—in season, of course. Yours will be in the latter price range. It's also got a three-hundred-person meeting place. You'll be amazed at the spectacular waterfront. If you ever get bored, there's also mountain biking, yachting, sail boating, whale watching, kayaking, tennis, a spa, and deep-sea diving and fishing."

Yìchén's eyes widened at the scenic view as Fred parked the SUV. For added privacy and security, the Agency had reserved the exclusive Cliff House on the Rosario estate, also known as the Rosario Suite. It was a separate cottage on the cliff near the Moran Mansion facing Cascade Bay and had all the amenities—TV, kitchen, fireplace, oversized bathtub, four-poster bed and a stunning bay view.

From the outside, it looked boxy, uninviting, even sterile, but the inside was decorated with bright, warm colors—gold couch with blue-and-gold-striped pillows, blue-and-gold-striped dinette chairs, a bamboo wardrobe and a bedspread with a yellow, green, blue and gold collage of trees and animals.

Fred helped Yìchén put his suitcases in the Rosario Suite and peppered him with non-threatening, open-ended questions to get him feeling comfortable and relaxed.

"Whaddya think of this place and America? Isn't it everything you imagined it would be, or do you miss Beijing already?"

Fred spit his wad of tobacco in a small wastebasket by the desk in the living room area, then took out his can of chew, pinched another portion and stuck it in his mouth. Yìchén winced at the disgusting habit but kept a blank look on his face.

I'll bet Yìchén figures that I'll leave soon and all he needs to do is stay calm and act polite.

"It's better so far. Just the fresh air alone. You might know I have health issues because of Beijing's pollution. You'll notice I don't seem to be coughing. I think I'll like it here as soon as I get acclimated to this new culture."

"How'd your family react when you told them about your move?"

"My mother was happy for me. Parents always want a better life for their kids."

"Kids? Hell, I thought you were an only child."

He yawned. "I am now. I'm a product of the one-child policy in China." There was pride in his voice. "I was born in 1990; the policy officially ended in 2016."

"Is it true that most people in China wanted boy babies?"

"Yes. Of course. Boys have more opportunities to earn money."

"Is it also true that Chinese officials knew when a girl's time of the month was and watched all women to see if and when they got pregnant?"

"My mother tried to hide it because she was pregnant with twins, but the state found out and took one of the babies away."

"Hell, that must've devastated your mother. What happened to the baby?"

"I have no idea. Just glad it wasn't me. My parents would have had to pay a hefty fine if they had kept it. I agree with the one-child policy. I grew up with total attention from my parents. Who wouldn't want that?"

Fred remained tight-lipped and smiled. *That dirty little bastard!*

Yìchén kept talking. "Besides, China is far advanced of America in collecting health information on its citizens. The technology is there. Why not use it?"

"Hell, most Americans'd be horrified that a government would know their personal medical information. They'd consider it an invasion of privacy."

Yìchén scoffed. "They're not living in the twenty-first century."

"You mean because of those damn apps that track your health?"

"Americans are easily fooled. One swipe or like at a time. It won't be long until China can glean health information on every citizen in the whole world."

Fred stifled the impulse to say "you little turd" and for once kept it professional. "You sound as if you're in favor of it."

"I have no preference really," he said, yawning again. "To me it's a fact of reality."

Yìchén looked like he'd fall asleep any minute now, but Fred continued peppering him with questions. He moved on to more serious topics now that—in Fred's eyes, at least—Yìchén seemed more relaxed and trusting.

"So, what did you bring us? Anything good?" Fred said.

"Most of it is all up here." He pointed to his head.

"That's horseshit!"

Yìchén glared at him with a stern look on his face. Clearly he was displeased but he remained polite.

"I have a thumb drive in my suitcase."

"I'll wait till you get it," Fred said.

"What I'd really like to do is get some rest. It was a long flight and I'm exhausted."

"In due time. Now, if you don't mind…"

He opened one of his suitcases and searched but couldn't find it. "It must be in the other one. Are you sure this can't wait?"

"I have all day."

Yìchén rummaged around in his suitcase and unloaded some items from it onto the carpet.

"Is that a Go board?" Fred said as Yìchén pulled a game from his suitcase.

"We call it *Weiqi*."

"I don't care what the fuck you call it. I'll challenge you to a game," Fred said.

"*You* know how to play?"

"I do."

"I've never played it with an American before."

"I'm sure I'd give you a run for your money."

"And what exactly do you mean by *that*?"

"It's an age-old expression. It means I might beat you."

He gave Fred a quizzical look. "Fat chance. I've played since I was little."

Fred smiled like a sadistic dictator.

Yìchén grimaced.

"Okay, give me a chance to get rested up, Mort, and I'll play a game with you." He unloaded more items, then searched in the pockets of the suitcase.

"Here it is." He handed the thumb drive to Fred.

"What's on it?"

"The same thing I put on the thumb drive that you Americans said you never got—proprietary information about Facebook's algorithms as well as a political assessment of Kentucky Republican Senator and Minority Leader Mitch McConnell's chances for reelection—plus, I added some strategic cyberspace plans. It was all I could get on such short notice. The rest is up here." He pointed to his head again. "I assure you my memory is almost photographic."

"I told you that was horseshit!"

"Then give me another handler. I refuse to deal with you!"

"I'm afraid you're stuck with me, cowboy."

It was clear from the expression on Fred's face he immediately regretted his words. He needed Yìchén to tell him about the activities, targets, equipment and personnel of the MSS. He tried a softer approach since a good relationship between a defector and his handler depends on trust and mutual respect.

"I have a bad headache," Yìchén said.

Fred gave him a Tylenol.

After taking it, Yìchén immediately vomited.

Fred's medical training kicked in. "Oh my, God!" he said. "I've seen that reaction before. You're probably allergic to Tylenol. Try this aspirin instead." He tried to hand it to him, but Yìchén refused it.

"I don't want anything you have to offer me. I'd rather suffer the pain."

Fred backpedaled. "I didn't mean to be unappreciative, Yìchén. The information you've given us has been incredibly invaluable. If it weren't for your help, why, we'd truly be at a loss of understanding between our two countries. There's plenty of time to go over that later. I've been given authorization to resettle you here in Seattle. You'll get used to the rain after a while. We'll go over housing options tomorrow. For now, you just need to get some rest."

Most resettlement cases did not get to choose where they wanted to live. That was decided at CIA headquarters and they determined it would be best for Yìchén, to live in Seattle's Beacon Hill where there was a large concentration of Chinese-born residents. But because Eastside's population included more people born in China than Seattle, officials decided he should live in one of the South Bellevue neighborhoods.

There were three possible neighborhoods—Eastgate, Somerset or Factoria. Of the three, Somerset was the highest priced, Eastgate medium range, and Factoria, the lowest. The CIA, through a retired FBI-agent-turned-realtor, found a four-bedroom house built in 1958 in Eastgate that rented for just under $3,000/month and a two-bedroom condo built in 1981 in Factoria that rented for less than $2,400/month.

It was no surprise that the U.S. government preferred the more reasonably priced property. It may have been a seduction at the beginning, but after Yìchén defected, he was at the Agency's mercy. Officials wisely decided to give Yìchén a choice to create the illusion that it wasn't being forced upon him.

The next day Fred stood nearby Yìchén at the Cliff House at the Rosario Resort as he helped him take a tour of each property on Zillow using his laptop.

"What was your home like in Beijing?" Fred asked. Fred was on his best behavior since he almost blew it with Yìchén yesterday.

"It was government housing. In Qianmen. What I liked most was that it was located near a shopping district."

"Factoria has the most shops," Fred pointed out. "Factoria Square Mall has a famous clothing store called Nordstrom's Rack, a drug store called Rite Aid and a low-cost department store called Target. There are also many strip malls nearby as well as an Asian market grocery store called Jing Jing."

"What is a strip mall?"

"It's a small shopping mall full of stores and restaurants typically in one-story buildings with nearby parking."

"So, what's Eastgate like?" Yìchén said.

"Mostly a residential area, but it also has some chain restaurants like Sonic Drive-In, Pizza Hut and Outback Steakhouse as well as a Starbucks."

"Hmm. I'd like the extra space, but the condo is newer as opposed to the sixty-year-old house in Eastgate."

"And the condo is closer to more shops. Plus, you might stand out more in Eastgate, whereas most people in Factoria keep to themselves. But it's really your choice."

"Isn't there anything else?"

"There's not a lot on the market right now, and these will be rented quickly if we don't act fast."

"Okay, I guess I'll take the condo."

He found out later LineageFinder headquarters was conveniently located a short distance away in northeast Bellevue on 110th Avenue. Chen Pao would be pleased.

After the deposit was made along with the first month's rent, Yìchén spent time furnishing it. He capitalized on the open and natural lighting in the living room's vaulted ceiling and chose a modern décor with sleek, clean lines—an uncluttered look. As a contrast to the hickory floors, he selected an off-white neutral color for his flat-pack sofa and chair. Above his fireplace, he hung a huge Miró framed print with a geometric shape floating against a celestial blue background. On another living room wall, he hung an oversized mirror.

When he finished filling his apartment, he turned his attention to finding transportation and, with his savings, bought a brand-new silver SUV so he could explore the nearby mountains. His next priority was sending a signal to Beijing to let them know he ended up in Seattle and would try to get information on LineageFinder. After that, he'd see about getting a pet.

May 2020

CHAPTER 12

The Special Agent in Charge (SAC) of the FBI's Seattle field office was retiring and a friend held a retirement party dinner in his honor at the thirty-eight-story century-old Smith Tower in downtown Seattle. Guests included anyone who had known or dealt with him over the past twenty years which included veteran CIA cases officers, including Donald Hughes and Fred Ainsley, and rookie FBI agents from the local field office, like Jenny.

The Observatory Restaurant & Bar, with its 360-degree views of Seattle, was located on the thirty-fifth floor of the Smith Tower and had room for eighty guests. The mood was festive and the crowd loud and boisterous. Most wore face masks. Jenny stood at the bar and ordered a glass of Chateau Ste. Michelle Chardonnay. She took off her mask, swirled the wine around in her glass and sniffed the pleasant aroma.

Dave chose his usual glass of Cabernet Sauvignon from Beaulieu Vineyards. Donald and Fred were drinking Manny's pale ale, which they chased with whiskey.

The food, served buffet-style, included the restaurant's signature deviled eggs—wasabi yoked egg, seared pork belly, and furikake—along with a main course of either smoked salmon or green curry chicken salad on a toasted sourdough baguette or miso beef on toast.

As luck would have it, Jenny and Dave found themselves at the same table as Fred Ainsley, a veteran case officer, who many referred to as "Fred Asshole." The reason quickly became obvious. After exchanging a few pleasantries, Fred launched into a tirade about his current assignment.

"I'm sitting in the Rosario Suite and I've managed to get this dumbass deplorable from one of the biggest countries in the world to spill his guts." He put a wad of Skoal snuff tobacco in his mouth and kept on talking. "One thing I'm good at—and I'm being modest—is breaking down people's defenses."

"How did you do that?" Jenny said, curious. She had heard of his reputation and wondered whether it was warranted.

"I just kept him awake. Wore him down. Pretty soon a motherfucker like that will tell you everything. Hell, you'd think I would've been promoted for it. But, no, headquarters didn't see it that way. Obviously, they don't know talent when they see it."

Boy, this guy really is full of himself, Jenny thought.

"How long have you worked for the company?" Dave said, trying to change the subject to something more pleasant and positive.

"Going on fifteen years. I've spent tours in Europe, the Middle East and Africa. This one is only temporary until I get reassigned somewhere else."

"How many languages do you speak?" Dave wanted to know.
"Five, including English. The others are French, Arabic, Mandarin and Russian."

"Jenny is fluent in Mandarin," Dave volunteered.

Jenny had lingering mixed feelings about being adopted—that discovery still gnawed at her emotions—but she was grateful, even proud, she learned Mandarin while growing up.

"Yes," Jenny said. "I grew up speaking it."

"*Wǒ hěn gāoxìng jiàn dào nǐ,*" Fred said. *I'm pleased to meet you.*

"*Kuàilè shì wǒ de*," Jenny answered. *The pleasure is mine.*

"Hey, I'll bet you know how to play the game Go." Fred said.

"Yes, you could say I'm familiar with it," Jenny said. "I've played it since I was a child. My parents called it *Weiqi*."

"Although I'm proficient at chess, I'm not very good at Go, I hate to admit."

"Where do you play it and with whom?" Jenny said.

"About the only club for it in the area is the Bellingham Go Club. They don't have a lot of members but sometimes have small meetups at different sites around the Seattle area. I have a date to play with the deplorable soon. Maybe you'd like to join us. Both of you, I mean."

"We're currently working on a hush-hush case," Jenny said. She turned to face Dave. "But we'd love to, wouldn't we, Dave?"

He nodded. "I'm about as good a player as you, Fred, but I think Jenny would give your guy a go for his money." He smiled. "No pun intended."

"Great, it's all set then. I'll text you with the details later. You should use your other identities, if you know what I mean."

Jenny raised an eyebrow.

"Hell, it doesn't hurt to be too careful," Fred said. "I've had many a case turn on me. The deplorable might be a double for all we know. I go by the name Mort."

"Nice to meet you, Mort," Dave said. "I'm Bret Haltgren and this is my wife, Charlotte."

I can see why he might've had a case turn on him, Jenny thought. *This guy is a truck with no brakes. Wonder what the deplorable guy thinks of him.*

———◆———

Later that week, Fred texted Jenny an address in Bellingham where a few members from the Bellingham Go Club, including Fred and Yìchén, were meeting to play some games. The downtown area was full of quirky shops and restaurants. The address Fred gave brought them to a 1924 white cottage-style house with dark brown trim on H Street in old Bellingham, near Broadway and Kearney Streets.

After heading up I-5 North from Seattle and driving eighty-nine miles, they reached Bellingham and parked the black SUV near the sidewalk out front, trudged up four cement steps to the small front porch and knocked on the door.

A young Chinese American man answered.

"Charlotte and Bret?" he said.

They nodded. Both wore black face masks.

"Come in. Fred told us about you."

"Well, look what the cat dragged in," Fred said as they entered.

Yìchén looked puzzled. "What? That must be an American expression," he said.

Fred's so old school, Jenny thought. *I bet he even irons his underwear.*

Jenny locked eyes with Yìchén. "Yes, it's said when someone arrives to express your dislike or disapproval of them, but I assume Fred is only teasing. Nice to meet you. I'm Charlotte." She held out her hand.

"Yìchén."

Even though both were wearing face masks, she felt an immediate chemistry with him but had no idea why.

The four of them were the only ones in the living room. Others occupied other rooms in the house.

"Let's switch partners," Fred said. "Charlotte is a much better player than I am. Yìchén, you play her and I'll play Bret."

"I've never played against a woman before," Yìchén said. "Since I'm probably the strongest player," he said, "I'll take the white stones and you can have the black."

"I wouldn't be so sure you're the strongest—we'll see—but I'm happy taking the black stones."

"Since you're the weakest player, you go first."

Jenny, aka Charlotte, placed her stone in the top right corner. Yìchén placed his next to Jenny's, with the hope of encircling her stones and taking prisoners, as well as filling in more empty spaces in order to control the territory.

Hiding her true intentions to keep Yìchén off balance, she began asking him questions to see if they had any common interests. The other reason was to get him to use up all his turns.

She held a black stone between the tips of her index and middle finger and placed it gently on a point on the board. "Where are you from?" she said.

"I was born in Shenzhen but spent most of my time in Beijing."

"What brings you here?"

"Fresh air. Also the American dream—to make money. How 'bout you?"

"I've lived mostly in Seattle. I like the music scene here. What type of music do you like?" she asked.

Jenny felt Yìchén liked her. He seemed to want to make a good impression. She noticed he had an eye on the board while he politely answered her questions.

He placed a white stone on the board while he talked. "My favorite is hard rock but I also enjoy rap music."

Jenny encircled his stones as she spoke. "I love rap music, too. Have you seen the Broadway musical *Hamilton* yet?"

She fought back tears, remembering she and her mother had planned to see it, yet she couldn't contain her excitement about the musical.

"I don't know what you mean by Broadway musical. I just arrived here a short time ago."

"It's a play that has music in it. The characters sing songs. In *Hamilton*, they sing rap songs. You'd love it. You'll have to get tickets to see it if it ever comes again to Seattle."

"Who or what is Hamilton?"

"He was a founding father of the United States who fought in the

American Revolutionary War, helped draft the U.S. Constitution, and served as the first Secretary of the Treasury. He was the founder and chief architect of the American financial system."

"I guess I'll need to read up on him, especially since I plan on becoming a citizen."

She smiled. "What's your favorite movie, Yìchén?"

"There aren't many American movies in China, but some that I liked were an adventure film called *Indiana Jones and the Temple of Doom* and a spy thriller called *Spy Game* that starred Robert Redford and Brad Pitt. Have you seen either?

"I share your love for the *Indiana Jones* movie. It's one of my all-time favorites. I haven't heard of the movie *Spy Game*. I don't think it was ever big in the U.S."

"It came out around 2001. It's still popular in China."

"What's it about?"

"Robert Redford is a CIA case officer who takes on a dangerous mission when he learns his former protégé and CIA operative, Brad Pitt, is a political prisoner sentenced to death in China."

Jenny was able to keep his attention and keep him off balance with her questions. Although the information she was gathering wasn't intelligence per se, it would help the Agency paint a clearer picture of him and was better information than Fred could provide them about Yìchén's personality. Besides, she found they had a lot in common. She also took three prisoners while he wasn't able to take even one.

After playing 100 stones, they approached the middle game. Jenny glanced at Dave, who was concentrating on his game with Fred. She continued to seek out her common interests with Yìchén.

"I'll bet now you're going to tell me your favorite book is *The Good Earth*."

He smiled. "I loved that book. It's one of the few American books China has no problem with."

After placing a black stone on the board, she asked, "What about art?"

He paused to answer her question before he put his white stone on the board. "I have a huge Miró framed print hanging on my living room wall. I also love impressionist paintings. I'd love to have an original Monet or Renoir, but I can't afford them."

I'm beginning to be spooked by this guy. We have so much in common.

"I inherited a Monet print after my mother died," Jenny said.

"What did she die from, if I may ask?"

"Car accident. I miss her a lot. I think of her every day. Are *your* parents both still alive?"

"My father died, but my mother is still alive."

Jenny kept encircling his stones as she talked. "Do you miss her?"

"I'm not a mama's boy, if that's what you think."

"I didn't mean that. I just think family is important, that's all."

"My parents wanted a better life for me." He looked away. "My mother is happy I moved to America."

"And you want to make her proud?"

"I'm my own person. I'm not living to make anyone else happy."

She smiled but kept a blank look on her face while she continued to encircle his white stones.

"That's a nice shirt you're wearing. I love the color red."

"Me, too. Red symbolizes luck, joy, and happiness in our culture. It's also worn by Chinese brides to ward off evil."

She smiled again and took a prisoner.

"What's your favorite food, Yìchén?"

"Anything hot and spicy."

"Have you been to Tian Fu?"

"No. I've never heard of it."

"It's a restaurant located in a strip mall on southeast Thirty-Eighth Street, not far from the Factoria Square Mall. It has authentic Sichuan food. Hot and spicy like you like. It's the only authentic Chinese restaurant in the area. It might remind you of Beijing."

"I live in Factoria. I'll check it out."

They were nearing the end game. Jenny wondered whether to let Yìchén win so that he didn't lose face. Or should she teach him a valuable lesson about the power of women? Maybe she'd rise in his estimation if she beat him. She decided to risk it. The next move was Jenny's. She passed. Yìchén did too.

Then each of them counted the number of unoccupied points surrounded by their stones and then subtracted the number of stones that were captured by the other.

Jenny, the clear winner, raised her eyebrows and smiled.

"You may have won this time, Charlotte," Yìchén said, "but I demand a rematch—and soon. Next week. My place."

"You're on," she said.

He gave her his address.

May 2020
CHAPTER 13

It was well after midnight when Jenny arrived at the safehouse near the Liu residence, as she had gone to the office to tell her boss and file a report to Fred, like he had asked, about her conversation with Yìchén so he could pass it along to the Agency. She undressed in a hurry, crawled into bed and snuggled up to Dave, who was snoring. He blinked open his eyes, gave her a hug, rolled over and went back to sleep. It wasn't long before she did also.

Morning came with light streaming in their bedroom window. Jenny woke up to Dave reaching for her.

"Good morning," he said, his voice sounding cheery.

She yawned. "What time is it?"

"Time to wake up. It's a new day! The sun is shining. The birds are chirping. I just heard the garbageman come and go, and a newspaper is waiting to be picked up on our front porch. Looks like another *great* day."

"So, what's on the agenda for today, Mr. Bossman?"

"I told you. I'm not your boss. How `bout I take you to dinner at the Il Bistro tonight?"

"Really? What's the occasion?"

"I have something important I want to tell you."

"What is it? Give me a hint."

"No, no, no. Not this time." He suddenly grew quiet.

Jenny's mind raced with wild thoughts. Il Bistro was well known as one of the three most romantic restaurants in Seattle. Was he planning to propose?

In addition to a date to play *Weiqi* with Yìchén again, Jenny was still assigned trash duty and scrutinized the Lius' trash each week in an empty garage in King County before it was dropped off at the dump. She wore a clean pair of khaki cargo pants and a long-sleeved purple sweatshirt with a Washington Huskies logo on it along with a black face mask to help avoid the smell. Like the previous weeks, with puncture-proof gloves, she opened the Lius' garbage bags and dumped them on a canvas tarp spread out on the floor.

As always, there were several bundles of wrapped newspaper with the remnants inside of a meal the Lius had eaten. Most were chicken bones. A few had tofu, rice and/or stir-fry vegetables. No dessert crumbs ever.

Next to several grocery receipts, there was a toilet paper roll, a gas receipt from Costco and a utility bill. The next item Jenny found was a paper Mr. Liu had written and torn into shreds. This piqued her interest because it was written in Chinese. Jenny pulled out the small squares, laid them out on a table, and pieced them back together.

Her eyes widened when she finished translating it. Clearly this was a shopping list for highly classified materials from Boeing that Mr. Liu was to supply to the Chinese government. She knew this list would be enough to convict Mr. Liu and put him and his wife in prison, where she felt they belonged. She'd tell her boss immediately but planned to give the good news to Dave tonight.

At 5:00 p.m. Dave drove the black SUV down to the heart of Seattle, where he and Jenny found a parking spot at Pike's Place Market, built in the early 1900s and the oldest public market still in use. A strong, salt-air, fish odor wafted through the market. It boasted over eighty varieties, which included mahi mahi, swordfish, and octopus. All were sold daily.

What a perfect night! No wind. No rain. A handsome man to have dinner with and he makes me feel like I'm the most beautiful woman he's ever seen, even though I still have a shaved head. It can't get any better than this. I'm sure he's planning to propose. Why else plan a dinner at Il Bistro?

Their vehicle was parked by a stall filled with a variety of citrus fruits and garden-fresh vegetables. As they walked past more stalls heading to the right, they came upon tulips, daffodils, and other dried varieties in silver buckets. The prices were very reasonable, and Dave asked Jenny if she would like some, but she declined, saying she didn't want to have to worry about carrying them.

The day's events ricocheted in her mind. *All my hard work is beginning to pay off. The boss was certainly excited to hear the news. I hope Dave will be too.*

Although he had been to Pike's Place Market many times before, Dave had never been to Il Bistro and found it difficult to locate. After they passed through the market stalls, they wandered over to the large, nearby Cutters Crabhouse restaurant, famous for its tantalizing seafood and spectacular view of Puget Sound sunsets and Olympic Mountains. After getting directions from someone there, they walked down a narrow renovated alleyway called Post Alley, where some ethnic restaurants were found—Kell's Irish Restaurant & Bar, a traditional Irish pub with live Celtic music, and the Copacabana, offering Bolivian cuisine.

They asked a waiter picking up broken bottles of beer outside the Copacabana for directions to Il Bistro, but he didn't understand much English, so they walked on. Finally, a passerby told them to go down some stairs and then to the left and then up to the right. There they stumbled onto a wall of graffiti, and across from it was a black sign with red pheasants, which touted the name, Il Bistro.

Jenny, in heels and a face mask, was grateful their search on the cobblestone alleyway was over. She turned around to face the alley and could hear voices echoing off the walls like she once heard on a gondola ride at the Bridge of Sighs in Venice. More distant, she could hear the buzz of the crowd at Pike's Place Market.

Entering the restaurant under the black sign with red pheasants, Jenny was greeted with something delightful, maybe a whiff of roasted lamb or fresh Dungeness crab. Whatever it was, she decided that dining in this restaurant would shock her taste buds into believing that good food was to be found only in small romantic settings.

Inside, the room had a soft glow to it. The lights were dimmed, and each round table had a white tablecloth on it, a glass with a lit candle in it and a vase with fresh flowers—pink and white tulips. Every detail was so perfect, Jenny felt like she was on a movie set.

There was something magical about getting dressed up, putting on one's best manners and dining in a romantic restaurant with a handsome man. Fairy tales were born of this. Most men in her life, like her father, were very businesslike and never got past her guard to find out she craved romance. Tonight was a night she would remember for a very long time.

A balding man with gold wire-rimmed glasses in a black-and-white checkered shirt came to take their order after they were seated. He could have easily been mistaken for a patron of the restaurant rather than a waiter. He introduced himself and asked if they wanted any wine or something else from the bar. Jenny ordered a Riesling and Dave ordered an expensive bottle of cabernet.

"I hope you like Italian food," Dave said, coaxing Jenny out of her daydreams. "I'm afraid I forgot to ask you."

"I knew it was Italian, and yes, I love Italian food. Good choice, Dave."

"So, what'll you have, sweetheart?"

"I think I'll have the rack of lamb marinated in rosemary and garlic with Sangiovese wine sauce. Or maybe the chicken breast."

"I want the cioppino. I love Dungeness crab, prawns, mussels and clams. My mouth is watering just thinking about the taste."

The waiter stopped by to take their order. They ate amid the seventy-five other patrons in the restaurant, totally unaware of anyone at the other tables. The food was superb. Many restaurants in Seattle cared more for presentation of the food than for taste or volume. Dave and Jenny thought Il Bistro's presentation was excellent, but they also liked the taste and it seemed to be the right amount of food.

"I have some news," Jenny said. "We won't need to live next to Charles and Elizabeth very much longer."

"We won't?" Dave looked puzzled.

"No. I found enough evidence today to convict both of them."

"That's great. Terrific news, really. I'd love to hear more about it when we're not in a public space." He raised his glass in a toast. "Congratulations!"

She reciprocated.

"Now tell me *your* good news." She smiled and looked at him expectantly. "The suspense is killing me."

He had a pained look on his face. "Jenny, I don't know how to tell you this, but here goes. I'm taking a leave of absence and moving back in with my ex-wife."

Jenny's core shook as if he had just dropped an atomic bomb. *He's abandoning me?* She wanted to run, but the fighter in her made her stay.

"What? How *could* you?"

"It's not what you think. She has cancer. It's terminal. She needs help."

Jenny didn't say anything.

"What was I supposed to do?" he said.

"What about *us*?"

His neck flushed beet red. "There will always be an 'us.' This is only temporary."

"Oh, like you expect me to wait around for you. How long will it be? What if she doesn't die?"

"Don't be cruel."

"I'm being realistic." She didn't tell him she felt nauseous this morning and suspected it might be morning sickness, although she hadn't had time to buy a pregnancy test from the pharmacy. She'd keep this secret for another time.

"I've finished dinner," she said. "Can we go?"

June 2020

CHAPTER 14

Yìchén checked online and found there was a shortwave radio site that anyone could use called the University of Twente in the Netherlands. But that would leave a footprint, which Chen Pao had advised him against doing. He took a trip to the library in northeast Bellevue on 110th Avenue, where he used a computer to find what he was looking for. He googled "shortwave radios to purchase" and found one on Amazon for thirty dollars. Now he just needed someone to buy it for him.

He was hungry and decided to have lunch at the Chinese restaurant Charlotte had recommended. Tian Fu on Thirty-Eighth Street. It operated in two shifts—the early one from eleven to three, and the late one from five to eight. The restaurant was located next to a dentist's office and a Jimmy John's sandwich shop. Across the street was a United Parcel Service package shipping store.

When Yìchén walked in wearing a face mask, he noticed there were only three customers in the restaurant—an older Chinese couple and a single man, a millennial, who was seated in the back of the room. A tall Chinese American young man, dressed in black pants and white shirt, smiled at him and said, "Right this way."

The thin man wore oversized black glasses, which Yìchén thought made him look intelligent. He stopped at one of many square tables with four large square heavy chairs—authentic furniture imported from China.

"Here we are," he said, as he motioned for Yìchén to sit. "Anything to drink?"

"Just water and tea."

"Very good. I'll come back and take your order when you're ready." The waiter went to the kitchen and was back at Yìchén's table several minutes later, bringing a napkin, a teacup and a glass of water without ice.

"Have you decided?"

"Yes, I'll have the Sichuan pork."

"Mild or hot?"

"Hot."

"It doesn't come with a side. Would you like rice or noodles?"

"Rice. Steamed."

He came back with the food as well as chopsticks.

"Enjoy your meal!"

"Before you go, I was wondering. Is this the only restaurant like it in Seattle?"

"If you're asking me whether this is a chain, the answer is no, but they are all owned by the same man. He named them all the same because it's better for advertising. The first one was in Redmond. There are currently four, but soon there will be six in the Seattle area." He smiled as if he owned the place.

"Is the owner from Sichuan Province?"

"No, but the chefs are."

"I'm from Shanghai." The waiter looked impressed which not only fed Yìchén's ego but also gave him the courage to continue asking questions. He was curious and wanted to know if the waiter had an interest in men, so he asked what he considered to be a non-threatening question. "What do you do in your time off?"

The wide-eyed waiter looked flabbergasted by the blunt question. "Excuse me?"

Now I've done it. I was too forward with him.

"I'm sorry. I don't mean to pry. It's just that I'm new here and haven't made many friends yet. Where's a good place to meet people?"

"Try the gym at the community center in Eastgate Park on Newport Way. It's not far from here."

"Thanks. I will."

After he finished his meal and paid for the food, Yìchén left the restaurant, got into his SUV and headed south on Factoria Boulevard and then turned left onto Newport Way. The snake-like street had clearly-marked bike path lanes and was lined with a variety of deciduous trees.

About ten minutes later he came upon a low sign on the right that said South Bellevue Community Center. He drove up the winding road to the top of the hill and parked his car in the good-sized parking lot.

He got out of his car and walked up the sidewalk to the gray-windowed entrance in the building with a light wood façade. Inside, he looked down from the roped-off balcony onto the reception area below. He saw a gold square chair and a brown boxy chair with an end table divider between them and like chairs opposite them.

He descended the stairs to the first landing and looked through tall windows on his right that overlooked a gym where two young men were playing a game. Yìchén had no idea what game they were playing but thought it was a cross between ping-pong, badminton, and tennis. It looked to him like a simple paddle game played with a small wiffleball. He hurried down the steps, wearing a face mask, and entered the gym to see what all the fuss was about.

"Hey," he yelled to one of the players. "What game are you playing? How do you play it?"

"Ignore him," a young guy on the opposite court said to the other. "You've got a dillball. Keep thwacking."

The other guy, also a teen, shook his head and walked over to where

Yìchén was standing on the side of the court. "Don't mind him," he said, giving a nod to his friend. "It's like tennis or ping-pong. Are you familiar with those?"

Yìchén nodded.

"The game is called pickleball. First one to score eleven points wins. Only the serving team can score points."

"How do they score points?"

"If the opponent doesn't hit the ball back or he wins the rally. Sort of like tennis. Where're you from? I don't recognize the accent."

"Shanghai. I just moved here. How 'bout you?"

"I grew up in Bellevue. I've lived here all my life. My name is John. What's yours?"

"Zimò." He made up the name on the spot.

"Care to play?"

"Thanks for the offer, but I don't think your friend would like it. I'll just watch for now."

They volleyed the ball back and forth when the young guy on the opposite court shouted, "Opa!"

John turned to Yìchén to explain as he kept whacking the ball across the net. "That means from now on it's okay to hit a ball out of the air. You're still forbidden to hit the ball into the kitchen—the seven-foot zone on either side of the net."

"Sounds confusing."

"It has some funny rules, but I'm sure you'll catch on quickly."

"Thanks for the tips."

"You're welcome. My opponent can be a little rude sometimes, but he's harmless. So, what brings you to the U.S.?"

"The opportunity to make money, like everyone else."

"What business are you in?" He kept thwacking the ball.

"Import and Export. I haven't started one yet, but I hope to soon."

John turned to Yìchén again and stopped playing. "I've heard you can make a ton of money in a business like that. You don't need a helper, do you?"

The open door I hoped for. Isn't he eager? This rich kid is probably bored with his life and wants a little excitement.

"I might." He arched an eyebrow. "Are you offering your services?"

He nodded. "I don't have anything else going on right now, so, yes."

"Listen, I need to purchase something on the internet and I don't have my computer set up yet. Is there a possible way you could get it for me? I'd pay you for it, of course."

"Sure. No problem. Let me know where and when."

Three days later, on Tuesday afternoon, Yìchén, aka Zimò, met John in the parking lot at the community center in Eastgate Park to pick up the shortwave radio which John had purchased for him from Amazon. Yìchén had chosen one that was Amazon's Choice in portable shortwave radios, which had over 6,000 positive reviews. The compact radio was so small it could fit in a shirt pocket and was built in five languages: Chinese, English, Spanish, Russian and Japanese.

The radio was capable of recording a voice; however, a TransFlash, or TF card—a memory card similar to an SD card, but smaller and more compact—was not included in the package, so he had also ordered that as well as an extended antenna. He gave John cash—twenty dollars extra for his trouble—and headed back to his condo in Factoria.

Yìchén sat down at his dining room table, took out the radio, and threw the box in the trash. The radio had a bandwidth of 4.75-21.85 MHz, and the instructions said reception was better at night or when an external antenna was connected. The instructions also cautioned to keep the radio away from fluorescent lamps, Wi-Fi, computers and TVs for best reception.

He planned to broadcast the same five-digit code numbers related to the message he was sending. He had been given the code on a one-time pad from Chen Pao in Beijing. He'd broadcast the codes tonight and every week at the same regular intervals—every Tuesday at 6:00 p.m. and 8:00 p.m., Pacific Standard Time (PST), —which meant it would be received on Wednesday at 1:00 a.m. and 3:00 a.m., Universal Time Code (UTC).

Listeners would first hear a set of gongs, like a grandfather clock, followed by a weird transmission of a metallic Chinese voice reciting what appeared to be a random set of numbers in Mandarin.

Although anyone in the world could hear the transmission, only Chen Pao in Beijing would be able to decode the numbers because Chen had the only other copy of the one-time pad.

Listening to a set of numbers over and over could be hypnotizing, if not downright infuriating because you didn't know what they meant. However, any rational person would not attempt to decode the numbers lest they become insane while trying to do so.

When Chen decoded the message, it would tell him where Yìchén ended up settling in America.

Yìchén remembered Chen telling him about a spy case in the U.K. where an agent was caught red-handed writing down messages in his kitchen while listening to a numbers station. Chen's warning to Yìchén was clear: "If you are ever caught, you'll need to prepare for the consequences, including jail time."

Yìchén was unwrapping the TF card when he heard a sudden knock on his door. He wasn't expecting anyone and wondered who it might be. He hustled to the front door to find out.

"Charlotte!" he exclaimed as he opened it. "What a surprise!"

"Can I come in?" Charlotte (aka Jenny), who wore a face mask, said after the shock registered on Yìchén's face.

Damn! Why did she have to visit right now? Will she see the shortwave radio? Damn! I wish I had put it away.

"Sure," he said, after a brief pause. "Come in. Come in." He ushered her inside.

"I was in the area and thought I'd stop and say hello, maybe play a game of *Weiqi* with you if you're not busy."

A drop of sweat rolled down his cheek. *We'll need the dining room table. How can I remove the radio from it without causing suspicion?*

"Sure," he said. "Please, have a seat. Let me just put a face mask on and clear off the table and get my magnetic game set."

His hands were shaking as he scooped off the radio from the table.

"I hope I didn't interrupt you listening to that," Jenny said, pointing to the radio.

"Not at all," he said, keeping the tone of his voice level so as to appear calm. "I can listen another time." *I hope she doesn't know it's a shortwave. What will happen to me if she finds out it is?* His hands were shaking as he put the radio in the hall closet and took out the game board and stones. Charlotte sat down at the table, her eyes following him the whole time, but she remained silent.

"Since you won the first game, thus making me the weakest player," he said, "I'll take the black stones and you can have the white. As you know, black goes first."

Yìchén placed his stone in the top left corner. Charlotte held a white stone between the tips of her index and middle finger and placed her stone next to Yìchén's.

Yìchén wondered whether, like his father, Charlotte's true intentions were to keep him off balance to get him to use up all his turns. No, he decided, she couldn't possibly be as smart as his father.

"Mort told me you worked for the MSS," she said, in a casual tone. "It must've been very interesting work. Can you tell me a little about that?"

With an eye on the board, Yìchén politely answered Charlotte's questions. Although she was just a housewife, he found her to be intelligent and curious, which had the effect of making him interested in impressing her with his knowledge. He placed a black stone on the board while he talked. "We recruited spies within an organization."

"What kind of organizations?"

"Like Facebook or Google."

"Interesting. What kind of people did you recruit?"

"Often, top-level people with vulnerabilities. Some had Chinese ancestors or other ties to China."

Charlotte was encircling his stones as she spoke. "Fascinating. What traits did you look for?"

"Greedy ones or someone who was down on their luck and suffering financial hardship. They weren't difficult to find. A lot of corporate traitors are motivated by power, greed, getting ahead or money. They'll do anything to realize the American dream or avoid bankruptcy."

Charlotte remained poker-faced and continued peppering him with questions. She also captured three stones while he wasn't able to take even one.

He told her details on Facebook's algorithms. He also mentioned a source for Boeing's new laser technology.

"I'm sure there were plenty MSS sources. It's not unusual for a foreign country to have sources inside the United States. I don't suppose you remember any of them."

"Yes, I do. Kathy Green, one of Facebook's executives and Charles Liu, a Boeing engineer."

Normally he wouldn't be this voluntary with information to a total stranger—especially an American—but the commonality between them had him trusting her despite his head not making sense of it yet. She was a curious soul, probably hadn't encountered anything enticing in a very long time.

After placing a white stone on the board, she said, "Well, again, I'm not surprised. Tell me more about the secretive MSS. Were you in the division that had the most clout?"

He paused to answer her questions before he put his black stone on the board. "The MSS is organized by bureaus. There are seventeen bureaus, ranging from number one, the Confidential Communication Division, which is self-explanatory, to number seventeen, the Enterprises Division, which operates and manages MSS-owned front companies. Bureau number one has the most clout."

"Which bureau were you in?"

"Three. The Political and Economic Division."

She nodded in approval. "Who did you say your boss was?"

There's no way this will get back to Chen. He's an ocean away and has a security detail to protect him.

"I didn't. His name is Chen Pao."

"And he heads Bureau Three?"

"Yes."

"What kind of work do they do?"

"They gather political, economic and scientific intelligence from countries around the world."

She kept encircling his black stones as she talked. "I'm trying to picture him. What does he look like?"

Yìchén paused again to answer her question, making eye contact with Charlotte. "He has black hair with a smidgen of gray near his temples and ears. He reveres Mao and looks like an authoritarian strongman with his large muscular hands, a protruding belly and broad shoulders."

"A man like that must wield a lot of power."

He nodded. "Sometimes he receives kickbacks to remain in power. I'm sure American officials have run across his type."

Charlotte remained poker-faced.

She switched topics. "What did you think about the Tiananmen Square massacre?"

"We call it the June Fourth Incident. I don't remember anything about it because it happened in 1989 and I was born in 1990."

Charlotte stopped playing for a moment. "Surely you must've heard your parents talk about it. My parents did. Deng Xiaoping declared martial law, sent in 250,000 troops to quash the student protesters, and ended up killing hundreds, even thousands, all because he felt the protest might provoke a civil war."

He nodded. "Yes, I heard that. It is true."

"The next year—the year you were born—the government cracked down further, closing twelve percent of all newspapers, thirteen percent of social science periodicals, and seventy-six percent of China's five hundred publishing companies, according to a report I read. The government also seized millions of books, banned films and punished almost a hundred thousand people who took part."

Yìchén frowned. "Even though I don't agree with censorship like that, it had no real effect on me. Sometimes you need to go along with policies in order to survive."

"By the way, what month and day were you born?" Jenny asked.

"August eighth."

"No kidding?" she squealed. "That's my birthday, too."

"I celebrate my lunar birthday. Every year it's a different day because of the lunar calendar."

"Well, anyway, we're the same age. No wonder we have so much in common. Both of our astrological signs are Leos. The signs are based on the month you were born."

"We have something similar in China; however, instead of being based on your birth month, Chinese zodiac signs are specific to a person's birth year." He placed another black stone on the board.

Jenny placed a white stone. "A person has certain traits according to their sign."

"So, what are the traits of a Leo?"

"Leo rules all the other signs. They believe in their royal right to rule friends and family and alternate between being energetically gregarious and beautifully lazy. They like an audience and like to live it up in style."

"Sounds like me. Maybe there is something to that."

"Did you know President Xi was born in June?"

"Why is that important? I don't understand."

"He was born June fifteenth, to be exact. That makes him a Gemini."

"What are Geminis?"

She stopped playing again to answer his question. "They are natural-born salesmen, sometimes two-faced, expert at double-talk, quick to adapt and often witty. They have a deep-seated need to disguise their true motives. Do you think this description fits President Xi?"

How should I respond? After all, she doesn't know I defected.

"I'm not sure that is a fair characterization. Most Chinese think he's an honorable man."

"Do you know what Xi's true intentions are for the U.S.? Does he believe, like Deng Xiaoping did, *tao guang yang hui*—hide your ambitions and build your capability—which is a favorite admonition from the Warring States period?"

Yìchén blinked but remained stone-faced.

"Maybe that's why he's secretly building up his Navy with new state-of-the-art aircraft carriers, thirteen-thousand-ton stealth guided-missile destroyers, Yuan-class submarines, merchant ferries to transport thousands of men as well as creating a maritime militia. Did anyone, maybe your bosses, ever talk about that?"

She's very intelligent. Seems to know a lot for being just a housewife.

"If they did, I wasn't aware of it. President Xi says he has no ulterior motive. He says China has been hampered in the past because of its backwardness in achieving economic growth. He supports freer trade. He's only trying to make up for lost time."

"That's what he wants us and you to believe. Are you aware that China's economy tripled in size within ten years after 1997 and continues to grow, and that it did so by stealing intellectual property from the West?"

Yìchén was aware of it and used to be in agreement with it, but not since his father was beheaded, yet he was afraid to let Jenny know.

"Xi says it's not his fault. It's the result of an open society." *Where is she going with this conversation? I hope she doesn't find out I plan to steal DNA files from LineageFinder.*

"Aren't Chinese citizens told to go to American colleges or travel to the West in order to bring back technologies for China?"

Yìchén was silent.

"You may have noticed how Xi tends to demonize America and manipulates China's currency. He also promised the U.S. that China would provide assistance against North Korea and Iran. The truth is Xi has been supporting and sustaining both regimes. And President Xi also has the power to stop the never-ending cycle of fentanyl from China being trafficked to the United States through the Mexican drug cartels; however, he looks the other way."

I like her, but maybe she needs to leave.

The room grew quiet until Yìchén plopped another black stone on the board.

Charlotte smiled and continued talking while encircling his stones. After a few more questions, she wrapped things up by saying, "What other things haven't I asked you that you think I should know?"

A simple question that elicited a simple answer, yet it made him feel uncomfortable.

He shifted uneasily in his seat. "What do you mean by 'other things'?" he said. A drop of sweat fell from his brow.

Charlotte shrugged as if to say she didn't know. She locked eyes with him.

He admitted to her he had a fetish for BDSM sexual relationships with younger men.

Charlotte (aka Jenny) googled it later and found out BDSM stood for Bondage/Discipline, Dominance/Submission, and Sadism/Masochism, and it centered on power exchanges within the context of sexual intimacy.

Although revealing something so personal clearly astounded her, she reassured him, saying, "I still care about you and hope we can be good friends. Let's not let these differences about Xi come between us. I don't need to remind you why you wanted to move to the West. You'll find out there is more freedom here. Things we Americans take for granted."

"Like what?"

"Like you can criticize the president without repercussions. Like belong to any political party you choose. Like read any newspaper or watch any news channel, not just what is approved by government leaders."

"Is that all?"

"We also have the right to vote and dual citizenship, which China doesn't allow. And we have access to Facebook and Twitter, not just WeChat."

"You forgot one."

"What's that?"

"Freedom to travel."

"Yes, that too."

"I've always wanted to go on a tour."

"Where?"

"I don't know. Europe. Maybe a safari in Africa. Maybe South America."

"Can you afford it?"

"I have some savings."

"South America would be the least expensive of those you mentioned."

Yìchén looked at his watch. It was getting late. He worried that Charlotte wouldn't leave before he needed to send a transmission burst on the shortwave radio.

Charlotte took the hint. Although she was poised to win, she played several stones in order to let Yìchén win this time.

A while later, she resigned from the game. "I need to go. Game's over. Let's count up the stones."

Although he was the clear winner, he didn't gloat.

She let me win this time. I've been too distracted to concentrate on the game. I don't have time to refute it today, but I'll make sure when there is a rematch that it'll be fair.

June 2020
CHAPTER 15

After Charlotte left, Yìchén hurried to the hall closet and retrieved the shortwave radio. From his training in Beijing, he learned number stations had been around since the First World War but became more prevalent in the Cold War. They were used to send messages back and forth from a government in a country, like China, to spies operating in foreign countries, all while the government denied having any affiliation with the numbers station. He found out there hadn't been even one government who had ever admitted to using them.

One of the most famous transmissions from a number station during the Cold War, Yìchén learned, was from a drunken Stasi officer trying to woo his agents after the opening of the Berlin Wall, who began his broadcast with, "to all my ducklings." He and Chen Pao shared a chuckle over that.

The numbers stations often had nicknames. One classic number station was nicknamed "Bulgaria Betty," who wasn't actually Bulgarian. She was Czech. Another tidbit Yìchén learned during his training was that Moby, an American musician, singer, and songwriter, once turned a number station into a song. *How cool was that?*

Yìchén also learned ham radio operators gave each station an enigma as a way to identify them or distinguish between several. These included E, G, S, and V stations, such as E21, G23, S16 or V22. Some were easily identifiable, like E for English, or G for German.

It was now 1700 hours and Yìchén had to scramble to practice sending numbers over the airwaves before he sent the transmission at 1800 to his station, V22, nicknamed "the Beijing station." He knew the lower the frequency he used, like 2 MHz, the farther the number/message would go. It could even bounce across two oceans, so reaching China was no problem.

Chen Pao had warned him that his house and car might be bugged, as the FBI had a habit of doing, especially in the case of a defector, so he needed to use the shortwave somewhere else. He took out a small book he had hidden in his suitcase and a cigarette lighter he had purchased at a drug store and threw them into his backpack, then took the backpack and the radio and drove to what he considered was a secure location—the community center parking lot in Eastgate Park.

Yìchén, aka Zimò, had made an appointment with John to play pickleball at 1830 hours. His iPhone said it was now 5:15, or 1715 hours.

Although there were other cars in the parking lot, no one else was around. He took his radio and his backpack and got out of his car and hid behind some trees several feet away from the parking lot.

He inserted the TF memory card, a secondary storage device similar to an SD card but not as bulky. He spoke into the Mic to record his voice. He created a metallic-sounding voice by using a delay, setting the time short and turning up the feedback till he got the bass sound he wanted.

His first attempt practicing hit a speed bump. The first recorded voice had a high-pitched squeal instead of the bass sound he wanted. The clock was ticking away. It was now 1730 hours. A drop of sweat rolled down his brow to his cheek. He tried three times before he got it right.

He pulled out the book from his backpack—a small Chinese holy book, called *The Lunyu*, known in English as *The Analects*. The book contained the most revered sacred scriptures of Confucius' teaching. It also contained loose-leaf pages of a one-time pad where numbers were written in invisible ink. Chen Pao in Beijing had the only other copy.

To reveal the numbers, he waved the paper over the flame from the cigarette lighter. He continued heating the paper until the message darkened to a golden-brown color. He memorized the numbers and got rid of the one-time pad by chewing up the paper and swallowing it.

He spelled the digits out in Mandarin Chinese and spoke them into the mic at exactly 1800 hours and repeated them twice after the recorded gongs.

Èr sì liù liù èr sì.

Èr sì liù liù èr sì.

Two four six six two four.

Five minutes later, he repeated the numbers. He put all his gear back in the trunk of his car and then went into the community center to play pickleball with John for an hour and a half. John won the game easily as Zimò failed to score any points and, thus, was "pickled."

When they finished, Yìchén waited until John drove off, then got out of his car, made sure no one else was around and opened the trunk to get the radio and other items and safely made another transmission at 2000.

Mission accomplished. Chen Pao would now know he ended up in Seattle. All he had to do now was wait for further instructions.

Jenny woke up at 4:00 a.m. Saturday, ruminating about the Liu case, her upsetting conversation with Dave Friday night and the back-and-forth she had with Yìchén the other day about President Xi as well as his revelation about Facebook and Boeing sources. She took some deep breaths, rolled over and tried to get back to sleep, lying in her blackout-shades bedroom, but it was no use. Anxiety coursed through her veins. She also felt nauseous.

She got up, petted Daisy, and went to the bathroom and took an at-home pregnancy test she had purchased from the pharmacy. After taking a sample of urine, she saw two colored lines on the strip.

"I knew it. I'm pregnant," she said out loud to her cat. *I wish Mom were here.*

Thoughts of Friday night and the painful silence between her and Dave during the long ride back to the safehouse ricocheted in her mind. When they returned to the house, he got out of the SUV, retrieved his clothes and Pax, and said, "Jenny, I hope you know this is only temporary. I'll be back if you'll have me."

Jenny didn't say anything, stifling her tears. There was an awkward silence. Dave started to reach out and hug her, but she pulled back, indicating she didn't want to be touched, so he got into the car and drove off.

Today, what should have been happy news that she was going to have a baby, was overshadowed by not being able to share the good news with the father. She wasn't concerned with how it might affect her career. Reaching one of her lifetime goals was more important right now. Resigning herself to be strong, like her mother, she put on her white Turkish bathrobe, went to the kitchen and made coffee. She opened the front door, picked up her copy of *The Seattle Times*, and threw the folded newspaper on the couch.

She went back to the kitchen and poured herself a cup of coffee and sat down at the kitchen table. She heard raindrops tap tap tapping on the roof. She sighed. *Today is going to be tougher than I thought.*

She put water and food in Daisy's bowls and fed her a treat, then went to the living room to retrieve the newspaper. When she sat down again and unfolded it on the table, her eyes zeroed in on a small article on page six with the headline: "Anonymous Company May Be Under Siege from China Theft."

Although the story didn't identify Boeing or the Lius directly, she wondered, *Who leaked it to the media before I even had a chance to brief my boss with the news that I had evidence to put the Lius behind bars? If the Lius see this, what will be their reaction?*

Jenny finished reading the article and then showered and downed another cup of black coffee before hustling out the door to go to her office.

When she arrived at 7:00 a.m. wearing a face mask, her boss, Matthew Woodruff, the case agent for the Liu case, was waiting for her. He was over 6 feet tall, and had dark brown eyes that could penetrate a wall of steel.

"Did you see the article in *The Seattle Times* today?" he said.

"I certainly did," she said. "Who leaked it to the press?"

"I don't know. I thought you did."

"It wasn't me. The only person I told was Dave and I can't imagine him doing something like that. He knew I had evidence to convict the Lius."

"What've you got?"

She showed him Charles Lius shopping list for Boeing's proprietary information about its new laser technology. She also briefed him about what Yìchén had said concerning Charles Liu being one of Beijing's primary sources for classified information about Boeing and Kathy Green providing intel regarding Facebook, and she mentioned her suspicions about the radio Yìchén had nervously put away in the hall closet as well as his admiration for President Xi.

John arched an eyebrow when he heard the last bit of news about Yìchén. They would discuss that later.

He took a few minutes to read over the list, then made eye contact with Jenny. "Although this looks like a slam dunk, it's actually more complicated than that. The SAC has been in private conversations with Governor Isaacs and Senator Murphy, who voiced their concerns about what this might do to Boeing if we arrested one of their engineers. The economy is bad enough as it is. Seattle depends on Boeing."

Jenny bristled. "Maybe one of them leaked it to the press. Maybe to gage what public reaction might be. What the hell ever happened to national security?"

"I hear you. All I'm saying is that there are other things to consider."

"Like the best interests of shareholders if Boeing's stock should plummet? Do you own any shares in Boeing?"

Silence.

"This is the breakthrough we've been hoping for all along. We need to do the right thing. Most people will understand if we are on the right side of justice. As I see it, we don't have any other option."

"There's more at stake. Do you know how many people depend on Boeing? Not only the employees but also companies that supply aircraft engines, aerostructures, components and parts, all major U.S. airlines and healthcare insurance companies. The list goes on and on."

"But national security is also at stake. Don't you see? China is stealing our technology right under our noses and it's got to stop. The Lius need to be punished. We need to make an example out of them."

"What good will that do?"

I can't believe what I'm hearing. Whose side is he on? Could he possibly be a double agent?

"It's hard for me to believe you would entertain doing anything else. Besides, based on the wiretap, we were already able to obtain a warrant for their arrest. You're going to tell me we're not going through with it? Really?"

After what seemed to Jenny like a long pause, John said, "All right. The arrest is a go. I'll send teams over to the Lius' house immediately."

"I want to go too."

"Fine," he said.

Four FBI agents, including Jenny, pulled up in the driveway at the Lius' house in Federal Way, got out of their vehicles and knocked on the front door.

No answer.

"FBI!" yelled one of the agents, who stormed in after the agents forced the door open and entered with their guns drawn.

Inside, the house was eerily quiet. They searched the living room, kitchen, bedroom and bathroom but found no sign of the Lius.

Jenny's heart raced. She checked the garage. "Their car is missing. They must've left for work."

"Or would they have gone to the gym?"

"No. They only go to the gym on Tuesdays and Thursdays. Let's report this to Woodruff and head over to Boeing."

What should have taken less than a half-hour drive to get to the Boeing facility on East Marginal Way South in Seattle from the Lius' house in Federal Way took over an hour because traffic was backed up on the twenty-mile stretch going north on I-5.

Jenny was on-the-edge-of-her-seat nervous about whether they'd find the Lius at the Boeing facility or whether someone might have tipped them off the same time they had tipped off the media for the story in *The Seattle Times*. If someone did, she hoped to God that someone wasn't Dave.

When they arrived at the Boeing facility wearing face masks, a receptionist guided them to where Charles and Elizabeth worked in the Airborne Laser Program. They were met by Charles' supervisor, Nathan Stiles.

"We have a warrant for the arrest of Charles and Elizabeth Liu," Jenny said after she flashed her badge.

"I'm sorry, but the Lius didn't show up for work today. I've tried calling them several times, but the call always goes to voicemail and it says their mailbox is full."

"Damn!" Jenny said. She excused herself from the group and called Woodruff.

"Okay," he said. "Let's do an airline search and check the passenger lists."

Jenny had another call coming in but saw it was spam, so she ignored it. "If they did get away by plane, I'm sure they wouldn't use their true names. I'm wondering if someone tipped them off."

"Check the passengers lists anyway and the TSA surveillance cameras. Also, alert the border patrol at the Canadian border. I'll send out an APB to the police to have them watch for the make and model of their car along with their Washington license plate."

Jenny let out a sigh. "This might take a while."

"We don't have any other option, I'm afraid."

June 2020
CHAPTER 16

Yìchén received a coded message the next day from Beijing via the shortwave to proceed with obtaining whatever information he could get about LineageFinder executives and its voluminous DNA database.

Genetic engineering was crucial to China's economic goals, and DNA was prized by the regime because China was determined to dominate the potentially lucrative biotech industry.

During his university training in biometrics and gene editing at the South University of Science and Technology in Shenzhen, Yìchén had studied under a biology professor who had worked on human gene embryo editing, controversial in the scientific community because of ethical considerations in trying to create superhumans.

The professor taught him that most people favored preventing inheritable diseases but objected to being coerced or forced by a government to edit out human embryo genes in order to make sure it happened. It came down to a fear of what else governments would require being edited out.

From his studies, Yìchén learned it was possible to isolate genetic markers in the DNA associated with several illnesses, like breast cancer, for example, using 10,000 DNA samples. He understood that with more samples statistical chances improved dramatically, which is why China had a goal of getting at least ten million or more samples. The race to dominate the market was fierce. By doing so, China hoped to one day control not only America's but the whole world's health care.

Yìchén never before thought about whether a national DNA database might invade people's privacy or tempt government officials to not only penalize dissidents and/or activists by withholding treatment but also punish their relatives, like what happened in the June Fourth Incident (the Tiananmen Square Massacre).

After googling LineageFinder and finding out overt information about the company and its executives online at the public library, posing as Greg Roberts, Yìchén planned to scope out its headquarters in northeast Bellevue on 110th Avenue later today and try to make some contacts to help him get hired or at least help him get inside information about the company.

He headed out westbound on I-90 and took the exit for 405 heading toward Renton/Everett, then followed the signs to 405 North Bellevue, zigzagging right and left several times until he reached 110th Avenue, where he saw a red, black and white sign that said LineageFinder. The front of the brick-red building was an entrance to a wide parking garage. On either side were tall green leafy trees and a smidgen of lawn as well as low bushes near the sidewalk.

He parked his SUV inside the parking garage. Dozens of license plates in alphabetical order said things such as Censure, Geishas, Giggles, Jezebel, Jillion, Kokanee, and Lovebug, to name just a few, adorned the wall adjacent to the parking garage, opposite the building entrance. Yìchén was puzzled by it and wondered if the plates were meant to be some sort of insider joke.

When he entered the building wearing a face mask, he noticed the modern painting of Marie Curie, almost cartoon style, on the lobby wall, as well as several others he did not recognize.

"Good morning. How may I help you today?" the stunning receptionist said.

He smiled broadly. "I'd like to put in an application to work here."

"Which division are you interested in?"

"I'm not sure. What are the possibilities?"

"What is your education or experience?"

He ran his hand through his hair. "I'm fresh out of college. I have a degree in biometrics."

"Then I would suggest our DNA division. Have you ever had a DNA test done?"

"No."

One eyebrow went up. She locked eyes with Yìchén. "I'd recommend it. It helps if you know our process. Do you currently have a membership with us?"

"No. Do I need one for a job application?"

"Not necessarily. I probably shouldn't tell you this, but a membership and a DNA test can give you the edge over another candidate. You can do all that online. Go to our website and click on 'membership' to join and then 'employment' to apply for a job. Fill out the basic stuff, like name, address, education and work experience. Then you'll be asked a series of questions to see if you're the right match."

"I'll do that." He smiled.

"What did you say your name was?"

"Edwin Wu. And yours?"

"Cassie Jones."

"Thanks very much for the advice, Cassie. Have a nice day!" He turned to leave.

"No problem, Mr. Wu. You as well."

———— ✦ ————

Jenny worked through lunch to try to find the Lius. At two o'clock she popped her head into Woodruff's office.

"Any news from the police or Border Patrol?" he asked.

"Zero. But I did get a hit from a TSA surveillance camera. The number of air travelers has dramatically decreased in the pandemic, so it was easier to find them. It looks like they were in line for an early morning Lufthansa flight headed to Vancouver."

"Are they on another flight to Beijing?"

"Not yet. Vancouver has several airlines that travel to China, but none have flights until Monday morning. According to the internet, some four hundred thousand ethnic Chinese, many of substantial wealth, live in Vancouver, which has a population of 2.5 million. The city proper has twenty-eight percent ethnic Chinese. Good place for the Lius to hide. I think China probably owns a safehouse there, which is where we might find the Lius. What do you think?"

"Sounds reasonable."

"Any idea how we might find them before Monday?"

"I'll call one of my contacts at the RCMP."

Jenny wondered if Woodruff would follow up. It would be a dereliction of duty if he didn't. She still had suspicions about his loyalties. After all, Robert Hansen, the biggest spy in the world and an FBI agent for twenty-five years, was a double agent who spied for Soviet and Russian intelligence services from 1979 to 2001. He was later sentenced to life in prison without parole.

Is Woodruff a spy for China? It was hard to know who to trust in this business.

She sighed. If Dave had been in close proximity, she would have confided her fears to him, but he was away in Oklahoma caring for his ex-wife, and she didn't know when he'd be back and didn't want to interrupt his care with a phone call. It might make her appear too needy. No, she should just buck up and be cautious about who she trusted. Duty. Honor. Loyalty.

She had a job to do and a responsibility to the American people for their safety and national security. She would find a way to make that happen and make her dad, as well as the baby she was carrying, proud of her at the same time. Somehow things had a way of working out.

Woodruff made eye contact with her. "Before I make that call, I want to hear more about what you told me about Yìchén. You said something about a radio. Why did that make you suspicious? What kind of radio was it? How big was it?"

"It was pocket-size. I'm not really sure what kind of radio it was. He just seemed nervous when he put it into the hall closet."

"Maybe he was nervous about playing *Weiqi* with you since he didn't know you well."

"What if it's a shortwave?"

Woodruff waved his hand dismissively. "I think you might be jumping to conclusions, maybe hoping for something that isn't there. Tell me more about what he said about President Xi."

Those penetrating eyes of his. Jenny felt like she was on trial.

She filled him in on their conversation, mentioning Yìchén's surprising responses and reactions.

"It's not unusual for someone to be loyal to their former government head. He's probably homesick or suffering from the loneliness that comes when you first move to a new place. You naturally miss your former home or country."

"Even a defector?"

Silence.

"Jenny, you're working too hard. This work really takes its toll on you. You have my permission to take some time off. You'll come back refreshed and renewed."

She wondered again whose side he was on. "Are you out of your goddamn mind? These are some of the most important cases of the century. I don't need to take time off. I need to put in more overtime to solve both of them."

He took a breath and exhaled slowly. "Fine. Do what you want, but just remember I gave you the option."

Yìchén, aka Zimò, invited John out for a drink after they played a game of pickleball at the gym at the community center in Eastgate Park. They went to Tian Fu in Factoria, not far from Yìchén's condo. Yìchén and John, both dehydrated from sweating it out at the gym, guzzled down a few beers. When John stood up and excused himself to go to the restroom, Yìchén slipped GHB (gamma-hydroxybutyric acid) into his drink. This date-rape drug was more commonly known by its street names: Grievous Bodily Harm, Liquid Ecstasy, or Cherry Meth.

Yìchén waited patiently for the drug to have its effect. He didn't have to wait long.

After settling the bill, Yìchén took an inebriated and drugged John, loaded him into the car, drove to his condo and carried him to his bedroom and had his way with him. He stripped off all his clothes, fondled his genitals until he saw an erection and then photographed him in the nude, using his iPhone. He turned him over and penetrated him from behind, leaving him there for the night, satisfied with his own orgasm.

"Where am I?" John said the next morning when he awoke and regained consciousness.

"Hello, pretty boy," Yìchén said, stroking John's hair.

"What the fuck?" John said. "Get away from me, man!"

"Easy, buddy. You're my property now."

"I'm no one's goddamn property. Get the fuck away from me!"

Yìchén got out his iPhone and showed him one of the photos. John reached for the phone but Yìchén was too quick for him.

"Nuh uh uh," Yìchén said as he took the phone away. "Aren't we testy this morning? You'd do better to cooperate. Then no one gets hurt. Otherwise, I'll show these photos to your parents. I'm sure they'd love to find out what a bad boy you've been. If you cooperate, no one has to know."

"What do you want from me?"

"I want you to apply for a job at LineageFinder. You can apply online."

"Why?"

"It's not for you to know why. Just do what I say."

While watching TV later that night, Yìchén came across an advertisement for LineageFinder, which claimed ninety-eight percent accuracy in finding your ancestors from a DNA test. *I wonder if they are as good as they say they are. Certainly wouldn't hurt to investigate. It might be worth the risk. Might help my reporting. Why not?*

Before he left Beijing, Chen Pao had warned Yìchén that the American government would keep close tabs on him, perhaps to the point of knowing which sites he visited on the internet, although that was becoming less common because of encryption.

It was becoming more common for the government to get a court order requiring a company like LineageFinder to tell them if someone, or a known IP address, had ever visited their site and to disclose what information that person provided.

He was also tech-savvy enough to take extra precautions to try to hide from government snoopers, like using a virtual private network (VPN) or proxy.

In order to get the DNA sample kit from LineageFinder, he gave them his email address, mobile phone number and home address. *What could it possibly hurt? I'm not doing anything illegal, so it should be okay.*

He was amazed at the fast service. The kit arrived in a couple of days. The following day he spit saliva into the tube and promptly returned it to LineageFinder. *Well, that was easy.* Now all he had to do was wait for the results.

He didn't need to work at LineageFinder, didn't really need the money as the Americans were giving him enough money to cover the cost of his living expenses and would use John to tell him everything he found out about LineageFinder's executives. John might initially act cooperative, but there was a chance he might not be helpful or reliable and could sabotage the operation later on, so it was better to use him only in the beginning.

June 2020

CHAPTER 17

A couple of weeks later, Yìchén, aka Zimò, drove to meet John in the parking lot at the community center in Eastgate Park to find out more information about LineageFinder's executives. John pulled up in a car and parked next to Yìchén.

"Get in," Yìchén said, as he motioned for John to climb in his front seat.

John looked uncomfortable and seemed hesitant at first, but put on his face mask, opened up the passenger door and sat down in the SUV.

"What did you find out?" Yìchén said, adjusting his own face mask.

"I was able to get some of the stuff you asked for while I was employed there. Research and development strategies, manufacturing and marketing plans and some customer lists. They were very difficult to get."

"I don't care how difficult it was. Where's the information?"

"Here in this folder I brought with me."

Yìchén didn't thank him. Got down to business right away. "What did you find out about all the major players?"

"James Anderson is the president. The VP is Rebecca Jenkins."

Yìchén knew both were mainly responsible for the day-to-day operations while the CEO was the decision-maker and visionary.

"What about the CEO?"

"Gary Parker."

A car pulled into the parking lot. A young woman got out wearing navy sweats and a pair of Nike tennis shoes. Yìchén waited until she went inside to speak.

"Do you know where any of them live?"

"Why do you want to know?"

"Don't ask why, just tell me."

"Okay, man. Anderson and Jenkins live on Mercer Island. Parker lives in Medina."

"I'm not familiar with those neighborhoods. Tell me more about them."

"Mercer Island is home to many of Seattle's billionaires though I've heard other big wigs who work for companies like Microsoft, Amazon and Starbucks live in Medina. It's allegedly the seventh richest city in the U.S. Most homes there are valued at around three million. Medina is rural-like and has lots of parks."

"Where are they located?"

"Mercer Island is an island on the southern portion of Lake Washington between Seattle and Bellevue. Medina is on a peninsula in Lake Washington on the opposite shore from Seattle. It's above Mercer Island."

"Are those gated communities?"

"Gated and pretty near all have alarmed homes. Plus, you can't drive more than twenty five miles an hour in those neighborhoods or you'll get stopped by the police."

"Anything else?"

"All three are Mormons and teetotalers. Parker is gregarious and drinks a latte from Starbucks every morning on his way to work, according to his secretary. He also hosts a golf fundraiser every year for the Humane Society. He owns a yellow lab, which he sometimes brings to the office. I wasn't able to get much else on Anderson or Jenkins."

"Any idea when Parker usually arrives at the office?"

"I saw him coming in one day around 9:30 a.m."

"Did his secretary happen to mention what kind of food he likes?"

"No."

"What was he wearing on the day you saw him?"

"Business casual. Khakis, a blue blazer, white shirt and no tie. Loafers."

"What kind of car did he drive?"

"An Aston Martin Valkyrie. I'd give my eye teeth to ride in a car like that."

Yìchén watched a man exit the community center, then get into his Honda Civic and drive off. After he left, Yìchén continued asking John questions.

"What does he look like? Does he wear glasses?"

"Why do you want to know all this? Are you planning to kidnap him or something?"

"Shut the fuck up! Just answer my questions."

"Sorry, man! He's about my height. Five-nine. Medium build. I bet he works out every day in a gym. He's also real tan with sandy hair and gray at the temples. Not sure what color eyes, but he doesn't wear glasses."

"Do you know his age?"

"I'd guess mid-fifties."

"What about his nose or hands? Are they large or small?"

"He's got big hands. His nose is A-line, not large or bulbous."

"Is he married? Any kids?"

"I assume he is. His secretary said the fundraiser is popular with his grandkids."

"Anything else you'd like to mention that I haven't asked you?"

"A French company is trying to buy out LineageFinder, but Parker is putting the brakes on the deal."

Interesting. Chen Pao told me the MSS hired a cutout—a French company—to purchase LineageFinder so the Americans wouldn't know it was really the Chinese who were buying it.

"Anderson is also beefing up security," John added. "They may start instituting polygraphs for everyone. If they do, I'm toast."

"You can always quit."

"I was planning to."

"Won't matter. Keep this between me and you. Then no one gets hurt. Now, let's go inside and play pickleball."

———•◆•———

Mort (aka Fred) met with Yìchén again at a secure location in Seattle to debrief him further about what President Xi and the MSS had been up to recently. After exchanging pleasantries and offering Yìchén a comfortable chair to sit in as well as a bottle of Pepsi and a small bag of Lay's potato chips to snack on, they got down to business.

"What do you know about the origin of the coronavirus?" Mort asked. He placed a wad of Skoal snuff tobacco in his mouth. "Was it from human contact with an animal or from a lab leak accident in Wuhan?"

"As you probably already know," Yìchén said, after taking a sip of Pepsi, "the Wuhan Institute of Virology Laboratory is a forty-minute drive from the wet market in Hunan where the initial infections occurred. Three researchers at the lab were treated at a hospital for the virus in November 2019. This was the first known virus infection. My boss said the virus escaped accidentally from the lab."

"Interesting. I thought Chinese party officials said the virus entered Wuhan in food shipments of frozen meats from elsewhere in China or Southeast Asia."

"That was one theory," Yìchén said as he munched on some potato chips. "Another, more probable, is that the virus spread naturally. It emerged from bats, then jumped to humans, and did not involve any scientists or laboratories. Even government officials don't know for sure and those who might know aren't telling."

"I guess we'll never get to the bottom of this. What other information do you have for me today? Do you know anything about China's buildup of its Navy?"

"I'm sure the CIA probably knows more than I do. Charlotte mentioned that Americans are aware that President XI is secretly building up China's Navy. I'm not so sure the destroyer is a secret. You can't hide a 13,000-ton stealth guided-missile destroyer. I do know it's larger and more powerful than most American, Japanese and South Korean destroyers."

"Are you talking about the Type 055 destroyer?"

"Yes."

"What about the Type 039 submarine?"

"China has seventeen of these already with plans to build eight more in the next three years. These subs are equipped with air independent propulsion, making them deadly silent and they do not need to surface frequently like other submarines. Plus, they are armed with anti-ship cruise missiles. What you don't know is that China was able to easily steal the technology from America to build most of it."

Mort spit some of the tobacco in a nearby wastebasket. "Can you provide dates and names who provided it?"

"Yes, in exchange for something I want."

"We'll talk about that in a minute. What else do you have?"

"These potato chips are addictive."

"Here's another bag." Mort handed it to him. "If President Xi goes after Taiwan, he'll no doubt need an invading force of more than a million men. Any idea how he might accomplish that?"

"Easy. By quickly converting China's massive fleet of civilian ferries for military use. They were designed with that in mind. China has also created a maritime militia—more than a hundred fifty or so commercial fishing vessels—to carry out its wishes in disputes in the South China Sea."

"Have some more chips," Mort said.

"Thanks, but I've had enough. Your government is probably also aware that we've been stealing proprietary intellectual property from

Boeing for at least fourteen years now. How do you think we were able to deliver our first-ever C919 to Eastern Airlines?"

"What is the C919?"

"It's a large mainline commercial jet—a narrow-body, 164-seater, passenger plane."

"Who manufactured it?"

"The state-owned Commercial Aircraft Corporation of China, also known as Comac. It took them fourteen years to produce it but now they can compete with their rivals, Boeing and Airbus."

"Can you name anyone at Boeing who gave away secrets?"

Yìchén took another sip of Pepsi. "I'll name one, but there are plenty of others."

"Who is it?"

"I think his last name was Liu. Can't remember his first name."

Mort put another wad of tobacco in his mouth. "Okay, we'll get the rest from you later. Now, what is it that you want?"

"I want permission to go on a guided tour. Charlotte suggested maybe South America because those tours are less expensive."

"I'll check with my boss and let you know."

———✦———

After consulting with his superiors, Mort gave Yìchén permission to take a short break and book himself on a guided tour under the careful watch of the Agency.

He looked online for tours in South America, and found one through G.A. Tours for Costa Rica: Rainforests, Volcanoes & Wildlife (nine days/nights) for under $3,000 which had a rating of four and a half stars. Group size was ten to twenty-two travelers. Another, Highlights of Central America—Costa Rica & Panama (eleven days/nights) cost over $3,000 but it only had a rating of four stars. A third was Ecuador & Galapagos Islands Cruise (eight days/nights), rated four and a half stars for close to $5,000. Group size was fifteen to thirty-five travelers.

The thought of being stuck on a ship with thirty-five passengers for eight days nauseated him, not to mention the fact that the cost was considerably higher.

He decided to check Europe for a comparison. *Okay. Two bestsellers. Now we're talking.* A week in Italy: Venice, Florence & Rome (seven days/nights), rated four and a half stars for close to $3,000. The other was a tour to London, Paris & Rome (nine days/nights), also rated four and a half stars for close to $4,000. Group size for both was fifteen to thirty-eight travelers.

"Hmm," he said out loud to no one. "Better to go with a bestseller. Won't draw attention for wanting to go on the tour." *The Italian trip has more travelers. I could easily get lost among them.*

He checked the itinerary. There was one free day in Florence and two in Rome to explore the city anyway he chose. He'd use them wisely.

Since it was Tuesday, he'd send another shortwave transmission tonight at 1800 hours and then again at 2000 to let Chen Pao know where he could meet an MSS agent.

He put all his gear in the trunk of his car and headed for the community center parking lot at Eastgate Park. Being mindful of possible surveillance, he pulled into the parking lot when he felt he was "black," meaning no surveillance was detected.

Quickly retrieving the radio from his trunk, he hid next to some trees, where he sent the various transmission bursts. Yìchén used a one-time pad to figure out the numerical digits, spelling out the numbers in Mandarin Chinese, then spoke them into the mic.

He sent two separate messages, five minutes apart, and repeated the string of numbers twice after the recorded gongs. Chen Pao would be able to decode the messages, which read:

Vatican. St. Peter's statue.

Friday, July 3 at noon.

Yìchén received confirmation the next day. The operation was a "go."

Jenny, who had moved back into her own home, got up Saturday, looked in the bathroom mirror at her hair which was beginning to grow back, then went to the kitchen and stuffed some saltine crackers in her mouth, chewing and swallowing them to alleviate the nausea she felt from morning sickness. She thought briefly of Dave. Still felt abandoned. Still grieved the loss. But she was beginning to heal from the relationship and getting better each day.

Even so, she wondered what he was doing at the moment and when he might be back. In a few months she'd be able to get an ultrasound to find out the sex of the baby. By then, it would certainly be time to let Dave know. She wondered what his reaction would be. Would he feel obligated to marry her so he could take care of her and the baby? Knowing Dave, he would. But how could she ever marry anyone who felt such an obligation? Would he feel stuck later on? Would she feel stuck?

It was a lot to think about.

Right now, she needed to concentrate on the Liu case. Charles and Elizabeth might be hiding in a Chinese safehouse in Vancouver before boarding a plane to Beijing, possibly Monday morning.

She dialed Woodruff on a secure line. "Any word from our Canadian friends yet?"

"They've located the house."

"Where is it?"

"It's on the West Side. It's owned by Su Bin."

"Who's that?"

"He's a Chinese national. He owns the house but spends most of his time in China. His wife and two children live in the Vancouver home."

"I read somewhere that Vancouver has a big problem with absentee Chinese landlords. The Chinese who were flushed with cash swooped in

Vancouver from the mid-eighties through the late nineties and bought up all the real estate. The natives were more than happy to sell it to them. I think I read where a house that normally would've sold for about $20,000, the Chinese bought for about $400,000 cash."

"I read that too. Problem is there are so many absentee landlords in Vancouver now and they often don't spend money on heat or lights, so the homes end up with a serious mold problem."

They were getting off-track. Jenny steered the conversation back. "So, what about Mr. Su? Do we know anything else about him?"

"Plenty. He's also used the names Stephen Su and Stephen Subin. He was arrested in the summer of 2014 in the Richmond suburb of Vancouver and was extradited to the U.S. He pleaded guilty to conspiring to hack into the computer networks of Boeing and other major defense contractors to steal secrets about the C-17 military transport plane and F-22 and F-35 fighter jets. He sold them to aviation firms sponsored by the Chinese government."

"For financial gain, obviously. Was he ever sentenced?"

"He was charged with one count of conspiring to gain unauthorized access to a protected computer and to violate the Arms Export Control Act. For that he got four years in prison and a $10,000 fine. Hardly seems worth the manpower and money it took to convict him."

"How can you say that? At least he was punished."

"Maybe this century belongs to China, just like the past century belonged to us. Maybe it's futile to try to prevent it. My gut tells me maybe we should just go along and get along. I don't know."

"Are you saying we should just let the Lius escape instead of arresting them?"

"I'm saying I'm tired of fighting. That's all."

She still suspected he might be a Chinese spy but didn't really have enough proof. Better to give him the benefit of the doubt. Force his hand, so to speak.

"I think our democracy is worth fighting for. China is doing everything it can to test our dominance in the world. Aren't you a little afraid of that?"

"What makes you think that?"

"I heard the Secretary of the Air Force speak on a talk show."

"What did *he* have to say?"

"That China has identified high-value targets for them to attack, such as our aircraft carriers, our forward air bases and our satellites in space. He also said China has begun a military modernization program and they have the resources, the strategic intent and capability and scale to test the U.S. and its dominance. Doesn't that scare you? It does me."

"We already have next-generation fighters that are capable of eliminating ninety-five percent of the world's air force."

No use arguing with a know-it-all. How did we get off on this tangent? Better to go back to the original problem. "So, what's the next step in the Liu case?"

"We're coordinating with the RCMP to make the arrest and extradite them to the U.S. They've got surveillance on the house as we speak. So, don't worry your pretty head about it."

Jenny hated Woodruff's condescending attitude, but didn't take the bait by giving him the satisfaction of a reply or a negative reaction. She still didn't trust him. She'd wait to see what happened with the case before she brought it to the attention of the SAC.

June 2020

CHAPTER 18

Jenny was busy getting ready for work to help with the extradition of the Lius back to the U.S. when the phone rang. She was running late but answered the call when she saw who it was on the caller-ID.

His voice was full of emotion.

"Linda just died. The funeral is tomorrow."

"I'm so sorry, Dave."

"None of us last forever. I expected it but had no idea I'd feel like such a damn piece of crap when it happened. I'm filled with such remorse and regret now for what happened in our marriage." His voice cracked.

"Don't beat yourself up. We're all human, and you did the best you could."

"That wasn't good enough. I made a promise that I'd do better in my next relationship. By the way, how have *you* been? I've thought about you a lot. I've missed you."

Not sure how I feel about our relationship now. Still have lingering feelings of being abandoned. My gut tells me to be cautious.

"I've thought about you, too. We've missed you at work. Charles and Elizabeth are being extradited to the U.S. The case is heating up."

"Sounds like I've missed a lot. I'd love to hear more about it when we can talk. We have a lot to catch up on."

"I was just about to head out the door when you called."

"I hope I'm not making you late."

"No, it's okay. I'd like to send flowers for the funeral. Text me later with the address."

"That's very kind of you, but a donation to the Leukemia Foundation would be more appreciated."

"Consider it done! Call me when you get back and we'll go over the case."

"Jenny…I…I still love you. I hope you know that."

She felt a catch in her throat and had trouble responding. *Damn! Why did he have to call right now? Just when I was feeling confident about my career. Now I'm reduced to mush.*

"I've gotta go. I'll talk to you later."

On Saturday, June 27, Yìchén boarded a Lufthansa plane at SeaTac airport for a direct overnight flight to Frankfurt, then transferred to a smaller plane to fly into Venice's Marco Polo International Airport. He arrived in Venice on Sunday, got situated in his hotel and met his fellow tourists, including ten Chinese Americans who looked similar to him, at an evening welcome dinner.

The next day, Monday, he played tourist, taking a guided tour with fellow travelers to see St. Mark's Square, St. Mark's Basilica, Doge's Palace, and the Rialto Bridge on the Canal Grande, and watched a glass-blowing demonstration—a beloved art in Venice.

He never said much, not wanting to draw any attention to himself. Only a casual comment or two here and there.

"Lovely day. Sunshine. Light wind. No rain. The weather couldn't be better."

"Yes, Italy is better than I imagined."

"I can see why glassblowing is so popular here. I need to get a photo of it."

In the afternoon he rode a gondola in the Venice Canal while taking photos of the Bridge of Sighs. He kept most of his comments to himself but did utter something when he came to the bridge.

"This bridge is so spectacular. I've seen pictures before, but they don't do it justice."

Traveling with the group by bus to Florence on Tuesday, he again played tourist, where he saw the Duomo, and the legendary Florence Cathedral and visited the Gallery of the Academy, which contained a notable collection of Florentine paintings as well as some of Michelangelo's most famous sculptures. Again, only casual comments.

"I've never seen anything like this," he said in front of the Florence Cathedral.

When he was standing next to the famous fourteen-foot marble statue of David, he handed his iPhone to a fellow traveler.

"Hey, can you take my picture next to this statue?" he said.

That night he had dinner with other Chinese American members of the tour. He was pleasant enough but again didn't say much.

"This food is delicious. I think I'll have another glass of wine."

Wednesday was a free day. He ate breakfast at his hotel, then took an excursion to San Gimignano, a small hill town in Tuscany, southwest of Florence, that included a triangular square in the center of the old part of town that was lined with medieval houses. He ate lunch and dinner in Tuscany, savoring crostini toscani and panzanella, with friends he had made on the tour.

"This food must be why Italians love this city. I'll never forget the taste."

So far nothing out of the ordinary that might arouse suspicion. Good.

On Thursday, he went by bus to Rome for a guided sightseeing tour to the Colosseum, stopped at the ruins of the Forum, and went on to Circus Maximus, the stadium where ancient Romans raced chariots.

When he returned to his hotel that night, he made a casual comment to the clerk.

"I can't remember when I've been so exhausted."

"What did you do today?" the clerk asked.

"I trudged around the streets of Rome for two hours with the tour group."

"You should sleep well tonight. Have a nice evening."

Friday, July 3rd, was a free day in Rome. He hurried to the Vatican and, pretending to be a new convert, went to St. Peter's Basilica and stood in line with dozens of other tourists to kiss the well-worn foot of St. Peter that millions of Catholics had kissed before him.

Yìchén wore sunglasses, and while standing in line, he saw in the distance an undercover MSS agent he recognized. He did not make eye contact with him. The agent was in an opposite line heading out while Yìchén was on his way in. As usual, it was so crowded in St. Peter's that the two lines bumped up against one another.

Yìchén engaged in small talk with an older lady who was in front of him.

"Do you know if Pope Francis will say Mass here today?" Yìchén said.

"I think our tour guide said he is in Castelgandolfo," the older lady said.

"What's Castelgandolfo?"

"His summer residence."

While Yìchén stared straight ahead and kept idly conversing with the woman, he succeeded in making a brush pass with the agent who also stared straight ahead, their hands touching no more than a second or two. Long enough for Yìchén to hand off a thumb drive to him that contained crucial information that John had supplied on LineageFinder—research and development strategies, manufacturing and marketing plans, several customer lists, as well as background and stalking information about its executives.

Mission accomplished. Now all Yìchén needed to do was go back to his hotel and wait for a phone call on his burner phone letting him know what to do next.

JULY 2020

When Jenny walked into her house close to ten o'clock Friday night, she was drained and mentally exhausted. She had been working overtime on the Liu case because of complications in their extradition from Canada. In the process, the RCMP requested full background details from the FBI before they would agree to release the Lius, which meant long hours and more paperwork for Jenny. But she was motivated to see this case through and get justice for the Lius. It wouldn't hurt her career either. If she accomplished her goal, she'd be on track for a promotion.

She petted Daisy and topped off water in her bowl, then changed into pajamas and put on some soothing music on the stereo to unwind. She selected Marconi Union's "Weightless," which neuroscientists pegged as the world's most calming song.

Her phone pinged. It was a text from Dave, saying he'd be back in Seattle tomorrow. She had mixed emotions. A tinge of happiness that he still wanted her in his life but also apprehension because she still couldn't get over the fact that he'd left her. The reason didn't matter. Could she trust that he wouldn't do it again? *Here is that trust problem again. I wish Mom was still alive so I could talk to her about it.*

She plugged in her phone in the kitchen to recharge it and then headed to her bedroom. Since she received updates on her dad from a friend she made at the nursing home, she powered up her iPad to see if her nurse friend had sent an email today.

Sure enough, there was one. Her friend wrote:

"Jenny, I know you have a lot on your plate right now and I'm sorry to be the bearer of bad news, but your dad has Covid. They put him on a ventilator this morning. Because of his other health issues, his prognosis isn't good. He's not allowed visitors but I'll help you Face-Time him. Just let me know when you're available. I'm so sorry."

A tear rolled down her cheek. She had known her dad her whole life. He was the one to play peek-a-boo with her in the window of their front door. He was the one to give her her first kitten. He was the one she ran to when she fell during kick-boxing practice at the gym or had a math problem in high school she couldn't solve. She loved him more than any man she had ever loved since, but now he was slowly slipping away. When he did, she'd be left without any family whatsoever.

She mindlessly clicked on a notice from LineageFinder that had been sitting in her in-box for a couple of days.

"You have a new clue in the Jen Hae Chu Family Tree."

These are always gimmicks to get you hooked on their service.

She clicked on it anyway and was directed to the website. Then she clicked on "Jen Hae Chu's DNA Matches" on the next page. Her eyes popped wide as she read.

Full Sibling:
Yìchén Zhang
Brother
57% shared DNA

"Oh my God!" she said out loud to no one. "I can't believe this. Yìchén must be my brother. I've wanted a sibling my whole life. Now I have one. *I have a brother!*"

I can't believe my luck. A baby, a brother, my career is off to a good start and even Dave is back in my life. It can't possibly get any better.

She sighed. "Yìchén and I must be twins."

Yet she wondered why it wasn't one hundred percent shared DNA if he was her twin. She googled it and found out that fraternal twins will only share about thirty-five to fifty percent of their DNA with each other, the reason being that each person inherits fifty percent from their mother's DNA and fifty percent from their father's.

After thinking about it more, she sighed again. "It makes perfect sense. The one-child policy. Oh my God, my God!" Her heart raced like wildfire. She wondered if it would explode. Her calico cat climbed on the bed. "Daisy, now I know why I have a trust problem. I was abandoned at birth."

Even though she switched off her iPad and turned off the light, she wasn't able to sleep for a couple of hours, ruminating about her dad and her biological brother. She lied in bed, listening to the calming music from the stereo, but her thoughts kept ricocheting in her mind, keeping her awake.

If Yìchén gets the same type of message, he won't know it's me because he knows me as Charlotte, not Jen Hae Chu. He couldn't do a simple name search on social media because I don't have a profile picture on Facebook or any of the other sites. I wonder how I can let him know without breaking cover. Or if I should.

July 2020

CHAPTER 19

Jenny reported to work early Monday morning for a conference with Woodruff and Dave regarding the Liu case. Dave got back late last night, and he and Jenny didn't have time to chat before the morning conference. Jenny was aware that coworkers had been speculating about her and Dave's relationship, yet they tried hard to keep up formal appearances to the contrary. No one in the office knew Jenny was pregnant, including Dave.

"Good morning, Ms. Chu," Dave said, smiling. His eyes hugged her above his face mask.

"Good morning, Mr. Kamakaris," she said. Her eyes smiled back at him above hers. "Ready to get back to work?"

"Ready as I'll ever be. So, give me the low-down on the Lius."

"I'll let Woodruff do the honors."

After Woodruff finished telling Dave about the case, Dave said, "What's the plan now?"

"Our team, including RCMP members, will be escorting the Lius from the Bin residence to the Vancouver airport to transport them back to the U.S."

"I assume Dave and I'll be a member of that team," Jenny said.

"Be my guest. I still say the money and the manpower on a case like this is a complete waste. They'll probably get off with a four-year prison sentence and a $10,000 fine like Su Bin."

"Who is this Su Bin you've mentioned?" Dave asked.

After Woodruff filled him in on Bin's background, Jenny said, "The punishment doesn't always fit the crime. At least he was punished and that sent a strong message to China to stop the theft."

"It only worked for a short time," Woodruff said. "They're back at it again. I'll be damned if they haven't already won this economic war."

"They're sure to win if we don't do anything to try to stop them," Jenny said. *Whose side are you on anyway?*

"Easy, Jenny," Dave said. "I don't think he means we should give up the fight."

She'd talk to Dave sometime in private about her suspicions about her boss. For now, she'd let it go and listen to Woodruff's plan.

After they finished, Dave walked Jenny back to her office and gave her some startling news.

"I'm friends with a local cop who phoned me late last night," Dave said. "We got to talking and, in the middle of the conversation, he told me the parents of a kid named John showed up at the police station yesterday complaining their son was blackmailed by a guy who called himself Zimò. Played pickleball with him at the community center at Eastgate Park."

"Why is that important?" Jenny asked.

"The kid found out from a property search yesterday Zimò's real name is Yìchén Zhang. Have you had any contact with Yìchén since I've been away?"

"Only once to play another game of *Weiqi*." Her face turned pale. "That little creep. To add insult to injury, I just found out from Lineage-Finder that Yìchén is my biological brother."

"Really?"

"Yeah. Sixty percent DNA match. Found out earlier from Yìchén that we share the same birth date, so that makes him my twin. I was excited about it until I heard what you just said about him. Are you sure it's true?"

"I've never known my cop friend to lie."

"I'm shocked that he would do such a thing. How did he blackmail the kid?"

"The kid thinks Yìchén put something in his drink. He blacked out, but when he woke up in Yìchén's apartment, Yìchén had taken nude pictures of him in a compromising pose and threatened to show them to his parents if he didn't do what he said."

"What did he want him to do?"

"Get a job at LineageFinder headquarters."

"For what?"

"In order to get inside information."

"To purchase their stock?"

"Maybe. Dunno. But he was real inquisitive about their executives. The kid wondered if it was to kidnap them for ransom."

"Holy moly!"

"I know. We need to get to the bottom of this. Maybe you need to pay him another visit."

"The last time I saw him, he mentioned that he wanted to go on a tour. Not sure if he did or if he's back yet."

"Where did he go?"

"I don't know. I mentioned that South American tours would be cheaper than Europe. I'm sure Fred and company keep pretty close tabs on him. We could ask Fred."

Yìchén paced back and forth with nervous energy inside his hotel room in Rome Friday night, anxiously awaiting a call on his burner phone from his MSS handler. His mind was flooded with thoughts of his grieving mother.

It pained him to think she was alone in her grief. She suffered the loss of not only her beheaded husband but also her son, whom she might never see again. He could almost smell the aroma in her kitchen. She often made him hot, spicy dishes like Sichuan pork and fried rice, two of his favorites. He never appreciated it until now.

He wondered what she thought when they told her Bohai was guilty of treason or whether he had shared with her anything about his clandestine life. He could still see the hurt look on her face when he told her the MSS was forcing him to move to America. She probably guessed they were up to no good.

He sighed, thinking about the futility of his life and what it had become—one giant lie—from which it would be difficult to escape without causing harm to his mother. Would his father feel betrayed by what he was currently doing? Why did he choose this career? He deserved better.

His thoughts returned to the problem at hand. He hoped the information he had provided the MSS was sufficient and that he wouldn't need to do more research. Also wondered what they would require him to do next.

He stopped pacing and sat on the bed for fifteen minutes before the phone rang. It was close to midnight when he received the call. He answered it on the first ring. They spoke in Mandarin.

"Good evening, Mr. Wu. I trust you'll sleep well tonight after the delicious meal served at your hotel."

Yìchén's ears perked up. "Delicious meal" were codewords that meant the intel Yìchén had given them about LineageFinder and its executives was excellent.

"I will. Any other news?"

"I must inform you the plans have been made. The surprise party for the CEO will be held next Wednesday. Your choice of drinks on the house. I hope you can make it."

"The surprise party for the CEO" was code for "eliminate him." "Your choice of drinks on the house" meant Yìchén could choose the poison for the CEO's drink.

"I'll be there," Yìchén replied.

He returned to Seattle the next day with the tour group and thought about his next move to murder LineageFinder's CEO.

July 2020

CHAPTER 20

Sunday evening, Jenny and Dave flew to Vancouver to extradite the Lius back to the U.S. early Monday. They met up with Fred at the bar in their hotel Sunday who was also in town for the Monday extradition.

"Drinks are on me tonight," Fred said.

"You mean it's on the government's tab," Dave said.

He laughed. "You know me too well."

"No harm, no foul," Dave said. "Hey, Fred, have you heard what the guy you call a dumb-ass deplorable did?"

"You mean that horseshit he did with a kid named John?" Fred said, placing a wad of Skoal snuff tobacco in his mouth.

"Yes. Sickening, isn't it? Jenny said.

"I've heard worse."

"I'll bet you have," she said.

"We—another FBI agent and I—went to Yìchén's house and questioned him about his blackmail attempts but he denied the whole thing. He said he didn't know anyone named John and never played pickleball at the community center in Eastgate."

"You do know he's gay, don't you?" Jenny said.

Jenny had been meeting regularly with Fred since she and Yìchén first met. But so much had transpired with Dave and the Liu case she couldn't remember what she told Fred.

"I assumed as much. I think you mentioned it in one of our previous conversations."

"The last time I spoke to Yìchén, he was planning to go on a tour," Jenny said. "Any idea where he went?"

"Italy. Nothing unusual, if that's what you're getting at."

"Did someone follow him?" Jenny said.

"Yeah. We paid a retired case officer. Nada."

"You're sure?"

"As sure as I'm Fred Ainsley aka Mort. Just so you know, you might want to keep tabs on the 'ol' deplorable for the time being."

"Why?" Jenny said.

"I put in for a transfer and my orders just came through yesterday. They haven't named a replacement yet."

"Where're you headed?" Dave said.

"Back to the Middle East. Can't say anything more. I'll need to bone up my Arabic skills for one thing. Then there's those minor details that come with packing shit."

"Good luck," Jenny said. "I think I'll pay another visit to Yìchén for you in the meantime."

"Great. You do that." He drained his glass. "Well, kids, I hate to drink and run, but I've got some things I need to take care of before the excitement begins tomorrow."

"Hasta la vista, baby," Dave said, raising his glass of whiskey.

"Toodles," Jenny said, raising hers.

After Fred left, Dave turned to Jenny and smiled. "I'm glad we finally have some alone time together."

"Me too," she said. "I've missed you."

He put his arm around her and gave her a hug. "I've missed you too."

She pulled back, remembering why he had left her. "How was it in Oklahoma?"

"Depressing."

"Yeah, it's hard to watch someone you love die."

She expected him to correct her, saying "loved," not "love," but he didn't.

"I wasn't talking about my ex-wife. I was talking about all the backwoods people who live there. One of her neighbors had an annoying young twit, maybe two or three years old, who came over to the house every day. The kid never shut up. I wanted to put a piece of duct tape on his mouth."

Jenny laughed. "I'm sure it wasn't as bad as that."

"Oh, no? I'd bet you'd have had the same reaction if you had been in my shoes."

"You might feel differently if it was your kid."

"I doubt it."

She had hoped to feel more comfortable telling him about the baby. No way now. It was obvious to her that he had an aversion to having children. A tingling of pain coursed through her veins. *I miss Mom. I wish I could talk to her about this.*

"Hey, whaddya say we continue this party up in my room?" he said, draining his glass. "Do the horizontal boogie and play hide the salami and all that?"

She couldn't help but smile at his crude sexual joke. She had gotten used to his crudeness at times. It wasn't that which bothered her. She just didn't feel like being close to him right now. Their relationship had soured as far as she was concerned.

"Maybe some other time. It's late and I need to be at my best tomorrow morning. I have a lot riding on this case. I hope you'll understand."

He had a hurt look on his face. "Yeah, I understand."

———— ✦ ————

Yìchén found out there were three possible Starbucks restaurants near Medina where Charles Parker, the CEO of LineageFinder, might buy a latte. He needed to find out which coffeehouse he usually frequented. John said Parker arrived at work around 9:30 a.m., so if he stopped on the way for a latte, that meant he'd leave his house at 8:45 or 9:00 a.m.

In his MSS training before he left Beijing, Yìchén learned spy tradecraft, like how to make dead drops, how to avoid surveillance detection as well as how to send transmission bursts via shortwave radio on a numbers station. He also learned about toxic substances and poisons.

He remembered his Chinese instructor telling the class how someone tampered with capsules of Extra Strength Tylenol in the Chicago area in 1982 and laced them with lethal amounts of potassium cyanide, which killed seven unsuspecting people. As a precaution in case he was ever caught, the MSS had given Yìchén two cyanide pills. Now he had a chance to use one of them. *These pills have come in handy. Definitely the right choice for the CEO.*

Yìchén drove over to Medina the next day, traveling the speed limit of twenty-five mph through the neighborhood, and got to the CEO's house around 8:45 a.m., just as Parker pulled his blue Aston Martin Valkyrie out of the driveway and headed toward Bellevue. Yìchén waited three minutes, then followed Parker's car in his silver SUV, leaving enough room between them to go unnoticed.

When Parker pulled up to the Starbucks drive-through, Yìchén's SUV was right behind him. Parker ordered, then paid for his drink and was quickly on his way. Yìchén was next. The smell of roasted coffee wafted from the drive-through window.

"What'll you have?" the female barista said in Spanish-accented English.

"The same latte the guy in the Aston Martin ahead of me ordered."

"He ordered a chai latte. Is that what you want?"

"Yes, please." He handed her a twenty.

She gave him his change and went to the latte machine and watched as it poured a chai latte into the cup. Then she put a lid on it and handed it to Yìchén.

He took it from her, then said, "You're very nice. Have you been working here long?"

"Just started last week."

"Is this store hiring? I could use a job."

"We're in desperate need of help actually. You apply online. It's a plus if you have prior cashier experience."

"Thanks for the tip." He smiled. "I hope I get to work with you."

Now all he had to do was get hired and wait for the right opportunity.

———•⁜•———

The RCMP, Fred, Jenny, Dave and other agents showed up at the Bin residence on the West Side in Vancouver, BC, at 2:00 a.m. with guns drawn to arrest Charles and Elizabeth. They planned to arrest them, take them into custody, then extradite them to the U.S.

Elizabeth, still in her pajamas and barely cognizant of what was happening, came out of the house and gave Jenny a hateful stare as she passed by, then spit at her. Although her blood pressure rose, Jenny remained professional and stifled the urge to slap her. Mrs. Liu was followed by her husband, Charles, who hung his head low as he was being handcuffed and taken away.

They were loaded into a police van and driven to the I-5 South entrance to the freeway toward Seattle. There wasn't much traffic at this hour. They arrived at the King County Jail in downtown Seattle in record time—less than the normal two hours and forty-six minutes. Taking the James Street exit from I-5, they turned left and then left again on Fifth Avenue, arriving at the tall multi-story building, which looked more like an outdated corporate office building than a jail.

No visitors were allowed at the jail as a precaution to limit Covid-19. However, professionals and new inmates were let inside if they wore face masks. Jenny remembered her dad telling her, "Be kind to others even when they are unkind to you."

Jenny visualized her own mother going through something like this. Her strong mother might've lashed out too. Jenny handed Mrs. Liu a face mask. "Please put this on," she said. "I'm sorry you have to go through this. I wish things were different."

"*Zhū!*" Elizabeth mumbled under her breath in Mandarin. She called her a pig.

Jenny's cell phone rang. "I need to take this," she said to Dave. "It's an emergency." She walked out of ear shot from the others.

When she came back to the group, Dave said, "What was it?"

"It's my dad. He's in the ICU at Evergreen Health Hospital."

"What's wrong?"

"Covid. He's on a ventilator. He's been on it for over a month now."

"I'm so sorry."

"The nurse said he's now suffering from Post-Intensive Care Syndrome, which includes symptoms like weakness, balance problems, and breathing difficulties. He also has difficulty concentrating, slowed mental processing and is suffering from depression and insomnia."

"Wow! That's a boat-load of shit."

"The nurse said he's mad at us for letting him live and he's angry at the whole world. I feel so helpless to do anything to comfort him."

"Are you able to visit him?"

"Yes. Immediate family only. The nurse said I should come as soon as possible."

"Jenny, I can handle this thing with the Lius. You should be with your dad."

"I've worked so hard on this case. I want to see that they get justice. I love my dad, but I need to work. Patriotism is more important than family."

"I just hope you don't regret that statement."

The following day, Jenny paid another unannounced visit to Yìchén. She was torn by mixed emotions. Love at finding out the revelation of him being her brother and anger at finding out about the blackmail/rape. *Which emotion is stronger?* She wasn't sure.

He was fixing himself lunch when she knocked on the door.

"Just a minute," he hollered.

"It's just me," she said, opening the door. "What's that I smell?"

"I'm making Sichuan chicken and rice for lunch. I have enough. Would you like some?"

"I'd love some. Why didn't you just go to Tian Fu and buy it?"

"They don't offer the chicken, only pork, and anyway, I like mine extra hot. My mother showed me how to make it. It's her recipe."

A pang of sadness came over her that he got to grow up with his biological parents while she was the child who was given up for adoption.

"That's how I like it too. We must have the same stomach."

He laughed. "Let me get another place setting. What would you like to drink?"

"Water is fine."

He went to the refrigerator. "I have a chilled bottle of Gewürztraminer on the white side. How about that?"

"Sounds good. Whatever."

As he was preparing the food and setting the table, she said, "Did you end up going on a tour?"

"I did."

"Did you go alone?"

"Yes. But there was a group of us. Maybe thirty-five people."

"Where did you go?" Fred had already told her, but she wanted to hear it from Yìchén.

They sat down to dish up and eat. Yìchén opened the bottle of wine and poured each of them a glass.

He took a sip of the wine. "Europe. Venice, Florence and Rome, to be more exact."

"Any photos?"

He took out his iPhone to show her some pictures of his trip. "Here's one of me in Florence standing next to the famous statue of David."

"Nice." She stabbed a piece of the chicken. "This is delicious."

"Glad you like it."

"What was your favorite part of the trip?"

"Probably the excursion to San Gimignano, a small hill town in Tuscany. The old part of town was lined with some fantastic medieval houses. I had lunch and dinner there. I ate something called crostini toscani and it was excellent, but, Charlotte, it wasn't near as good as my mother's Sichuan chicken."

She had almost forgotten he knew her as Charlotte. She smiled and held up her glass of wine in a toast. "To your mother!"

"Yes, to my mother," he said, raising his glass.

"What is she like?"

He wiped his lips with a napkin. "She's the type of person who lights up a room with her presence. She's a strong woman with passionate ideals. She's also gregarious and funny."

My heart still has a hole in it for my adoptive mother, but I wish I could meet my birth mother.

"Do you miss her?"

"What kind of a question is that? Of course, I miss her. But I'm making a better life for myself here."

His tone of voice made it sound like he didn't believe his own words.

He put down his fork and took a gulp of wine. "I found out my twin is still alive. I wonder if she's anything like my mother."

Jenny was surprised at this but remained poker-faced. She wasn't about to reveal her true name. No reason to right now.

"How did you find her?"

"I did a DNA test on LineageFinder. I'm not sure where she lives, but her name is Jen Hae Chu."

Jenny stared at him blank-faced. "I thought you said you were an only child."

"Because of the one-child policy the state had found out and taken one child away. They abandoned my twin at the train station. My mother carried guilt over this her whole life."

Jenny's eyes teared up. *So, my biological mother did care after all. That makes me so happy.*

She quickly recovered. "Yìchén, what are your plans now?"

"I'm bored sitting at home. I want to get a job."

"Don't you need a work visa?"

"Mort was able to obtain one for me."

Good ol' Fred. At least he's useful for something.

She took a sip of wine. "What kind of job?"

"I want to start out small and get some practical experience. I'm hoping for a job as a barista at a coffee bar. It will give me more people contact."

"Like Starbucks?"

"Maybe. If they'll hire me."

July 2020

CHAPTER 21

After two interviews, Yìchén got hired as a barista at Starbucks and became fast friends with Carmen, the drive-through barista. Their shift ran from 4:00 a.m. till noon. As new recruits were rarely asked to work the drive-through, Yìchén needed to work fast and make few mistakes in order to prove himself. He was a quick learner, so it didn't take him long.

His first goal, however, was to secure a weapon in case there were complications from poisoning the CEO. He had done his homework about purchasing a handgun that couldn't be traced back to him, e.g., a ghost gun. Gun shows and gun shops required registration, background checks and U.S. citizenship. There was a website called ghostguns.com which seemed a better option. However, purchases from that site also required U.S. citizenship.

He was focused solely on the CEO/handgun right now, and since John had quit, he decided he needed to enlist someone else to help. Perhaps that person could be Carmen who was the right age and, spoke English well even with Spanish accent, and was a full-blooded American.

Carmen was shorter and thinner than Yìchén and had long dark hair, eyes to match, and a nose ring and tongue ring. Yìchén liked working with her because she was efficient and fast.

"I'm thinking of maybe going somewhere for drinks tonight," he said one Friday morning. "You interested?"

"Heck, yeah! My boyfriend is out of town and I'd rather not sit home pining for him. Where?"

"Where would you suggest?"

"How 'bout a dive bar near where I live?"

"Where do you live?"

"Belltown. Not far from Pier 66."

"What's a dive bar? Is that like a pub?"

"Pubs are usually larger, cleaner and more friendly to those who didn't grow up within a three-block radius of the bar. I'm sure you'll like it."

"Sounds good. Give me the address and I'll meet you there at eight."

Friday night, Yìchén headed west on I-90 from Factoria and then weaved through streets in Belltown to get to the Screwdriver Bar, a dimly lit basement dive bar with a rock 'n' roll jukebox, pinball machines and live rock shows. He had to show his ID card at the door to get in. Carmen arrived not long after.

The inside looked almost psychedelic to Yìchén. He had never seen anything like it. Music memorabilia and artwork hung on the walls and ceiling, oblong tables stood in the center, bull horns adorned the brick fireplace, and colorful paint-splashed chairs surrounded one bar while round salmon-colored vinyl bar stools surrounded another.

Yellow records and hundreds of yellow plastic 45 rpm spindle adapters were embedded in one bar top. One piece of art that stood out was a black-and-white photograph of a black man with an Afro haircut, large nose, thin mustache and big lips with trails of smoke coming from his lit cigarette, which graced a brick wall in the center. Higher up on the wall were copies of black vinyl records.

The bar, founded in 2016 by Dave Flatman and Chris Jones as a rock and roll utopia designed for the music and art enthusiast, was known to be LGBTQ+ friendly. However, Yìchén noticed he was the only Asian in the room and Carmen the only Latino. But the atmosphere was so warm and inviting Yìchén relaxed.

Next door was the Belltown Yacht Club, launched by Flatman and Jones in 2019, which showcased rock 'n' roll, punk, and rhythm and blues music performances. Carmen had gotten tickets for them to see a punk rock band show later that night.

"What'll you have?" the bartender said as Yìchén and Carmen slid onto vinyl bar stools.

"Make mine a gin and tonic," Carmen said, smoothing her long flowery dress. She wore her hair up in a bun on top of her head with ringlets of hair cascading around her temples and gold hoops adorning her ears.

"And I'll have Scotch," Yìchén said.

"Glenfiddich?" the bartender asked.

"What?" Yìchén said.

"That's a brand of Scotch," Carmen said.

"Okay," Yìchén said. "I'll take it."

"I could use a drink after today," Carmen said in her Spanish-accented English.

"What happened after work?" Yìchén said.

"My fiancé called. He's in Vegas. Due back day after tomorrow. He keeps pressuring me to switch jobs."

"Why?"

"Says being a barista is not a career. He wants me to get a more professional job."

"What does *he* do for a living?"

"He's an accountant."

"Is your relationship serious?"

"Yes. We're engaged. Plan to marry in the fall. We're just waiting on his annulment."

"So, he was married before?"

"Yes." She smiled. "Yìchén, you'll have to excuse me. I need to use the restroom."

"Go ahead. I'll wait."

While she was gone, Yìchén slipped GHB into her drink—the same date-rape drug he had used on John. He hated doing this, hated the Chinese government for forcing him to do it, but couldn't see any other way. It was how the MSS had trained him.

Yìchén waited for the drug to have its effect. It wouldn't take long. He suddenly realized they wouldn't get to see the punk rock band show after all. *Pity.*

After settling the bill with the bartender, Yìchén took an inebriated and drugged Carmen, loaded her into his SUV and drove back to his condo in Factoria. He got her out of the car and led her into the house to his bedroom. He stripped off all her clothes and photographed her in a compromising position using his iPhone. Women weren't his sexual preference, so he didn't penetrate her, although he did take a selfie of her with lips on his dick and himself inserting his fingers into her vagina. Both would be enough to blackmail her. He was certain his plan would succeed since it had with John.

"Where am I?" Carmen said when she awoke and regained consciousness the next morning. She panicked, trying to find her clothes. "What just happened?"

"Don't you remember? I took you home last night."

"Please tell me you're joking."

"I'm not. We had a very good time together. I've got pictures to prove it. Want to see them?"

He took out his iPhone and showed her some of the compromising nude photos.

"Those are disgusting. How dare you!"

"I'm sure your fiancé would agree."

"I can't believe this is happening. What do you want from me?"

"I want you to purchase a ghost gun for me off the internet and I want you to keep it a secret."

"Why can't you purchase it yourself?"

"You need U.S. citizenship."

"And if I say no?"

"Then I'll show the photos to your fiancé. I'll also show them to him if you tell anyone, especially the police, about it. Simple as that. If you cooperate, no one gets hurt."

Carmen started crying and reaching for her clothes.

He stared at her. No way he was going to back down now. "I'm afraid crying won't help. Cooperation will. Don't be too hard on yourself. No one has to know."

She paused, letting that sink in. "Oh, all right. I'll do it."

"That's my girl."

"I'm fucking *not* your girl. Don't ever say that again!"

"Put your clothes back on and come out to my computer. I'll get the website up for you. Let me know when the gun will be delivered."

July 2020

CHAPTER 22

While driving home from the King County jail, Jenny's mind raced with thoughts of Mrs. Liu spitting on her. She wondered what her adoptive mother would think of her new career, especially when it came down to jailing people with Chinese ancestry. It wasn't something she signed up for. Although Jenny felt the Lius deserved to be in prison the rest of their lives, she had self-doubt in her heart for putting them there. Justified she decided.

When does this job get easier?

Jenny looked out the window and saw pedestrians crossing the street with their umbrellas at the stoplight in the unrelenting rain. That freedom which the Lius would no longer be able to enjoy. She had full faith that the U.S. government would seek justice at the Lius' espionage trial. But what if President Xi intervenes to get them out of jail before it happens?

In early July, when Jenny was eight weeks pregnant, she had an ultrasound performed by a sonographer in her doctor's office, which showed the baby's head, body and heartbeat surrounded by amniotic fluid. *Oh Mom, I wish you could see this!*

At this point Jenny couldn't feel the baby move—that would come at twenty weeks. She was, however, awestruck and elated by the picture of the one-inch fetus. Her heart bursting with joy, she wondered what the sex would be and wished she could have shared this special moment with Dave.

Today, she had a sudden intense cramp in her lower abdomen which extended to her pelvic area and lower back. It made her anxious and fearful about the baby. When she arrived home and used the bathroom, she found out she was spotting. Not a good sign.

Oh, God, no! Why did this have to happen now? It's probably nerves or stress, but I need to call Dr. Wang to make sure it's not a miscarriage.

She dialed her number.

"Calm down," Dr. Wang said. "Are the cramps severe?"

"No."

"You're not having chills with a fever, are you?"

"No."

"No blood clots or lots of bleeding?"

"No."

"Then I'd say don't be unnecessarily alarmed. I remember warning you this might happen. It's common for some women."

"Whew! That's a relief. Thanks."

After she got off the phone, she quickly changed into blue jeans and a purple sweater and rushed over to Evergreen Health Hospital to see her dad. The last time she had seen him, he was on a rollercoaster ride of highs and lows, sometimes lucid enough to know who she was but other times telling her that he was divorcing her for another woman or that he thought she was his mother. She had wanted to tell him he was going to be a grandfather. No chance of that now.

Today he was in the ICU hooked up to tubes and a ventilator amid the usual hospital smell. It broke her heart to see him like this, and besides having regrets that she hadn't Face Timed while he was still cognizant, she had an overwhelming sense of helplessness to do anything to help him. She pushed up her face mask and took his hands in hers and squeezed them. He didn't squeeze back.

Her thoughts momentarily drifted to Dave. Why had their relationship soured? Was it worth saving? What kind of man was he that he didn't like kids? She could never be close to someone like that. She wondered if she should still tell him about the baby anyway.

Her thoughts returned to the present when her father's chest quit rising up and down. He was the only dad she had ever known. She couldn't have hoped for a better father. She remembered playing *Weiqi* with him in her childhood and sitting on his knee whenever they had visitors. He had always protected her. Now she needed to protect him.

Jenny panicked. "Nurse! Come quick!"

"What's wrong?"

"I'm not sure. I think he stopped breathing."

The nurse took his pulse, then shook her head.

Jenny began to cry. "He needs to be resuscitated," she said with a pleading look in her eyes.

"Did he sign an order?"

"Yes."

"Code Blue!" the nurse said, calling the resuscitation team.

The team worked on him for what seemed to Jenny like an hour but got no response.

"I'm sorry," the nurse said. "It's no use."

Jenny felt a tinge of guilt for continuing to work after the nurse had first called. *No one could prepare me for that kind of regret,* she thought, even though Dave mentioned she might feel this way.

Her father's sixtieth birthday was Thursday. Now instead of planning a birthday celebration for him, she'd be planning his funeral.

A tear rolled down her cheek. *My life seems to have taken a turn for the worse. It just sucks!*

Yìchén received the ghost gun from Carmen on Saturday afternoon and returned to work at Starbucks in Seattle, near Medina, on Monday morning, acting as if nothing had transpired between them. He wore gray casual clothes underneath a company-issued green apron.

"Good morning, Carmen," he said in a cheery voice. "I hope you slept well."

She looked at him in disgust but didn't say anything.

He hated himself for what he had done to her, but he hated the Chinese communist government even more for forcing him to do it.

The manager came and gave them their orders. "Carmen, you're on the drive-through. Yìchén, the front counter."

"Yes, sir," Yìchén said.

Be patient, he reminded himself. *You'll get your turn soon enough.*

Three hours in, at 7:00 a.m., Carmen told the manager she had a migraine.

"Okay, go on home," he said. "Yìchén, you take the drive-through and I'll man the front counter."

"I'd be happy to," Yìchén said. "I hope you feel better, Carmen."

His first customer wanted two vanilla lattes. Yìchén handled the order with ease, impressing the manager. He remarked about how polite Yìchén was with them.

There was a steady flow of customers after that. Boom, boom, boom. One after the other. Yìchén had no problem keeping up. *Being on the drive-through is easier than I thought.*

Then at 9:10 a.m. Gary Parker, LineageFinder's CEO, pulled through the drive-through in his Aston Martin. He ordered his usual chai latte.

Damn! I don't have the cyanide capsule today.

Yìchén collected the cash from Gary and fixed the latte, and Gary was on his way.

The next day Carmen was out sick, and because Yìchén did such a stellar job on the drive-through the day before, the manager asked him to be on it again today.

The morning was so busy for Yìchén that he didn't have a moment to rest. The majority of people wanted a venti-sized dark roast coffee or a vanilla latte, but others ordered a mocha Frappuccino or espresso.

A drop of sweat fell from his brow, not only because he was working so hard but also because he thought of the cyanide capsule in his pocket. The MSS told him it sometimes has a bitter almond smell, but it does not always give off an odor, and, anyway, not everyone can detect it. Neither he nor any of his coworkers seemed to notice any smell. *Good.*

At 9:05 a.m., Gary Parker pulled up in the drive-through.

Now is my chance.

"What'll you have?" Yìchén asked.

"Chai latte."

He collected the money and handed Gary his change from a twenty.

Yìchén went to make the latte, looking around to see if anyone was watching. No one was. *Good.* Before he put the lid on, he slipped in the cyanide capsule. The hot liquid would dissolve the capsule in no time. He handed the drink to Gary and watched him as he drove off.

Yìchén knew from his MSS training that cyanide takes about fifteen minutes to work, so he continued servicing customers for twenty more minutes. Then he took a Tylenol pill, knowing full well he was allergic to it and would have the same reaction he had when Mort had given him one several weeks ago.

He immediately vomited.

"My word!" the manager said. "I thought you looked pale. You've probably got Covid. You need to get tested and go home. I'll clean up this mess."

Yìchén did as he was told. *Safe for now, but not for long.*

As he drove home, he saw a pileup on Interstate 405 and noticed Parker's Aston Martin was among them. Looked like it was totaled. *Good. The police probably won't discover his death was by poison until they do an autopsy. That will buy me some time before they catch me.*

Yìchén needed to send a shortwave transmission burst tonight to let Chen Pao know the mission was successful and that he was waiting for further instructions.

He thought of his mother. He was doing this for her. From the first dirty diaper until his graduation from college, he was always the focus and center of her life and wondered how she would cope with the loss. Imagined her sobbing uncontrollably now from grief. Maybe in his transmission burst he would ask about her. He hoped she was safe and longed to be reunited with her. Soon.

I'll call in sick tomorrow.

August 2020
CHAPTER 23

Jenny slipped on an ivory silk shirt and twill pants to match underneath an expensive black blazer to get ready for work early Tuesday morning. Then she began applying ruby red lipstick. While she was curling her lashes, her cell phone rang. She retrieved her phone from the kitchen. The caller-ID said it was Dave.

"Hey, Jen, I plan to stop at Starbucks this morning. Want me to get a vanilla latte for you?"

She knew it was his way of trying to get close, which she didn't really want right now, but then no one should ever refuse an act of kindness, should they?

"I'd love that. Thanks."

"How are you doing, by the way? I mean, after your adoptive dad's funeral?"

"I'm still sad and miss him a lot but I think he'd want me to carry on with my life. He always cared about me and wanted me to be happy."

"I want you to know, Jenny, I'm here if you ever need anything."

"That's so sweet."

"I mean it. Hey, did you happen to read *The Seattle Times* today?"

"Haven't had a chance. What's in it?"

"Big story about LineageFinder's CEO involved in a car crash on 405."

"Sorry to hear that. Was he killed?"

"Yes," Dave said. "My cop friend told me they're doing an autopsy."

"Why? Investigative and toxicology reports can take up to three to five months to complete."

"You can get a preliminary report within twenty-four hours. Anyway, they're doing it as a precaution. My cop friend said Parker had just visited the Starbucks near Medina."

"The last time I spoke to Yìchén, he was trying to get a job as a barista, possibly Starbucks. Wonder if that's just a coincidence since the guy John said Yìchén was so inquisitive about executives at LineageFinder. You don't think...?"

Dave cut her off. "I don't know what to think. You tell me."

"Call it intuition, or maybe it's mental telepathy because he's my twin, but I have a hunch he's hiding something."

"Maybe you need to pay him another visit."

She frowned. "I doubt he'd be upfront with me. He never mentioned anything about John."

"Then let's spy on him when he least expects us to. Like maybe stake out his house to see where he goes."

Jenny shook her head. "Wouldn't the Agency have someone who does that?"

"I doubt they have anyone watching him twenty-four seven. Probably only in daylight hours. I'm talking about an unauthorized surveillance at night. I'm game if you are."

"Won't I get in trouble for doing it?"

"Maybe. But it'll ease your anxiety about him."

"You're right. I'll do it tonight."

Dave raised his voice. "I'm coming with you. You'll need backup just in case."

"That's not necessary. He doesn't have a weapon. I can handle it."

"I'm not taking no for an answer."

Tuesday at 5:30 p.m. Yìchén drove over to the community center in Eastgate Park. Jenny and Dave followed behind him on Newport Way in a rental car. It had rained earlier in the day, so the pavement was wet, and dark clouds still blanketed the sky. Dressed in jeans, baseball caps and t-shirts, they kept enough distance between them so Yìchén wouldn't suspect he was being followed.

Eastgate Park was a fairly heavily wooded area full of deciduous trees with a baseball field, tennis court and community center amongst the trees. Yìchén turned right at the sign for Eastgate Park's community center and wound his way up the small hill to get to the top where the parking lot was located. He saw several cars in the lot but waited a few minutes till the others went inside the gym and he was by himself.

Now is my chance.

He quickly got out of his SUV, taking his shortwave radio and backpack with him. Inside the backpack was his ghost gun and also the holy book, *The Analects*, containing loose-leaf pages of one-time pads Chen Pao had given him that had groups of digits necessary for use in encrypting the messages.

Yìchén hid behind the same grove of trees as before that was several feet away from the parking lot and on the left as you exited the main building.

He froze when he heard another car pull up behind. He kept silent but strained his ears to hear their conversation.

"Let's go inside and see if he's there," a man said. Yìchén heard their footsteps on the pavement fade away as they got closer to the community center.

Yìchén felt a greater sense of urgency now to send the transmission burst on the shortwave radio and do it quickly before someone else showed up or exited the center.

He spoke into the mic to record his voice, which he altered to have a metallic tone. Like before, he did the same drill, tuning into the same frequency he used before for V22, the Beijing station, then spelling out the digits in Mandarin Chinese and speaking them rapidly into the mic at exactly 1800 hours and repeating them twice after the recorded gongs.

Qī sān èr èr sān qī.

Qī sān èr èr sān qī.

Seven three two two three seven.

Five minutes later, Jenny and Dave came out of the center.

"Did you hear that?" Jenny whispered to Dave.

"No, what?"

"It's very faint, but I hear someone reciting numbers in Mandarin. It must be Yìchén."

"Why would he be reciting numbers? I don't get it."

"He's probably on a numbers station. Shortwave radio. It's how spies communicate."

"Where is he?" Dave whispered.

"I think behind those trees on the left."

As they walked over near the bank of trees where Jenny thought Yìchén was hiding, Dave in front of Jenny, both had their Glock 19s drawn.

Dave shouted, "FBI! Freeze! Come out with your hands up."

"Yìchén! It's me, Charlotte," Jenny said.

Just as she said it, Yìchén drew his Glock 43 single stack 9mm pistol, and fired several shots in their direction. The sounds were just a soft *pop, pop, pop*.

Dave fired two rounds, but missed because Yìchén ducked behind trees.

"You sly piece of shit!" Dave shouted.

In a split second, Yìchén broke cover and fired again.

He missed again.

Having trained in live simulations at the FBI Academy, Jenny and Dave were relying on reflexive muscle memory now, firing back several shots each at a moving target because they didn't know Yìchén's precise location, and he moved quickly behind several trees.

Yìchén stopped to return fire.

"Drop the weapon," Dave commanded as he inched his way towards Yìchén.

"Stay back," Yìchén said, "or, I'll shoot you both." He dropped the empty magazine and inserted a full one with another ten rounds.

"Why are you doing this, Yìchén?" Jenny asked. "What is it that you really want?"

Yìchén didn't answer.

Seconds ticked by.

Yìchén fired several more shots. All misses, except for one that grazed Jenny's left ear.

"Ow! I've been hit," Jenny screamed.

Dave shot a quick glance at her but stayed focused on his target. He fired off more rounds.

Yìchén panicked, squeezing the trigger on his Glock ghost gun, firing more shots. This time the rookie got lucky. *Unbelievable.* A bullet hit the male FBI agent in the chest.

He dropped to the ground.

A grunt, like an animal in distress, emitted from the man's throat.

Charlotte let out a blood curdling scream. "Noooo!"

Her scream made Yìchén stop in his tracks as he stepped out from the trees. She pointed her gun at him while she hustled over to where the man was lying a few feet away, blood dripping from her ear. "How could you do this, Yìchén? I'm pregnant. He's the father of my child."

The man smiled. His voice was weak and barely audible, but he mumbled, "I am?"

He groaned and then faded into unconsciousness.

She had a split-second decision to make whether to call paramedics immediately. She decided not to take her sights off Yìchén in case he would shoot at her.

It was so quiet in the parking lot, Yìchén could hear himself breathe.

"It's just you and me now, Yìchén," Charlotte said. "I don't think you want to jeopardize our friendship further, so drop the gun. I'll see to it that you're treated well if you do."

"Are you really FBI?"

"Yes, afraid so. But our friendship was never based on that. You've got to believe me."

"I don't trust you."

"You'll never get away with this. You've got blood on your hands, so give yourself up now before anyone else gets hurt."

"I don't want to hurt you, Charlotte, but if I have to…"

She had him in her sights as he moved back toward the trees and pulled the trigger on her Glock.

He fired back as he slumped down from the bullet wound in his leg.

Charlotte fired again, this time hitting him in the upper chest, near his shoulder.

"Give up?" she said.

Adrenaline coursed through Yìchén's veins. Sweat poured from his brow as he weighed his options. At the moment, there was only one as he was too injured to muster up any further resistance.

He threw his gun out to her on the parking lot's pavement.

She put him in handcuffs and called 911. "This is Agent Chu with the FBI. Suspect is wounded and in handcuffs. My partner has a chest wound and is fading fast. Get two ambulances here quick! Community center at Eastgate Park."

Yìchén didn't hear her say 'Agent Chu' as he was reeling from the pain in his shoulder and leg. He thought of his mother. *What will she think of me now? This will only add to her grief.* He also thought about the other cyanide pill, which he hadn't used. He regretted not carrying it on him at all times. Especially now.

"Where did you get the gun?" Jenny asked.

Silence.

"Are you working for the MSS?" she said.

Silence again.

"Did you have anything to do with LineageFinder's CEO's car accident?"

He didn't answer any of her questions.

"What will happen to me now?" Yìchén asked after a long pause.

"You're headed for the hospital first to get patched up and then to the King County Jail. I'll see to it that you get a fair trial." She questioned him again why he did this, but he refused to answer.

A crowd began to form in the parking lot. Curious onlookers from the gym. On top of losing this gunfight, their scrutiny was too much for Yìchén to bear.

He had lost face and now wished he was dead.

———•✦•———

They heard sirens as two ambulances showed up. One took Yìchén away while other EMTs loaded Dave onto a gurney and put him in the back of the other ambulance. He regained consciousness.

Jenny climbed into the ambulance with him.

She cradled Dave's head in her arms and stroked his face.

Leaning down close so he could hear her, she whispered, "Hang in there, sweetheart. You're going to be okay now."

His voice was faint. "Jen, why didn't you ever tell me you were pregnant?"

She pulled him close. "You said you didn't like kids."

He let out a sigh. "Jenny…I didn't mean my own kids. I'm happy about the baby."

"You are?" She smiled and kissed him. "You're going to make a great dad."

"And you'll make a great mother. Is it going to be a boy or a girl?"

She touched her tummy. "Don't know yet. Not far enough along to get an ultrasound."

"I hope it's a girl and that she's like her mother."

She kissed him again. "And I hope it's a boy who is like his father."

His breathing slowed. "I want to ask you something."

She nodded. "Go ahead. I'm listening."

"I should've asked you this a long time ago. I just never found the courage."

"What?"

"Will you marry me?"

Her eyes teared up. She wasn't prepared for this. She felt a lump in her throat and could hardly speak. "I…thought you said being married was like a jailhouse sentence."

"I did say that, didn't I?"

She nodded.

"Well, I've changed my mind." He paused. "So, what's your answer?"

"Yes, you silly nutcase. Yes. Yes. Yes." She kissed him again.

He kissed her back. The color drained from his face. "That makes me so happy. So very happy. I…love…you…Jen," he whispered, before he groaned and stopped breathing. He was fading away right before her eyes, and it scared her.

"Dave! Dave!" she screamed. "Don't die, Dave! Please don't die!"

The EMTs took over then and tried to resuscitate him but pronounced him dead before they arrived at the hospital.

Jenny broke down and sobbed uncontrollably for the next several hours.

August 2020
CHAPTER 24

On Monday after Dave's funeral, Jenny went back to work at the FBI building on Third Avenue in downtown Seattle. The drab gray building and cold rain added to her depressed feelings. She was full of regret—that she didn't get to tell Dave how much she really loved him, that she didn't tell him about the baby prior to the shootout, and that she even let him be a part of it, knowing full well she was capable enough handling it by herself.

She had mixed emotions about her biological brother. She was glad to know she now had a sibling but felt a strange sense of grief knowing how a family member had betrayed her since Yìchén was responsible for shooting the father of her child.

Today, wearing a suitable black mourner's attire and a face mask, she had to fend off well-meaning coworkers who wanted to extend their condolences and sympathy.

"I'm sorry," they each said. She heard it so many times she wanted to scream.

Sorry won't bring him back. Never realized until now she'd feel this way or that one day she'd be like a grieving spouse. *I didn't sign up for this.*

She sat shuffling papers at her government desk when the SAC called her into his office.

As she stepped inside his office, he was about to say, "I'm sorry," when she cut him off.

She held up her hand, palm forward. "Don't. I've heard it enough today."

"Okay," he said. "Actually, I have some good news. Have a seat."

The aroma of coffee wafted in the air. She helped herself to a cup from a carafe on his credenza and sat in the chair directly in front of his desk. "I can certainly use some today."

He looked her directly in the eyes. "You're being promoted to a case agent."

She looked away. "Not sure I want a desk job. I like undercover work."

"It's more pay and less dangerous."

"Is this because of Dave?"

"Does that upset you?"

"I just want to earn my own way," she said, taking a sip of coffee.

"You've more than earned it on the Liu case."

She smiled. "Thank you."

"By the way, I've fired Woodruff."

Her eyes widened. "You did?"

"Yes. You were right about his loyalties. Thank you for bringing it to my attention."

"No problem. What's my next case?"

"I'd like you to work on the Charles Parker case."

"The recently deceased LineageFinder CEO?"

"Yes. His car accident and death look suspicious. The autopsy found he had cyanide in his system."

"I'll get on that right away. I have my own suspicions of who might have done it."

"Who?"

"I don't want to point any fingers until I do a complete investigation. I plan to pay a visit to someone who is currently inside the King County Jail."

He stood up. "I need to leave. Do whatever you have to. We're getting pressure from the governor and other executives at LineageFinder to get to the bottom of this in a hurry."

"I'm on it," she said, draining her cup and rising from her chair.

"Dismissed. Let me know if you want the new job."

She headed for the door. "I will."

———— • ✦ • ————

The next day, Jenny put on a pair of jeans and a teal blue cotton shirt and headed out to 500 Fifth Avenue in downtown Seattle to visit Yìchén at the King County Jail. Although in-person visitation to the jail was suspended as a precaution to limit COVID-19, there were no restrictions for professionals.

She donned a black face mask and went inside. Yìchén, in a red, two-piece, scrubs-like jump-suit, came out to the interview room looking dirty and disheveled. His hair was sticking up all over, and he had bags under his eyes as if he hadn't slept in weeks. The odor wafting from his body either smelled like a dirty latrine, or maybe it was a musty odor. She didn't know which.

"Yìchén, have a seat. I care about what happens to you."

He pulled up a chair and sat down. There was hatred in his eyes. "Why should I believe you?"

She stared at him. "Well, for one thing, who else came to visit you?"

"It's your job. You only want to find out information."

"That's not the only reason. It's more than that."

He gave her a look that said he didn't trust her. She tried a different tack. "How do you spend your time in here? Do you have any good books or magazines to read?"

Silence.

"How's the food?"

He looked away.

"Would you like me to get a letter to your mother? I'm sure she must be worried about you."

His eyes perked up.

"You know," Jenny said, "my adopted mother who raised me gave me more love than my biological mother ever did but I don't harbor any ill will towards her. Every human has flaws, even me. The point is we should learn from our mistakes and do better. Don't you agree?"

"Go on. I'm listening."

"I want to believe in you, Yìchén. I really do. But there's a lot I don't understand."

He jutted out his chin. "Like what?"

"Like what were you doing behind those trees at the community center?"

"Wasn't it obvious? You confiscated the radio."

"I think you were sending transmission bursts on the shortwave."

"So?"

"To whom?"

"Who else?"

"Stop answering my questions with a question."

"Then stop asking them. I think we're through here." He stood up to leave.

"Please, sit back down and for once in your life be honest with me."

"And what about you—Charlotte? I doubt that's your real name."

"And if it isn't?"

"I'll be honest with you when you start being honest with me."

She paused, thinking. *There doesn't seem to be another way to get him to confess. Besides, he's my flesh and blood, the only family I have left. If I don't tell him now, when will I get another chance?*

"Okay, Yìchén. I could get fired for telling you this, but my real name is Jen Hae Chu."

He stared at her, shocked.

"You mean…the match on my DNA test…You're my *sister*?" He shook his head. "I don't believe it."

"Your twin, to be exact."

"No. You must be mistaken. It can't be."

The overhead fluorescent light flickered.

"It's true. We have the exact same birthdate, and our DNA matches. I didn't believe it at first either, but the puzzle pieces fit. You told me because of the one-child policy the state took one baby away and abandoned your twin at the train station. You said your mother carried guilt over this her whole life. I was the twin they abandoned."

His eyes widened. "No way. I can't believe it's you."

She reached across the table to squeeze his hand. "Believe it. I'm your flesh and blood. You're also going to be an uncle." She looked down at her belly.

"Wow! This is a lot to take in. And that guy…I shot…He was the father?"

"Yes."

"You must hate me," Yìchén said.

Jenny shook her head. "Hating people is a waste of time."

"I'm sorry for your loss."

"I've heard that a lot lately. It won't bring him back. What's done is done. Your turn. Who were you working for?"

"The MSS."

"Thought so."

"It's not what you think though. They forced me to do it."

Her eyes pierced his like a bolt of lightning. "Why?"

"When they found out my father worked for the Americans for thirty years, they cut off his head in front of me, then said they'd do the same to my mother unless I cooperated."

She gasped. "Our dad? I just lost my adoptive father and now this. It pains me to hear it. What a horrible death! How did our mom react?"

Jenny felt funny about calling her birth mother "Mom," so soon after her adoptive mother's death but she was determined to get used to it. It was her way of moving her life forward. She knew her adoptive mother would've wanted it that way.

"It almost killed her."

"I'm so sorry."

"She's a very strong woman."

"Did the MSS tell you to poison Gary Parker?"

"Yes."

"Why did the Chinese government want him dead?"

"A French company is trying to buy out LineageFinder, but Parker was putting the brakes on the deal. My boss, Chen Pao, told me the MSS hired a cutout—the French company—to purchase LineageFinder so the Americans wouldn't know it was really the Chinese who were buying it."

"Why are the Chinese so interested in DNA testing?"

"In order to hack or manipulate humans. China hopes to build a profile on every human on this earth. They've already started doing this, starting with their own citizens. No one travels to China that they don't have extensive background on. It helped that they hacked the records of the Office of Personnel Management in America at the end of 2013."

"Yeah, our government is well aware of that."

"With an individual's DNA, they'll be able to control who gets sick, or they may expose them to a disease or a life-threatening virus. In effect, they will control who lives or dies. Their plan is not to take over immediately but rather gradually over time so that most Americans won't be alarmed or even fight back."

His words actually brought bile to her throat. She realized her fingernails were clawing into her closed palm and released her fist. This man—her own brother—under China's guidance, was capable of more harm than she had previously realized. "Do you believe in this plan?"

"At first, yes. But not after they killed my father."

"How did the MSS communicate with you after you moved to the U.S.?"

Yìchén cleared his throat. "Mostly through shortwave radio. I also met an MSS agent in Rome on the European tour I took. I put the research I had done about LineageFinder's executives on a thumb drive and handed it to him near the statue of St. Peter in the Basilica. The agent later called my hotel room with a code. Please don't tell anyone this. I'm already worried what Chen Pao might do to my mother because of my silence on the shortwave. I love my mother and don't want to see her harmed."

"She won't be. I assure you. Your secrets are safe with me. We'll find some way to get her out of China."

"You could do that?"

Jenny reassured him. "My government can."

"I'd be forever grateful."

"Right now, I need to work on getting you out of jail. Wonder if the MSS knows you're here."

He smoothed his hair. "They probably suspected something because I never sent the final transmission. Usually, I send the numbers again two hours after the first transmission."

"No one can contact you here, besides professionals, because of precautions for COVID-19. They'd have a difficult time getting you out of jail. You'll have a better chance if you cooperate with us."

"I'll do anything for my mother. Whatever you ask."

August 2020

CHAPTER 25

Jenny knew she had to come clean with the Bureau about Yìchén, so she called the office and made an appointment to see the SAC. She went home first, put water and food into Daisy's and Pax's bowls, petted them, then changed into a new bright red maternity dress she bought at Macy's. She could never say no to a red dress. Besides, she remembered Yìchén said, "Red symbolizes luck, joy, and happiness in the Chinese culture. It is also worn by Chinese brides to ward off evil." The color was sure to get the SAC's attention today and maybe even ward off the possibility of her getting fired.

The light rain this morning made her hair look stringy, and she was determined to look good for her important meeting with the SAC. It would also help boost her confidence, so she pulled her black hair into a ponytail and painted her lips ruby red. She decided to also dab on some Dior Hypnotic Poison perfume, the irony not lost on her.

All she needed now was more confidence. She rehearsed over and over what she wanted to say, but butterflies were dancing in her stomach on the ride to the drab FBI office building on Third Avenue. Along the way, she noticed several people with colorful umbrellas waiting at an intersection for a green signal to cross the street. She thought about stopping at Starbucks for a vanilla latte but decided against it because she didn't want to chance being late for her meeting.

She parked the car and took the elevator up to the SAC's office. When she got there, his secretary asked her if she wanted a cup of coffee.

"Thank you, yes. You're a godsend."

"How do you take it?"

"With cream and a little sugar."

"Coming right up."

After the secretary handed Jenny the cup of coffee, she stuck her head into her boss's office and announced, "Agent Chu is here to see you."

He motioned for her to come in. "Have a seat." He pointed to a chair directly in front of his large government-issued desk. "What's up? I know this isn't a courtesy call."

She sat down, put her coffee cup on his desk, and took a breath. "I have the answer you wanted about who poisoned the CEO of LineageFinder."

"Great! Who was it?"

"Yìchén Zhang. He's currently sitting in the King County Jail. I just got him to confess."

"He's the guy you and Dave had a shootout with?"

She took a sip of coffee. "Yes. He's a Chinese defector, an Agency asset."

"How do you know that?"

"It's a long and complicated story."

"I have time. Start from the beginning."

"Fred Ainsley introduced me to him. Fred was Yìchén's resettlement handler. They were playing a game of *Weiqi* at the Bellingham Go Club, so Fred invited Dave and I to join them. I had great rapport with him, so Fred asked me to continue contact."

"Keep going. I'm listening."

"Yìchén and I played *Weiqi* twice more at his condo in Factoria. He shared personal information with me that he didn't share with Fred like the fact he's gay. I reported all of it to Fred."

"I assume he ended up in jail for shooting Dave. Right?"

"Bear with me. I'm getting to that." *Where should I start? Should I go in the order it happened or in the order I found out about it?*

She decided on a combination of the two. "Dave told me his cop friend told him the parents of a guy named John came to the police station complaining that their son was blackmailed by a guy who called himself Zimō. John later found out his true name was Yìchén."

"So, is that one of the reasons he ended up in jail?"

"No. It gets more complicated than that. Yìchén told me he planned to go on a tour. I found out from Fred that he went to Italy. The Agency had a retired case officer follow him, but they didn't notice anything suspicious. Turns out he had been in communication with the MSS and made a brush pass with an MSS agent in Rome at St. Peter's Basilica. He gave him a thumb drive loaded with information about the executives at LineageFinder. The MSS agent later talked to Yìchén on his burner phone in code and told him to get rid of the CEO allegedly because the CEO was stopping a deal with a French cutout to buy LineageFinder."

"Holy shit! He told you that?"

She took another sip of coffee. "Yes, during his confession."

"Does the Agency know about this?"

She shook her head. "I haven't told them yet."

"Why not?"

"Because there's more to the story."

"What else?"

"Yìchén also told me the MSS forced him to become a double and move to the United States after they found out his dad had been spying for the Americans for thirty years. He watched them behead his dad, and they said they'd do the same thing to his mother if he didn't cooperate. He loves his mother and doesn't want any harm to come to her."

"I can see why you said this is complicated. But we already suspected he was a double. When the police processed the shootout scene, they discovered the shortwave radio and the book with the looseleaf one-time pad pages with the codes. The police notified the Agency of their findings and Fred pieced together that Yìchén might be a double."

"That's not all." She took a deep breath. *Here goes.* "I found out from a DNA test on LineageFinder that Yìchén is my twin."

"You're kidding, right?"

She shook her head. "I wish I was."

"How could that be?"

"You might recall there was a time during the one-child policy in China when adopting a baby girl from China who was abandoned at birth was popular in the U.S. I was one of them. My American parents adopted me and never told me. I only found it out through the test. Yìchén also did a test, but he knew me as Charlotte so he didn't realize we were related."

"I hope you didn't tell him."

"I had to tell him my true name in order to get him to confess."

He slammed his fist down on the desk. "*Jesus, Chu!* You've just violated one of the cardinal rules. I could fire you for that."

She shrugged, then sighed. "I know."

"So, besides those bombshells, what else have you got?"

"Yìchén, at one point, told me he planned to get a job as a barista, possibly at Starbucks. When I learned from Dave through his cop friend that the CEO stopped at a Starbucks near Medina before his accident, I put two and two together, and that's why Dave and I decided to follow Yìchén to the community center at Eastgate Park."

"And that's when all hell broke loose?"

She nodded. "Uh-huh. I didn't think Yìchén had a gun, but he fired several shots and got lucky, hitting Dave with a bullet to his chest. I was able to arrest him then."

"Where did he get a gun?"

"It was a ghost gun. He had someone he worked with buy it for him off the internet."

"So, what do you plan to do now?"

"Let the Agency know. I also think I need to tender my resignation. Before you fire me, that is."

Silence.

"Oh…one other thing. I promised Yìchén the Agency would help get his mother out of China."

His voice rose. "My God! That was pretty presumptive of you, don't you think? How do you suppose they'll accomplish that? China is locked down tighter than a three-hundred-pound woman in skinny jeans."

"Did you ever watch the movie *Argo* the true story about a brilliant CIA operative named Tony Mendez, who was able to rescue some of the hostages at the U.S. Embassy in Iran back in 1980? He had the group pose as a Canadian film production team scouting locations in Tehran. Tony has died but I think another CIA operative could arrange a similar scenario and rescue Yìchén's mother."

"What kind of weed are you smokin'? Just because it happened once doesn't mean another operative could pull off another stunt like that."

"With all due respect, sir, I disagree. You just need to have a vision like I do."

"Fine. We'll just see how you fare with that imagination of yours."

August 2020
CHAPTER 26

When Jenny informed Fred's replacement as to what happened with Yìchén as well as her thoughts regarding extracting his mother from China, the Agency paid for her to fly back to the CIA Headquarters in Langley, Virginia, for further discussions.

Jenny wondered what kind of reception she'd receive there. Her parents were liberals and she spent most of her life among liberals in Seattle. Those currently in power in Washington, DC were die-hard conservatives. Although she kept her political views to herself, never uttering a negative word to anyone about this administration, she didn't like the current President and didn't think she'd like the conservatives in the upper echelon of the Agency either. But she was willing to do what it took to get her and Yìchén's mother out of China.

After flying into Reagan National airport the next day, she rented a car and drove to a moderately priced hotel in Tyson's Corner. Early the next morning, she changed into a simple sleeveless black maternity dress. The hot, humid weather made the dress feel clammy when she was outside in the elements but not when she was sitting in her air-conditioned car or hotel room. Then she almost needed a light sweater.

She climbed into her rental car, headed down 123 and arrived at the headquarters building in Langley during rush hour traffic. Security whisked her through the gate and told her to park in the VIP lot. Walking from her car, she passed the Nathan Hale statue and entered the front entrance, noticing the huge CIA seal on the glossy floor. To her left she saw stars carved in the white wall for fallen CIA heroes.

A secretary from the DCI's office came to escort her up the private elevator to the director's office and secure conference room on the seventh floor.

When she got there, a man in a blue suit introduced himself as Samuel Klein and shook her hand. "You can call me Sam," he said.

There were two other women in the conference room. One was a thin, middle-aged woman who had shoulder-length brown hair parted in the middle with no bangs.

"Pleased to meet you, Jenny," she said. "I'm in the Operations Directorate. You can call me Karen."

Jenny learned she was originally from Kentucky, her father served in the U.S. Air Force, and she had risen from the ranks to the job as Director, amid controversy. When she said her name, Jenny realized who it was who stood in front of her. There was a fuss in the press about her because she had overseen a secret CIA prison in Thailand, code-named the Cat's Eye, which housed Al-Qaeda suspects, and used torture techniques, such as waterboarding.

Oh my God! What have I gotten myself into?

"And I'm also in the Operations Directorate," the other woman said. "You can call me Connie."

Obviously, the Agency isn't the old-boy-network anymore. Good.

"Would you like a cup of coffee?" Karen asked.

"I'd love one, thank you," Jenny said.

"Black?"

"Cream and sugar," Jenny said.

Karen asked her secretary to get it for her. The secretary came back and handed Jenny the cup.

"So sorry about Dave," Karen said. "I heard you're pregnant. When's your baby due?"

"February. Thanks for asking."

"You have a tough road ahead of you as a single mom. If there's anything I can do, just let me know."

It's worse than you know. I might not have a job left when I get back. Maybe these conservatives aren't so bad after all. At least she has a heart.

The atmosphere in the conference room was tense, and it was so quiet, Jenny could hear herself breathe and feel her heart pound. "Well… you can help get my biological mother out of China."

"A complicated history you have," Karen said. "We might not be so apt to do it for the son—someone who has been funneling secrets to China, murdered two people, including Dave and Gary Parker and blackmailed and sexually assaulted a teenage boy—but Yìchén's father was a crown jewel for us and we'd do anything to help his wife escape."

"Yìchén might also provide valuable information now that he's been flipped."

"We took that into consideration. That's why we brought you here. Sam may have some ideas. Go ahead, Sam, the floor is yours."

"We obviously can't have a repeat of using a Canadian film production team to scout locations like we did in Tehran," he said.

"Understood," Jenny said. "So, what *can* we do? What else?"

"First, we need a false flag operation to divert attention away from the mother's rescue effort. Maybe something to do with Taiwan since that is such a touchy topic for China. Maybe a naval exercise or a missile launch."

"I don't think the president would go for that," Karen said. "He wouldn't risk a major showdown with China over the mother of someone who murdered an FBI agent."

Jenny winced. She had mixed emotions and felt torn between her love and grief for Dave and her hope of getting to see her biological mother and seeing to it that her brother was released from prison. She sipped her coffee and remained silent for the moment.

"Then what about something involving fentanyl?" Sam said. "Maybe we could stage an interception by the U.S. Navy in the South China Sea of a ship coming from China that is loaded with fentanyl. Then there is fake news that a child of someone high up in the U.S. government dies of a fentanyl overdose. The U.S. government pitches a fit, accusing the Chinese government of complicity. Things get ugly, then mom can fly out under the radar."

"The Chinese usually use a cutout. They ship it to Mexico, and we can't intercept a ship going to Mexico," Karen said.

"How about a major trade war with China?" Sam said.

"Now, that's a possibility," Karen said. "I think the president would agree to that."

The others nodded in agreement.

Jenny stirred her coffee. "Now that that's settled, what about the rescue?" she said. "How will that go down, Sam?"

"We get an executive from one of the big firms, like Google, Microsoft or Apple, to travel to Shenzhen with his wife on a private plane. There are a lot of tech companies in Shenzhen. Then Yìchén's mother switches places with the wife on the return trip back to the U.S."

Connie interrupted to clarify. "We know from Yìchén's father's history that the family has relatives in Shenzhen."

Jenny nodded. "Yìchén told me his mother visits their relatives at the end of September every year. But how will we get word to her? The MSS probably watch her like a hawk."

"Don't worry. We have ways," Karen said.

"Sam," Connie said, "how do you propose we get an executive from one of the big firms to go along with this?"

"Nothing good ever comes easy," Sam said. "Difficult, but not impossible in my book. As Mark Zuckerberg has said, 'The biggest risk is not taking any risk…In a world that's changing really quickly, the only strategy that is guaranteed to fail is not taking risks.'"

"Which executive?" Karen said. "Bill Gates is too well known. Tim Cook is gay. Google's CEO is Pichai Sundararajan, an Indian-American. If he's married, I'm sure his wife isn't Chinese."

"Maybe someone below them," Sam said.

"I think Apple is our best bet. Its brand is so well known all over the world. There would be little opposition to a proposed meeting in Shenzhen, the tech capital of China."

"Tim Cook will never go for it," Karen said. "Too much flak if something goes wrong."

"Then we won't tell him," Sam said.

"Samsung, which is headquartered in Korea, is better known," Jenny said. "However, if I remember correctly, Apple sued Samsung in 2011 over patent infringement because they copied the iPhone design."

"They aren't the only Asian country to steal intellectual property," Karen said, shaking her head. "Tencent, whose headquarters is in Shenzhen, is the world's largest online video game company, but it also has a reputation for stealing ideas from competitors and creating counterfeit copies. Its founder and chairman, 'Pony' Ma, famously said, 'to copy is not evil.' He is known in Asian circles as 'a notorious king of copying.'"

"He might feel differently if he was the creative genius behind the original idea," Connie offered. "I also heard Jack Ma of Alibaba Group said, 'The problem with Tencent is that all of their products are copies.' In order to undo the damage to its reputation Tencent has begun aggressively acquiring other companies, rather than trying to duplicate their products."

"There is a big difference between American companies and Chinese firms," Karen said, pulling a strand of brown hair back behind her ears. "Chinese companies often get startup or 'seed' money in their initial stages from the Chinese government, unlike American companies who succeed or fail based on their own efforts. Tencent allegedly received funding from the MSS early on."

Jenny nodded. "It's a wonder American companies can compete at all, but one thing they'll never take away from us is our genius-like creativity or innovation because of the freedoms we enjoy. God bless America for that!"

Sam agreed. "We just need to secure our competitive edge," he said.

Karen drummed her fingers on the conference table. "As you may know, the president signed two executive orders early this month directed against TikTok and WeChat."

Sam looked at her. "I'm familiar with TikTok. I think it's owned by a Chinese company called ByteDance, isn't it?"

"Yes," Karen said, nodding. "It's an app used by the younger crowd to show short videos of themselves dancing, singing, performing comedy, or lip-syncing,"

Sam arched an eyebrow. "So, what is WeChat?" he asked.

"WeChat is part of Tencent," Karen said in a matter-of-fact tone. "It's a phone app with voice and text messaging and timeline. It's the most popular social mobile app, in China mostly, with over one billion monthly active users. Sort of an alternative to Facebook, which is banned in China."

"Why did the president go after WeChat?" Sam said with a quizzical look on his face.

"Not exactly sure," Karen said, shrugging, "but I think it was over allegations of censorship of politically sensitive content and surveillance issues with the app."

Jenny looked at her watch. "To get back to the question of finding an executive in one of the big five firms," she said, "I have a professor friend from my college days who is high up in Apple. He might be a possible candidate. If something goes wrong, it won't affect him because he's thinking of changing jobs anyway."

"Is he married?" Sam asked.

"Yes."

"How old is he?"

"Mid-fifties."

"What's his name?"

"Paul Duncan, and his wife's name is Angie."

"What does his wife look like?"

"She's a petite Asian-American and suffers from alopecia. She wears a wig."

"What color?"

"I'm not sure."

"What's your friend Paul's political affiliation?" Karen said.

"Pretty sure he's an independent. Doesn't get involved in politics."

"Any military service?" Sam asked.

Jenny took a sip of coffee. "He doesn't have any, but his dad was in the Army. Fought in the Vietnam War. From what he said, their family moved around a lot when he was a kid."

"Is he trustworthy?" Sam said. "Do you think he and his wife could keep a secret?"

"No question, they could. They're pretty much introverts."

"What's his position at Apple?"

"He's one of the chief engineers. Not sure of his job title, but he travels for business a lot."

"What if he says no?" Karen said.

"You introduce me, Jenny, and I'll make the pitch," Sam said. "He won't say no."

"Let's get to work," Karen said, rising from her chair.

"One more thing before we go," Jenny said, draining her cup.

"What?" Karen asked, sitting back down.

Jenny's eyes searched Karen's face. They locked eyes. "What should I tell Yìchén? Will he get out of jail?"

"Tell him we're working on it. Nothing more. Now, if you'll excuse me, I have other work to do." She got up to leave.

"Thank you," Jenny said, rising from her chair. "Thank all of you so much. This means the world to me."

She boarded an Alaska Airlines flight that afternoon back to Seattle and felt a sense of calm come over her that things had gone well so far, mixed with a tinge of uncertainty and anxiety about the future.

September 2020

CHAPTER 27

On Monday, Jenny and Sam boarded a two-hour nonstop Alaska Airlines flight from Seattle to San Jose, California, the closest airport to Silicon Valley, so she could introduce him to Paul and Angie Duncan.

Paul worked at Apple headquarters, known as Apple Park, in Cupertino in what looked like a giant circular spaceship amidst the lush flats that sprawled across 176 acres of land. He and Angie owned a Tudor-style mansion in nearby Menlo Park, which is where Jenny and Sam were headed, hoping to catch Paul after he arrived home from work.

They rented a car at the airport and arrived at the Duncan residence at 7:00 p.m. They rang the doorbell.

Paul opened the door. Distinguished-looking, he was of medium height with short cropped premature gray hair and a trimmed beard. His ice-blue eyes lit up his face. "Always good to see you, Jenny." He gave her a hug. "Who's your friend?"

Sam held out his hand. "Samuel Klein. You can call me Sam."

Paul shook his hand. "Welcome. Come inside. A friend of Jenny's is a friend of mine. This is my wife, Angie."

Angie was a petite woman with a heart-shaped face and pale complexion. She wore a black pageboy wig with bangs, straight hair on the sides and ends turned under, completing a look similar to Anna Wintour, the editor of Vogue magazine, except her hair was coal black instead of sandy blonde. She even wore large sunglasses like Anna. She hugged Jenny.

"This is my friend, Sam Klein," Jenny said.

"Glad to meet you," Angie said.

"The pleasure is mine," Sam said.

"Come," Paul said as he closed the door. "Sit down. Would you care for a drink? We were just about to have a glass of brandy."

"None for me," Jenny said as she sat down on the sofa. "Thank you."

"I'd love one," Sam said.

After a bit of small talk, Paul asked, "What brings you two here?" He handed Sam his brandy snifter, then poured a glass for himself and his wife. "Business or pleasure?"

"My friend has a proposition for you," Jenny said. "Go ahead, Sam. Tell them."

"I trust you can keep a secret," Sam said.

"Our lips are sealed," Paul said.

"We have a situation," Sam said. "I actually work for the CIA."

"Oh?" Paul said.

Sam told them about Yìchén being forced to watch his father's beheading and the fact that the father had worked for the CIA for thirty years and how the MSS threatened to do the same to his mother if he didn't cooperate. "We need help in getting the mother out of China."

"Where is Yìchén now?" Paul asked.

"Sitting in the King County Jail, I'm afraid," Sam said. "He murdered an FBI agent. It's a complicated story."

"Try me," Paul said, taking a sip of the brandy.

"I'll tell them," Jenny said.

She cleared her throat and told them about Yìchén poisoning LineageFinder's CEO and Dave getting killed in the shootout.

"Dave was not only my partner," Jenny said. "He's also the father of my unborn child."

"I'm so sorry, Jenny," Paul said. His wife echoed his response.

"Thanks," Jenny said. "It is what it is. That's not all. I also found out from a DNA match on LineageFinder that Yìchén is my twin. His mother is my biological mother."

Jenny noticed the shocked look on their faces.

"So, now you know why we need your help in getting the mother out of China," Sam said. "Will you help us?"

Paul was stunned and looked at his wife for her reaction. Angie nodded.

"What do you want us to do?" Paul asked.

"Yìchén's mother goes to visit relatives in Shenzhen every year at the end of September. We'd like you to schedule a meeting there with your counterparts around the same time. You and your wife will fly in a private plane, of course. On the return leg of the trip, we'll switch out Yìchén's mother disguised as your wife."

"And how do I get back to the U.S.?" Angie said.

"You'll board a later private plane to Seoul, South Korea," Sam said. "Paul's plane will be waiting to pick you up there."

"Where will we switch identities?" Angie said.

"Perhaps a safehouse or maybe in the bathroom of a restaurant," Sam said. "Somewhere that doesn't draw a lot of attention to you or Yìchén's mother."

"Let us have a few minutes alone," Paul said. He and Angie went to the kitchen.

What will it feel like if the mission doesn't happen and I never get to meet my birth mother? Or worse, what if something goes wrong? How will I live with myself? What will I tell Yìchén?

After Paul and Angie returned to the living room, Paul said. "Sam, Jenny, we've made our decision."

Jenny couldn't breathe. She looked at them expectantly.

"We'll do it," Paul said.

Jenny felt like her heart would burst. She got up from the sofa, went over to where Paul and Angie were standing and gave them each a hug.

"Thank you so much, you two. You don't know how much this means to me. How can I ever thank you? I'll be forever in your debt."

"It's getting late," Sam said. "I don't want to keep you two much longer, so let's quickly go over some of the details."

Jenny turned to Mrs. Duncan. "Angie, we'll need the name of the hair salon where we can get a duplicate sandy-blonde wig for you and a black wig for Mom as well as the store where you buy your sunglasses. We'll also need a recent photo of you and the outfit and shoes you'll be wearing. And we'll need a copy of your passport photo if you still have one."

"And, Paul," Sam said, "we'll need the type of private jet you'll be using as well as Angie's plane. Have either of you been to Shenzhen before?"

"I have," Paul said. "I do a lot of business there."

"Are you familiar with the Window of the World tourist attraction?" Sam said.

He was talking about a 118-acre theme park in western Shenzhen that housed almost 130 small-scale reproductions of the world's most famous landmarks, including the Statue of Liberty, the Eiffel Tower, Buckingham Palace, Mount Fuji, the Egyptian Pyramids, and many more.

"I've been there many times," Angie said. "Always had time to kill when Paul was in meetings. I took the Metro to get there."

"Excellent," Sam said. "You'll make the switch with his mother in the restroom of a restaurant inside The Westin Hotel in Nanshan on Shennan Road. There are several restaurants inside the hotel, but the one you want is a buffet restaurant called Seasonal Tastes."

"What type of food?" Angie said.

"Asian cuisine—cuts of smoked fish, seabass, sashimi, lobster, razor clams, that sort of thing—but they also have Western food in their breakfast buffet. A lot of people go there for breakfast or brunch. The buffet is good, but it's not cheap."

"Where is it located?" Paul asked.

"The Westin is across the street from or north of the Window of the World. Just so you know, we'll have surveillance on you the whole time."

"Great! When do you want us there?" Paul asked.

"We'll let you know the exact date later," Jenny said, "but it will be sometime the end of September, when Mom is there visiting relatives."

"I can hardly wait," Angie said, with a tinge of sarcasm in her voice.

"It'll be okay. I promise," Jenny said. *I hope it will, anyway.*

September 2020

CHAPTER 28

Virginia was sitting in the Chief of Station's office at the U.S. Embassy in Beijing, when his secretary poked her head in the office to show them an important cable that just came in from headquarters.

"What's this about?" the COS asked his secretary.

"It's about a meeting at headquarters concerning CACANINE. It's flagged high priority."

They both knew CACANINE was Yìchén's pseudonym.

"Let me see that."

"Here," she said, handing it to the Chief.

He read it and said, "Holy crap!" and handed it to Virginia.

The message read:

TOP SECRET
TO: COS, BEIJING; COB, GUONGZHOU.
FROM: WASHINGTON.
MI COTTONTAIL
MTG WITH TOP OFFICIALS AT HQS REVEALED REASON CACANINE'S FORCED DEFECTION. SUBJECT WITNESSED CACLIPPER'S BEHEADING. GOVT THREATENED KILL MOTHER IF SUBJECT DID NOT COOPERATE. SUBJECT POISONED CEO AND KILLED FBI AGENT. SUBSEQUENTLY IMPRISONED. TWIN, ALSO FBI

AGENT, HELPING GET CACANINE OUT OF JAIL.
BASE TO CONTACT CACLIPPER'S/CAPANZER'S RELATIVES SHENZHEN TO ASSIST CAPANZER'S ESCAPE. CONTACT TO SWITCH PLACES AT RESTAURANT INSIDE WESTIN HOTEL ON SHENNAN ROAD.
FURTHER DETAILS TO FOLLOW.
LF HORSETROT
TOP SECRET

"I warned you about that little mother-fucker," Virginia said.

"CACANINE had some relatives in Shenzhen, didn't he?" the COS asked. "Do you remember who they were?"

"Yes, an uncle. His dad's brother."

"Any on his mom's side?"

"She had a sister who lived there."

"Get on the horn and contact Ernie."

"The Chief of Base?"

"The one and only."

"On it, sir."

Jenny arrived back in Seattle late Monday night and the next morning she put on a pair of black casual slacks and a black cotton designer maternity shirt with gold trim, and swept her hair back into a ponytail.

Daisy rubbed against Jenny's leg as she was getting dressed, requiring her to use a lint roller to get the fur off her pants. Then she looked at Pax. On prior occasions when Dave brought Pax over to her house, the dog would usually go full attack blitzkrieg mode if Daisy dared get near him, even worse if Daisy came within ten miles of one of his treats.

Jenny had taken Pax in after Dave died. The dog usually sat by the window, looking sad and forlorn, his food untouched. A neighbor had looked after him while she was on the trips to Washington and Silicon Valley. Took him for walks. But no one could get him to eat.

"Come here, Pax," she said. He stared into space. She rubbed his back. "I know, buddy. I miss him, too." Her eyes teared up. She ran to the bathroom for a tissue. "You've gotta eat, Pax. He's not coming back."

I know…I'll give him a treat.

She went to the kitchen cupboard and pulled out a bag of beef jerky for dogs. The crinkly noise from the package aroused Daisy's curiosity, and she came into the kitchen. Jenny opened the package, held out a piece and let her sniff.

As soon as Pax saw the cat encroaching upon what he considered his territory, he made a beeline to Jenny and gobbled up the piece of jerky before the cat could get it.

"Good boy," Jenny said, petting him.

Then he stood stationery while Jenny put the harness and leash on him to take him for a quick walk outside before she had to leave to go to the office on Third Avenue in downtown Seattle to clean out her desk and meet with the SAC one last time.

After they returned from the walk, she said goodbye to Pax and Daisy, grabbed her purse and car keys and climbed into her SUV. She hoped they wouldn't destroy each other or her house while she was gone.

As she drove in the bustling traffic, she turned on her windshield wipers to blot out the morning rain. The humid smell of rain tickled her nostrils. She passed a kid on her right who was wearing a bright yellow poncho riding his bike in the bike lane.

She stopped at the Starbucks near the office and ordered a vanilla latte in order to boost her energy to sort through the material on her desk and say her goodbyes to her coworkers.

After parking but before she left her car, she put on an N95 face mask. Then with latte in hand, she entered the box-like building, clicked the elevator button to take her to the fourth floor and arrived at her office before 9:00 a.m. Her secretary let her know the SAC wanted to see her as soon as she got in, so she put her purse down on her desk, took her latte and headed to his office.

The door to his office creaked when it opened as she walked in. He was on the phone and motioned for her to take a seat directly in front of his desk. She didn't have to wait long before he hung up.

"How was your trip to DC, Jenny?" he said.

"Good," she said, taking a sip of her latte.

"What did you learn?"

"That the CIA isn't the enemy the Bureau makes it out to be. That conservatives are pretty decent people, too. That many in Corporate America are as patriotic as we are and will go beyond what seems impossible to help someone get freedom."

"What about Yìchén and his mother? What's the plan?"

"She's my birth mother, too. The Agency said not to divulge any details about it to anyone."

"Understood. I don't need to know. I trust you've got things under control."

"I wish I was as confident."

"So, how do you feel now about resigning? What will you do about money to live and to care for your baby?"

"I never thought I'd choose family over patriotism, but my gut tells me it's the right thing to do. Somehow, I'll manage. I think I've proved I'm a survivor."

"I have full faith in you. In fact, I have so much faith in you, I'm not going to accept your resignation."

"What?"

"No. I want you to take a leave of absence instead."

"You do?"

"Yes. I had my secretary prepare all the necessary paperwork. All you need to do is sign on the dotted line."

"Are you serious? I can't believe this is happening. I expected the worst. I was prepared for it."

"I'm totally serious. After hearing about the complicated circumstances, the director gave his approval."

"What a relief! How long is it for?"

"Three months, but you can take as long as you need."

"You've just made me the happiest woman on the planet. I feel like hugging you."

"No need. You deserve it. Now, get out of here. I'm sure you have work to do."

She collected her purse and headed out of the building to go visit Yìchén in the King County Jail in downtown Seattle. The rain turned into a light mist.

After circling the building several times, she found a nearby parking spot for her SUV on the street, walked a few feet to the towering jail, and went inside.

A guard ushered red-jump-suited Yìchén to a table in the interview room where Jenny was seated. He was more alert this time but had bruises on his face and a black eye.

"My God, what happened to you?" Jenny said with a shocked look on her face. "You look terrible."

"Jen, it's worse than you can imagine. If you have any love whatsoever for your twin, you'll get me out of this hell-hole quick."

"I wish it were that easy. We're working on it."

"So, what's this visit for?"

"I did want to check up to see how you're doing, but I came today to show you something. She took out a photo from her day planner and showed it to him. Recognize these two?"

"Mom and Dad! How did you get it?"

"The Agency provided me with this copy. I know you aren't allowed any possessions in here, so I'll keep this for you for when you get out.

Mom sure is pretty, isn't she?"

She said the word "Mom" on impulse.

It feels awkward to call her that, even painful, but it's overshadowed by the joy I felt in finding my birth mother. It brought new meaning and peace in my life after Mom's tragic accident and death. From now on I'll just refer to my birth mother as Mom. It doesn't mean my adoptive mother was any less important and it might make Yìchén get used to the idea faster.

"You remind me of her when she was younger. You look similar. Are you attempting to relocate her?"

"We're working on it is all I can tell you right now. You need to trust me that I'm doing everything possible to help you."

He nodded. "I don't have a choice."

"I wonder how Mom is coping," Jenny said, changing the subject.

"She's been withdrawn after dad's death. Maybe when she learns she is going to be a grandmother, she'll come alive again. Mom would be so pleased to know she is going to have a grandchild. She's an extrovert. Never hid her true feelings. Always told me she wanted me to marry so she could have a grandchild."

Jenny smiled. "She actually said that?"

"Yes."

"Did she know you were gay?"

"What's the term you use for telling someone you're gay?"

"Coming out?"

"Yes. Coming out to my parents was hard on them. I'm sure it drove a spike into her heart, but later she was okay with it. She still wanted me happily married and said I might always be able to adopt one day."

"She sounds like a wonderful person. I can't wait to meet her. What was Dad like?"

"He was a man of few words. Introverted, I think. He taught me how to play *Weiqi*. We played often."

"So that's the reason you're so good at it," Jenny said, smiling.

"He taught me a lot more than that. He was very wise. I remember him cautioning me to 'Never take your eyes off the goal of encircling your enemy. Don't let your opponent keep you off balance,' he'd say. He was the best friend that I could ever hope for." His eyes teared up.

Jenny changed the subject to improve his mood. "Did you ever take vacations as a family?"

"We didn't travel much, but every year we'd go to Shenzhen to visit Dad's brother, Uncle Feng and mom's sister, Aunt Jia."

"Are they aware of what happened to Dad?"

"Uncle Feng called Dad a traitor but Aunt Jia was more forgiving."

"Why?"

"Uncle Feng works for the local police. Aunt Jia is part-owner of a video gaming company. She doesn't see America as an enemy. She helped Mom a lot after Dad's death."

"Why did Dad work for the MSS?"

"He was very patriotic. He loved his country. Why did *you* join the FBI?"

"Same reasons." She smiled. "Why did Dad end up working for the CIA?"

"He never told me. Like I said, he never said much. I never knew he worked for the Americans until the MSS told me at his beheading. I was shocked."

"So, there wasn't any indication that he grew disaffected with the Chinese leadership?"

"I remember commenting to him that authoritarian regimes outlast democracies. I was so naïve. He told me I had been brainwashed and that I had learned deceit too well. He asked me if I believed everything the Chinese government told the Americans, that the Chinese government had no strategy at all or that we had been muddling through the last three decades with backwardness and are just rising out of poverty. He said few Chinese believe that."

Jenny sighed. "Wow! What else did he say?"

"He said they were all lies and he didn't want any part of that and that he craved freedom. I should have known then that he had switched sides."

"Don't you think that was his way of trying to influence you?"

"Yes. I couldn't see it at the time, but now I do. I thought he wasn't a risk-taker like I was. I was so wrong."

"Sounds to me like he loved you a lot."

"He did. He even said he hoped I would move to the West and that he and Mom wanted nothing more than happiness for me. And now I've put Mom in danger." His voice cracked. "I don't deserve parents like that."

"Yes, you do. You're a good person, Yìchén. We all make mistakes. I just hope I can get you out of here."

He smiled. "I wouldn't mind if you'd hurry."

September 2020

CHAPTER 29

The next day, Jenny returned to the towering King County Jail. This time she brought along a government-issued tape recorder as well as two bottles of water. She quickly ducked inside to get out of the rain and a guard ushered Yìchén, dressed in a red jump suit, to the same table in the interview room where Jenny met him yesterday.

After exchanging pleasantries, Jenny turned on the tape recorder.

"Yìchén, just so you know, I'm recording our conversation today. It might help getting Mom back."

"I'll do anything to help her. I have nothing more to hide."

"I understand we have relatives in Shenzhen. Can you tell me about them?"

"Uncle Feng works for the police and lives in a 500-square-foot apartment in Luohu. He is the one who called Dad a traitor. Aunt Jia is part-owner of a gaming company and lives in an equally small apartment in Futian."

"Why do they live in an apartment?" Jenny asked.

"They aren't poor if that's what you're asking. Poverty rates fell from about three hundred fifty million in 1978 in China to seventy million in 2017."

"I didn't mean to infer that they were poor. I just wondered why they didn't live in a house, especially Aunt Jia."

He leaned forward in his chair, touched his bruised face, and took a deep breath. "Most Chinese in large cities live in furnished apartments. The only single-family homes you'll see are run-down and located in rural areas. I'm sure Aunt Jia is a millionaire. Even millionaires live in small apartments in China. Shenzhen has the most millionaires. Forty-four million, I've heard."

"Why do you suppose that is?" Jenny asked. She was hoping to get him feeling comfortable in sharing his thoughts.

"Probably due to its proximity to Hong Kong. At the Futian Railway Station, you can take a fourteen-minute bullet train to Hong Kong."

"Hong Kong is capitalist, isn't it?" Jenny said. She knew the answer was "yes," but wanted to get his viewpoint.

"That's an interesting question," he said. "The British ruled Hong Kong for over one hundred and fifty years until July 1997. Back then it had a free market economy. Limited government. No price-fixing, no minimum wage laws, and no capital gain taxes. And there were no tariffs or other restraints on international trade."

"And now China rules Hong Kong, doesn't it?" Again, she knew the answer, but wanted Yìchén to feel that he knew more than she did.

"They established it as a special administrative region for the next fifty years, operating as one country, two systems, agreeing to maintain the existing structure of government and economics."

She ran her fingers through her hair. "Sounds like it was good for Hong Kong."

"Not anymore. In June of this year China increased its influence by passing the Hong Kong national security law. I'm afraid it will have a demoralizing effect on Hong Kong."

"Well, at least I can see now why Hong Kong initially had such an influence on Shenzhen."

Yìchén twisted the cap off a bottle of water Jenny offered him and took a sip. "Shenzhen grew at a phenomenal rate. Ever since 1980. There's still a lot of construction going on today. New buildings, highways, tunnels, subway lines, skyscrapers going up. I have always been amazed at its transformation. Also, the city has a lot of green spaces—trees everywhere—in the parks and on the streets."

"What's it like where Aunt Jia lives?"

Yìchén wiped his mouth off with the back of his hand. "Futian? It's a district of Shenzhen and is the main business and administrative center. The tallest building in Shenzhen, the Ping'an International Financial Center, is located there. The district is full of bars, cafes and restaurants as well as shopping centers."

"Sounds like my kind of place."

"It's one of the most exclusive and expensive districts. I'm not surprised Aunt Jia lives there, although now it's more popular with younger single working professionals."

"Is that where Window of the World is located?" Jenny said, taking a sip of water from her own bottle.

"No, it's in Nanshan, a more popular tourist area. Nanshan is referred to as Shenzhen's 'garden district' because it's clean and has easy access to its green spaces. Futian is situated directly east of Nanshan. The Luohu district, where Uncle Feng lives, is one of the oldest districts in Shenzhen. That's where you'll find luxury designer clothing, pricey antiques and smaller apartments."

She wanted him to feel like an expert. She gave him a quizzical look. "What's a typical Chinese apartment like?"

"Light and airy living room furnished with a sectional couch. No clutter. Near the living room might be a sun-room where a person might hang their clothes or use it as a book nook."

"What about the kitchen?"

"It's tiny compared to American standards. And in China they have gas stove tops and no oven or dishwasher or garbage disposal. People in China rarely bake, so they don't need ovens, and they don't cook many dishes at the same time, so they only need a few burners."

"What's Mom's specialty?"

"She likes to make hot spicy dishes. My favorite is her Sichuan pork."

"I remember you telling me she gave you that recipe. Her kitchen must've smelled wonderful."

"It did. My mouth is watering, thinking about all the good food she cooked."

She smiled, then changed the subject. "I'm curious. Is there smog now in Shenzhen like that in Beijing?"

"No, it's less. Years ago, there was an ocean of bicycles on the streets of Beijing, then cars took over, which brought heavy smog. Before the Summer Olympic Games in 2008, Beijing citizens were told not to drive their cars so the smog would be less during the Games. The Chinese weren't concerned for the athletes, however. They were more concerned about reporters."

"That's funny," Jenny said, chuckling.

"I'm glad I got a laugh out of you," Yìchén said.

Jenny felt she had gained his trust and now it was time for the government to cash in on the investment they had made.

"Yìchén, can you tell me anything you haven't already told us about how the MSS operates? Something we might not know. It might help your case—and Mom's."

He paused as if he was thinking. "Years ago Chen Pao told me the biggest misconception the Americans have is that they believe the MSS operates like Western intelligence services."

"By Western intelligence services, do you mean America and its NATO allies?"

"I also meant to add Russia to that group. For example, Russia's intelligence service, the FSB, is involved in spy operations mostly designed for cyber-attacks or to flip CIA officers in order to gain classified information."

"And you mean to tell me that's not the goal of the MSS?"

"The real power lies in the MSS's Social Investigation Bureau. It operates as if it's playing a game of *Weiqi*—encircling its enemies by focusing on the long game of building dozens of influence-peddling united front groups, like the China Reform Forum, and other networks and inserts spies into these groups and companies."

"Wow!"

"It also targets America's weak spots, including think tanks like the RAND Corporation, retired politicians, retired military officers and retired academics as well as unsuspecting business executives. They get them to champion China's interests or engage them in activities they will profit from."

"Incredible. Can you recall any names?"

"Not offhand but if I saw their names, it would trigger my memory."

"That would be awesome. We'll run a list past you. What else?"

"MSS officers are inserted into all kinds of groups who have dealings with China."

"What kind of groups are you talking about?"

"Just about every kind you can imagine. Music, literary, scientific communities, political organizations, the media, academia. MSS officers become poets and legitimate scholars or experts on China, even filmmakers, commentators, book publishers, cultural exchange officials and businessmen."

Jenny's eyes widened. "My God! They're geniuses. It makes perfect sense. Law enforcement or the FBI won't go after them because their influence would be hard to prove in a court of law. Instead, the FBI targets Chinese spy activities or technology theft where they might be able to get a conviction."

"Exactly. Typically, these MSS officers speak English or other foreign languages well, have master's degrees from prestigious universities in America, Britain or France and are deeply embedded in Western capitalist countries. Unlike their diplomatic counterparts in embassies who serve a three-year term, these MSS agents maintain their international connections for a longer stretch of time, some for ten or twenty years or more."

"Another important difference between our two countries. As you probably know, American strategy isn't often long-term. What else?"

"Their biggest coup was turning the West's dream of a more democratic and liberal society in China into a powerful weapon against them to quietly surpass America as the leader of the world. The MSS tasked some of its best undercover officers to convince foreigners that China would gradually liberalize. They're often known as China experts in non-governmental organizations like think tanks or in academia."

"Did Dad ever discuss this with you?"

"Dad said at that time the MSS lacked the skill in clandestine operations like the CIA or Russian intelligence services but it was way ahead of the game in influence operations. Its priorities for influence operations were America, Hong Kong, Japan, Germany and France. He said it was all a lie that China would become a more open society, that nothing could be farther from the truth. At the time I didn't believe him but I do now."

Jenny nodded. "The MSS is certainly patient. I give them credit for that."

"It has paid off for China handsomely. America and its western allies are easily fooled and downplayed or misunderstood the threat. Take, for example, Katrina Leung, who the FBI recruited and thought she was a star paid-informant on China for eighteen years. She was also a star in the eyes of the MSS. Chen Pao told me the information she passed on sometimes went straight to the White House."

"Yes, I heard of her case. She was later arrested and prosecuted but got off on a technicality. Anything else?"

After a short pause, Yìchén said, "America has had a long history of gun violence. As far as I know, the Americans haven't been able to prove that China or Russia is behind some of it but both definitely help cheer it on, especially by influencers they have in the news media, in academia or by influencing politicians. They would love to see laws enacted restricting gun ownership in America."

Jenny shrugged. "Most Americans are sick and tired of gun violence. I know I am."

"All the more reason to put pressure on politicians to enact gun laws. Russia and China will be the real winners if that happens. Their influence campaigns work."

"You may have a point," she said. *He's really opening up to me. Good.*

"I know I do. After the Pearl Harbor attack in 1941, there was absolutely nothing stopping the Japanese from invading America's west coast. Yamamoto strongly advised against it and said—I think this might be a direct quote— 'There will be a gun behind every blade of grass.' Furthermore, the first thing Hitler, Stalin, Mao, Castro, and Chavez did when taking power was to remove guns from the general population and instead arm their revolutionary cadres."

"It makes perfect sense," she said. "I often wonder what would have happened and how the world would be different today if someone had taken Hitler out during the mid-thirties. I truly wish guns had never been invented but since the genie is out of the bottle, I guess we're stuck with gun violence."

"Gun violence is the responsibility of the individual, not the gun. Just as automobile accidents are the responsibility of the individual, not the car."

"But we have automobile liability insurance for vehicles. Hmm. I'm thinking out loud here. Maybe we should require gun owners to have gun liability insurance. The pricier or higher capacity of the gun, the more insurance a gun owner would need to pay and the cost would be prohibitive for a person with a mental illness. Well, okay, that's enough arguing about gun violence for today. What else?"

"The MSS is also using Buddhism as a tool of its influence operations. Unsuspecting foreigners are led to believe in the holiness of Xi Jianping's ideology."

"How do you know this?"

"Dad told me. He said he quit going to Buddhist temples and quit practicing Buddhism because of it. At the time I thought he was nuts but now I feel differently."

"I envy you knowing Dad as well as you did."

"He's still very much on my mind and in my heart."

Jenny smiled. "That about wraps it up for today. "

"Wait…one more thing I think you should know."

"What is it?"

"I'm sure Chen Pao knows something happened since I didn't send the second transmission. He's apt to send some of his goons to rescue me when he finds out I'm in jail. Like I said, the MSS has spies everywhere—in the music industry, the media, the arts, think tanks, academia. It won't take long for Chen Pao to find out. I'm sure he is aware of it already."

"We'll be ready for them if he does."

"All I'm saying is watch your back and be careful."

"Don't worry. I'll keep working on your case and also Mom's."

When Aunt Jia read her emails today, she found one from a subsidiary of the China Birdwatching Society. Aunt Jia was a birder. She had belonged to the society for over twenty years. There were 1,300 species of birds in China and 500 in Beijing alone. The society shared news of bird sightings throughout the year via WeChat, email or eBird.

She opened the email and saw it was signed by a Mr. Jihun Huang.

The email talked about a sighting of the Gray-Haired Canary Flycatcher, also known as *culicicapa ceylonensis*, possibly only the third record or such a sighting. At the end of the last paragraph in the email, it said *hǎo xiāo-x,* which translated to *"good news."* She hadn't received one like this in a long time, not since before Bohai was beheaded.

She had at one time been an intermediary for Bohai to receive secret letters written in invisible ink from his American handler. The letters appeared at her doorstep a day after she received the note with "good news" at the end. They were dropped off at her apartment by an unknown person when Bohai made his annual visit to Shenzhen in September.

They were written to her. Always postmarked from Beijing with a fake return address from the China Birdwatching Society. Inside was always a fictitious open-text letter about birding, written in Mandarin and signed by a Mr. Jihun Huang.

She was surprised when she received an email like this today because Bohai had died several months ago. She wondered if it was a mistake or if his American handler was not aware of his beheading.

Sure enough, someone dropped off a letter to her apartment the next day and knocked twice and then left, alerting Aunt Jia that the letter lay by the front door. Jia opened the door and snatched the letter quickly, brought it inside and shut the door behind her.

She retrieved a cigarette lighter from a drawer in a credenza in her office. Jia had watched Bohai once when he waved the letter over the flame from a cigarette lighter and continued heating the paper until the message darkened to a gold or brown color in order to read the secret message. She did the same.

The message read:

Dear Mei,

Your son asked for help for you to escape China and join him in America. It is urgent that you do so immediately, not only for his safety but also your own.

If you agree, you will trade places with an American woman and will fly to America on a private jet with her husband. She will take your place in Shenzhen and board a later flight to South Korea, then to America.

Make contact with her inside the ladies' restroom at the Seasonal Tastes buffet restaurant inside the Westin Shenzhen Nanshan Hotel on Shennan Road near the Window of the World. Meet inside the restroom at 10:00 a.m. She will be wearing a black pageboy wig. You ask her (in Mandarin), "Pardon me, are you hoping to find Mrs. Sojun?" She'll answer, "Yes, you must be Jing." We will have the necessary passport for you as well as a change of clothes and a wig. Do not take any luggage with you or your phone.

If you agree, leave a signal—a yellow piece of tape outside on the left side of the entrance to your white apartment complex, near the middle—the day after you arrive. If the answer is no, leave a black piece of tape, and if there is imminent danger, leave a red one.

For your safety, do not tell anyone about this.

Good luck!

Signed,

Archibald

Bohai had once confided to Jia that Archibald was a pseudonym his American handler used.

Jia expected Mei to arrive tomorrow. She'd keep this letter hidden in her safe until then.

September 2020

CHAPTER 30

Jenny left the King County Jail on Fifth Avenue and got into her SUV to drive home. Drops of rain splatted her windshield. As she was pulling out of the parking space, she noticed two men in a black Mercedes behind her. *Didn't I just see these two walk past me earlier at the entrance? The ones carrying briefcases. Watch your back and be careful.*

She headed out Sixth Avenue and took the ramp onto I-5 South. Looking in the rear-view mirror, she saw the black Mercedes following several feet behind her. She changed lanes twice, then took Exit 163A toward West Seattle, driving three miles on the Jeanette Williams Memorial Bridge.

For the next ten minutes she played a game of cat and mouse with the Mercedes driver—speeding up, slowing down, changing lanes. However, the Mercedes remained hot on her tail.

Who are these men and why are they following me, or are they? Are they MSS agents? You're paranoid, Jenny. No, I'm not paranoid. They are following me. Maybe they're hoping to scare me. I don't scare easily.

Jenny's defensive driving course training at the FBI Academy kicked in. When she came to Alaska Street, she wove in and out of side streets, making a series of right and left turns, hoping to lose her Mercedes tail.

She sped up. So did the Mercedes.

Her head ached and her stomach was doing somersaults. She feared for the baby inside her. She feared for herself. *God, please help me!*

Her prayers were soon answered.

She drove several blocks which seemed to her like an hour had passed without catching a glimpse of the Mercedes. As soon as she was sure the Mercedes was nowhere in sight, she drove to her home on Forty-Eighth Avenue, pulled into her garage and breathed a sigh of relief.

Thank God! I lost them.

She heard Pax barking as she entered the house through the kitchen door from the garage.

"You hungry, buddy?" she said. *That dog sure can eat!* She opened the pantry door and scooped out a bowl of dog food for Pax and cat food for Daisy. When she put them in their respective dishes, her Ring video doorbell rang.

Jenny wasn't expecting anyone. The Ring video doorbell showed two Chinese men—one tall with a goatee, the other short with a clean-shaven face and slits for eyes—standing outside her front door. Pax went into attack mode, growling and barking as if he was a cornered grizzly bear.

"Who are you? What do you want?" Jenny asked.

"We're friends of Yìchén's from the Bellingham Go Club. Can we come in?"

Jenny remembered Yìchén said MSS agents were everywhere—in the music industry, the arts, the media, etc. It's quite possible they were also at the Bellingham Go Club.

"I saw you briefly at the jail. Why did you follow me here? Why not just talk to me there?"

"The corrections officers are paranoid about people hanging out there, especially now because of Covid. Are you Yìchén's lawyer?"

"None of your business."

"Sorry, didn't mean to pry. Can we come in and talk about this?"

"What're your names?

"What's yours?"

"I asked you first."

Suddenly, all hell broke loose.

The two men busted down the wooden door, guns drawn.

Pax let out a ferocious growl and bit the short man with his sharp teeth, knocking the gun out of his hands. Then Pax went after his throat and neck, his sharp teeth drawing blood.

Meanwhile, Mr. Goatee locked eyes with Jenny, pointing his gun at her.

"Say your prayers, sweetheart!" he said.

"You'll never get away with this," Jenny shouted. She kicked the backside of her right foot to his middle, knocking the gun out of his hand. She immediately followed this with another right-foot kick to his head.

He reached for his gun but not before she spun around and kicked her right foot to his head again, followed by an immediate right-foot kick to his stomach.

While Mr. Goatee groaned in pain, the short one put his hands up to his bloody throat. He was able to free himself from the hold Pax had on him and with bloody hands reached for his gun. Pax jumped up on him and with another angry bite, his sharp teeth tore off part of the Chinese man's nose. The man, screaming in pain, squeezed the trigger on his gun and a bullet grazed Jenny's head. She fell to the hardwood floor, dazed, blood dripping from her temple.

Jenny struggled to get on her feet, slipping on the small pool of blood on the floor from her head wound. *Oh my God! Don't let this be the end!*

The short man took aim at Jenny again, but not before Pax charged at him once more, going after his throat again. The short man quickly kicked the dog out of the way but Pax charged again and bit him in the leg. After kicking the dog hard again, and now with blood dripping from the short man's throat, he set his immediate sights on Jenny.

The dog's attack bought Jenny enough time to get up off the floor. *Sweet Jesus, keep my baby safe! I'm not through with these thugs yet!*

She flipped around in a split second and kicked the short man's head with the back of her right foot and repeated it. Then a second later, she kicked his stomach with both feet in succession. He was out cold.

Mr. Goatee suddenly came back to life, gained his equilibrium and walked over to where his gun had landed. He picked up the gun and subdued the dog first with a bullet in the dog's chest.

Jenny doubled down with a right-foot kick, a left-foot kick, then two feet in succession twice, knocking the gun from his hand again. Mr. Goatee reeled back, then headed toward his gun and Jenny.

"Fuck you, Miss Pussy! You're dead!" he shouted.

Jenny did what she had done before to that little punk on the trail. She stepped back, then ran toward Mr. Goatee, throwing herself on him at the waist, and put her legs backward over his head to topple him to the floor.

Thirty seconds later, after Jenny applied more brutal force to Mr. Goatee's ribs and a final right foot kick to his head, she picked up both their guns, put both men in handcuffs and called the police.

"This is Agent Chu with the FBI. I have two suspects who are wounded and in handcuffs. Possibly undercover MSS agents. Get two ambulances here quick!" She gave them her address on Forty Eighth Avenue in southwest Seattle.

Jenny leaned forward, touched her belly, then the wound on her head and said a prayer of thanks to the heavens as she caught her breath. She was still on an adrenaline high from all the trauma in the last few minutes. She breathed a sigh of relief and walked over to where Pax was lying. His low whimper barely audible.

As she petted him one last time, the dog stopped breathing.

"Dave would be so proud of you, Pax!" she said as her eyes teared up. "I never thought I'd say this, but I'll miss you, buddy! I'll really miss you!"

She called the SAC then and reported everything that had just happened.

An hour went by, then two. It was almost four o'clock when she received a call from the SAC with news about the two suspects.

"You were dead right, Jenny. They were undercover MSS agents. The Agency just confirmed it."

"Any news about Mom?"

"The last I heard Ernie drove past Jia's skyscraper apartment building and noticed there was a yellow piece of tape out near the front entrance. He promptly sent a cable to those in the know at headquarters, reporting that the op was a 'go.' You know more about the op than I do. Maybe you'll hear more from some of your other contacts."

"God, I hope everything goes as planned!"

"I've been in this business a long time. Trust me. Nothing ever goes as planned."

After Jenny made arrangements to have Pax cremated, she was about to heat some leftovers in the microwave for dinner when she received a frantic call from Paul Duncan.

"I'm afraid Angie's come down with Covid. She won't be able to make the trip. I'm sorry."

Jenny's heart sunk. *This can't be happening. Not now!*

"Paul, you know what this means to me. It's our only chance of getting Mom out."

"I know. I'm deeply sorry."

We were so close. Breathe Jenny! Breathe! Her mind was racing, grasping for a glimmer of hope. *Who was it that said 'When a door slams shut in your face, always check the window.' Dave, if you can hear me in heaven, what's the window? What's the damn window?*

"Wait a minute," Jenny said after a long pause. "Angie just needs a substitute. I'll fill in for her. Or, maybe I could pose as your sister instead of your wife."

"Brilliant. You get it cleared with your boss and I'll send my private jet to pick you up before our flight to Shenzhen tomorrow. Have you heard anything from Sam or anyone else?"

"Nothing except that it was a 'go.' Keep your fingers crossed."

The Agency will need to accomplish a small miracle to get my new fake passport ready before my overseas flight, but I have full faith they can pull this off. I'll contact Karen now.

Sam was too well known in intelligence circles to be the lead on a surveillance detection route for Aunt Jia and Mei in Shenzhen. In order to keep those who knew about the operation to a bare minimum, he enlisted help from a good friend he had known almost his whole life. His parents were diplomats and he met Kwan-Jun Lee at the international school he attended in Switzerland and they kept in touch.

Kwan, her nickname, was a Korean national who later worked in counterintelligence inside Korea and China for practically her entire career but had retired five years ago and was now a part-time adjunct professor at the University of Miami, a private college in Coral Gables, Florida. The University had a known connection to the CIA in the past, as it had leased some of its buildings to them in the 60s.

Sam trusted Kwan as if she was his own cherished mother and he had the Director's permission to use her. Kwan knew the drill well as she had been involved in numerous SDRs during her undercover career. She was also familiar with Shenzhen as she had lived there for almost ten years, spoke fluent Mandarin, and still had friends living there, some of whom worked in the gaming industry for Tencent. Sam hoped to confuse the MSS with her presence in Shenzhen. He had full faith that Kwan would do whatever they asked. She would head up a seven-member surveillance team that included case officers from the base at Guongzhou as well as some retirees.

As planned, Kwan flew to Shenzhen on a commercial flight, booked herself into the Ritz Carlton Shenzhen hotel and set out the next morning to trail Aunt Jia and Mei to the Westin Hotel on Shennan Road via the Metro from Jia's twenty-floor apartment building in the Futian residential district, south of Binhe Boulevard.

The Ritz Carlton was northwest of the district and the tall Ping'an International Financial Center building was a little further west. Various apartment buildings were tightly packed inside the residential area, almost as if they were on top of one another. Kwan weaved in and out of the maze, acting as if she were on her morning walk, keeping her eyes peeled on the target apartment building for any signs of life.

She was dressed like a tourist—white t-shirt and blue jeans and white Nike sneakers. She also wore a pair of dark sunglasses under a black newsboy hat.

At 9:00 a.m. sharp, she saw Jia and Mei step outside the front entrance. She followed them discreetly at a distance to the nearest Metro stop, close enough not to lose sight of them but far enough back so as not to arouse their suspicions. When they arrived at the Metro stop, they put on black surgical face masks, purchased a ticket, put the ticket into the turnstile, then hopped on a train on Line 3 for a short ride to the Shopping Park station.

Kwan and two other members of the team got on the same train. She found a seat several passengers away and pretended to read a Korean book she brought with her while scanning the area around Aunt Jia and Mei behind the sunglasses she wore, looking for any signals, any subtle movements, and listening to any and all conversations. She radioed her team members that she did not detect anything out of the ordinary. So far, so good.

Jia and Mei got off at the Shopping Park station and changed trains to Line 1, riding for six more stops. Kwan and two members of the team followed close on their heels. The train was crowded, so Kwan opted to hang onto a pole near where Aunt Jia and Mei were seated. She was within earshot of them but did not make eye contact with either of them.

Kwan noticed two young men in the train car, seated not far away, as well as an older man sitting next to them. The two young men kept looking up from their phones now and then to glance at other passengers, including Jia and Mei.

"I got a good price for pork at the market yesterday," Kwan heard Aunt Jia say. "I plan to make won-ton with it for the party this weekend."

"I love your won-ton," Mei said. "Sorry I'll have to miss it."

"I'm sure you'll be having a party of your own that's far better."

Mei smiled. "I can only hope so. Perhaps the weather might be an indication of things to come. The sun is shining. No wind. It's going to be an all-around good day. I'm sure of it."

"I'm sure, too," Jia said. "Even the smog doesn't seem so bad today."

Kwan's mind was on heightened alert, silently photographing the two young men in her mind, trying to remember if she had ever seen them before, and committing them to memory so she could report it to Sam. One was tall and lanky, the other a solid mass of lard. Both had black hair and wore nerdy-looking glasses. Maybe mid-twenties.

Lanky looked up from his phone and then briefly glanced at Jia and Mei then back down to his phone. Two minutes later, Lard did the same.

Are they just annoyed at the two old ladies' conversation which might have interrupted the games they were playing on their phones? Or, are they MSS agents?

One could never be too careful when it came to countersurveillance.

Kwan saw Lanky nod to Lard. *Was that a signal?*

Several minutes later, when the train car arrived at the Zhuzilin station, two beefy men in blue uniforms hopped on board and looked at Lanky who nodded at the older Chinese man sitting nearby. They handcuffed the man and tried to quietly escort him off the train car.

The man tried to wriggle free but they overpowered him.

He protested, speaking in Mandarin, saying, "Let me go. Where are you taking me? What crime have I committed?"

They didn't answer. Only hurried him off the train car.

Aunt Jia and Mei looked up when all the commotion started but remained silent for the rest of their ride.

Another passenger, hanging onto a pole close to the one Kwan was hanging onto, tried to engage her in conversation.

"Excuse me, don't you work in the gaming industry at Tencent?" he said in Mandarin.

Kwan's stomach tensed up but she opted not to speak. She stared back at him blankly as if he were from a planet in outer space, then gave him a quizzical look as if she didn't understand what he had said to her.

"I'm sure I've seen your face before?"

Kwan shook her head. She remained polite. "I assure you we've never met," she said in Mandarin. "You must've mistaken me for someone else."

"No, I never forget a face, and especially someone with an accent like yours. Where are you from? What's your name?"

How can I get rid of this man? Is he MSS? Maybe a pervert?

"Gun kai!" she said. Get lost.

All eyes and ears were on them, including Jia's and Mei's.

"Don't be so sour, old lady!"

"Gun kai!" she repeated in a harsher tone.

"Sorry," the man whispered. He got off the train at the next stop, which was Qiaocheng East.

Kwan radioed her team members, letting them know about those two brief interactions and that she felt the coast was clear for Jia and Mei.

Aunt Jia and Mei got off the train at the Window of the World station and trudged over to the Westin Hotel on Shennan Road. Kwan followed them at a reasonable distance. She did not detect anyone else following them and gave them the pre-arranged signal they were "black."

Once inside the restaurant, Aunt Jia and Mei sat at a table on the far wall, then helped themselves to some Asian food at the buffet.

The Seasonal Tastes buffet/restaurant inside the Westin Hotel was decked out in orange, modern chairs and faux white marble tabletops. A wooden partition with slats as well as several large cut-out circles divided the middle of the room, and one just like it graced the far wall.

Paul and his "sister," Jenny arrived early and helped themselves to the daily breakfast buffet which featured both Asian and Western food, tea, coffee, and fresh squeezed juices. Jenny surveyed the room and spotted Aunt Jia and Mei sitting at a table on the far wall.

Mom! I'm your daughter. I'm so glad we finally meet. She longed to go over to Mei and give her a hug and kiss but if everything worked out as planned, that would come later. For now, she would remain professional.

She did not make eye contact with either of them, only glanced at them a second or two.

Paul stood in line for the buffet and selected won-ton and noodles as well as fried eggs, hash browns, a huge bowl of fruit and coffee. Jenny selected a croissant, scrambled eggs, a small bowl of fruit, tea, and a bottle of water.

They sat down at a table near the middle of the room and quietly ate their meal. After they finished, at 9:55 a.m., Paul remained seated while Jenny excused herself to go to the ladies' room. She took her satchel and bottle of water with her. As she headed in, Mei approached her.

"Pardon me, are you hoping to find Mrs. Sojun?" Mei said in Mandarin.

"Yes, you must be Jing," Jenny replied.

Because the restroom was in a western hotel, the bathroom had western toilets in addition to the hole in the floor, common throughout Asia. The bathroom included graphics depicting instructions on how to use western toilets, like the fact that a person was expected to sit on the toilet seat, not squat above it.

Jenny went inside the stall closest to the bathroom entrance. Mei followed her lead and went into the stall next to it. While they continued engaging in small talk, Jenny passed Mei some clothes underneath the stall as well as a black wig along with her purse and a duplicate satchel. Mei passed hers to Jenny.

"So glad to finally meet you," Jenny said. "My daughter-in-law told me a lot about you. She said you were having breakfast here today."

Mei was savvy and quickly caught on regarding their "fake" conversation. She began undressing, putting on the new skirt, blouse and shoes Jenny had brought her. "How is she?" Mei asked.

"She's doing well."

"And the children?" Mei said.

"Energetic as ever."

Jenny poured water into the toilet from her bottle of water to simulate she was peeing. She suspected several women were in the restroom. She heard water running in the sink and thought some women must be washing their hands.

Jenny reached for an aerosol container inside her pack, which the Agency's OTS had given her. She pushed the button on the top of the can, letting out a stinky aroma—a mix of gorgonzola and limburger cheese with some rotten eggs thrown in for extra measure. This raunchy odor was sure to result in the other women leaving the restroom in a hurry, or at least not lingering, in the hopes that the occupants' minds were totally focused on the pungent odor and not on two women spies in the stalls.

"Ewww!" Mei said. "What's that smell?"

"Just me," Jenny said. "Have trouble with my bowels sometimes."

The trick worked. Jenny heard the door to the restroom open and close several times. She and Mei, now the restroom's sole occupants, hurriedly changed their clothes.

A few minutes later, the door opened again and a woman came in.

"Oh my God, the stench *is* bad!" she said, as she sprayed a sweet-smelling aerosol.

Jenny panicked and froze.

"Everything okay in here?" the woman said.

Jenny was speechless, but luckily Mei spoke up. "Suffering from gas and indigestion, I'm afraid."

"Hope it wasn't anything you ate," the woman said.

"No, the breakfast was fine. It was last night's fish."

Jenny heard the door open and close again, so she cracked open the door to her stall and peeked out. The woman had gone. When she saw the coast was clear, she knocked on Mei's stall door. "Go!" she said.

Mei quickly dashed out of the stall, adjusted her wig and makeup in the mirror, and was out of the restroom in a flash—for such an old woman that is—all while holding her breath.

Jenny stayed in the restroom, ran water in the sink to wash her hands and adjusted her wig and makeup. She'd wait several minutes until she was sure Paul and Mei left the restaurant. Then she would join Aunt Jia at her table.

September 2020

CHAPTER 31

Unlike with commercial airliners, Paul and Mei went through security in a private jet terminal which allowed them to board quickly, though it was equally secure. They didn't have to wait in a long line amidst the roar of hundreds of other people, as officers came on board the Gulfstream jet to check their passports.

Mei had her fake passport and visa ready and handed them to the passport official. He glanced at the documents only a second or two before he handed them back to her. Next came the Customs agent. She had nothing to declare.

Safe for now.

When they were finally in the air, Paul relaxed in his seat and tried to make Mei feel comfortable, hoping to allay her fears.

"That wasn't so bad, was it?" he said in Mandarin.

Mei was glad to learn Paul spoke her language. It made her smile. "My father always told me that when your life seems darkest, to remember the sun will shine again." She continued to smile.

"A very wise man, your father. What else did he say?"

"Don't be a victim of circumstance. If you want a happy life, you've got to make your own fun, make your own happiness. Yìchén is my life now. That's all that matters to me. Getting to see my son again."

"I don't know much about him. I just know he lives in Seattle."

"Is that where we're going?"

"After we pick up my sister in Seoul, we're heading to California. Then you'll board a private plane to Seattle. I assume your son will be waiting for you." Paul did not say anything about Jenny being Mei's daughter because Jenny asked him not to. She wanted to reveal that secret in Seattle.

Mei looked out the window of the plane. "Do you have any kids?" she asked.

"No, my wife could never have kids."

"I'm sorry."

"Don't be. I taught history in college for several years and my students became my kids."

"What made you and your wife decide to help me?" Mei asked.

"A former student who I dearly love reached out to me. I'd do almost anything for her. I'd also do anything for someone who wants the freedom I have experienced in my lifetime. I'm sure you'll find there is no other way to live once you've tasted it."

"My husband, Bohai, used to say the same thing."

Paul didn't want to bring up an uncomfortable subject for Mei so he changed the subject. "I'm curious to know what you've heard about America—especially California."

"I've heard of Silicon Valley with all the high-tech companies. It's like Shenzhen I'm told."

"That's where my wife and I live."

"What type of work do you do?"

"I'm an executive at Apple. Are you familiar with the iPhone?"

"Yes, I know it. I had a smartphone made by Huawei, but they said to leave it behind."

"Well, we'll have to remedy that situation. When we get to California, I'll give you an iPhone."

"Very kind of you. Thanks."

"We'll also buy you some new clothes. I'm sure my sister can help you pick out something you'll wear."

"You're too generous. How can I ever repay your kindness?"

"It's nothing. Just happy to help. Is there anything else you'd like us to get?"

"A gift for my son?"

"Believe me, you're the gift he wants. I'd love to see his face when he sees you."

"I can't wait. I never imagined this would happen."

"It won't be long now."

Jenny left the restaurant with Aunt Jia and returned with her to her apartment in Futian. At two o'clock in the morning, a black SUV pulled up out front. Jenny waited in the lobby, this time wearing a sandy-blonde wig. The SUV driver flashed his headlights on and off three times, signaling her that it was safe. He was the same man who drove her and Paul to the Seasons Taste restaurant at the Westin Hotel. Without saying a word, she exited the apartment building, got into the backseat of the black SUV and headed to the Shenzhen airport where she would catch a flight to Incheon International Airport in Seoul, South Korea.

Before she left California to go to Shenzhen, the Agency had provided her with a new passport which included a photo of her wearing the sandy-blonde wig, along with the fake name of Ashley Davidson and airfare from Shenzhen to Seoul on a private flight. She also had a fake California driver's license with the same name and photo. She left behind her black wig at Aunt Jia's house, as well as Mei's purse and her cell phone which she had given Jenny in the restroom at the Seasonal Tastes restaurant.

The driver was at the private jet terminal in no time. Jenny got out of the SUV and walked to the terminal. She knew, like Paul and Mei, she wouldn't have to wait in a long line with hundreds of other people, as officers came on board the Gulfstream jet to check her passport.

Jenny nervously handed her fake passport to the passport official. Her brain was overloaded with things that could go wrong, yet she remained calm on the outside.

The passport official looked at her passport and then back at Jenny.

"Ms. Davidson…"

"It's Mrs."

"Okay. Mrs. Davidson, it's odd that a wealthy lady like you would be traveling alone. Where is your husband?"

Her stomach was churning and her pulse quickened. She had anticipated this question. "He had work to do. I often travel alone. Otherwise, I'd be stuck at home. I'm sure you'd agree in this pandemic, it's not good to be isolated and alone. Travel gives me joy and enriches my life."

"And you're not afraid of getting Covid?"

"If I get it, hopefully I won't die from it because I'm healthy."

"Okay, you're cleared. Have a good flight."

"Thank you. I will."

Jenny relaxed and breathed deeply.

Then the customs agent came. He spoke English. Asked her if she had anything to declare. She told him she didn't have anything.

"Come on," he said. "A lady like you must've purchased something."

"Young man, I told you I don't have anything of value to declare. For your information, I spent my money on hotels and restaurants."

"Okay, okay. I believe you."

Dodged that bullet. Dave would be proud of me.

Three and a half hours later, she arrived in Seoul and was met by Paul and Mei in the private jet terminal.

Jenny had told Paul earlier that she decided to keep it a secret that Mei was her mother a little while longer until they were reunited with Yìchén in Seattle. She wanted Yìchén to join in on the surprise.

After an almost twelve-hour flight, they arrived in California, where she and Mei boarded another plane to go to Seattle.

After the directors of both the CIA and the FBI agreed to the conditions for Yìchén to be released from prison, Jenny was responsible for completing and expediting the paperwork and securing his release. Although she still harbored mixed emotions about it because of Dave's death, she decided Dave would have wanted her to be happy and move forward with her life. She completed the paperwork on Tuesday, and by nothing short of a miracle the corrections officers at the King County Jail were able to release him two days later.

Jenny arrived there early to pick him up. She put her arm around him as they walked out the door together.

"Yìchén, how are you feeling right now?"

"Excited. Happy. Relieved. Like I could kiss you for all you've done for me. Like I don't deserve any of it. Like I have a future now, thanks to you."

Jenny's eyes teared up. "And I have a family again. The family I've always wanted." She hugged him. "I don't know what the future holds, but I'm glad I've got my brother and our family will soon be reunited."

The sun was shining with only a few white clouds in the sky. Pedestrians were scurrying across the street when Jenny unlocked the car doors. "Get in," she said. "Mom is waiting for us at my house. Let's go!"

While they headed south on I-5 for the twelve-minute trip to the Jenny's home in southwest Seattle from the jail, Jenny steered the conversation to something light to ease the tension.

"Do you like pets?" she asked, adjusting the mirror.

"I had a golden retriever named Gǒu that I had to leave behind. I miss him. I'd love to have another dog."

"What happened to him?"

"I hope Mom kept him, but don't know for sure." He rolled down the car window a bit to breathe in some fresh air.

"Well, I can tell you this, she didn't bring him with her. There was no way she could. I have a cat named Daisy and I inherited Dave's dog, Pax, but he was killed recently by some MSS thugs who barged in my house and tried to attack me."

Yìchén's eyes widened. "They went after you?"

"Yes. I'll explain some other time. Let's talk about something more pleasant."

"What type of dog was Pax?"

"Chesapeake Bay Retriever."

"I'm not familiar with that breed."

Jenny kept her eyes on the road while talking. "Dave said you can train a golden retriever, distract a Labrador, but you negotiate with a Chesapeake." She smiled, remembering him. "They can be quite a handful. Pax loved to tease and torment Daisy."

He laughed, then changed the subject. "I have a question."

"Go ahead. Ask me anything."

"Did you get fired for telling me your true name?"

"I handed in my resignation, so I wouldn't be. But my boss got approval from the director to keep me on because of the circumstances. He let me take a leave of absence."

"That makes me feel so much better." He closed the car window.

"It's a strange business you and I were in. Late nights, long hours, sometimes terrible working conditions, often working for assholes, great responsibility but little recognition. Why did *you* do it?"

"I loved my country. I still do."

"Even after what the MSS did to Dad?"

"There are assholes everywhere. Dad wasn't one of them."

"He would be so proud to hear you say that."

They were on Fauntleroy Way now, not far from where she lived. Jenny was silent as she concentrated on maneuvering the side streets.

Within minutes she pulled her SUV into her garage. She and Yìchén got out of the car and entered the house through the kitchen door from the garage.

Yìchén's eyes lit up when he saw Mei. He ran to her, throwing his arms around her, kissing her and hugging her tight. They stood there embracing each other for what seemed to Jenny like an eternity.

Jenny cautiously moved toward them.

When she was a few feet away, she heard Yìchén say, "Mother, did Jenny tell you our secret?"

Jenny shook her head.

"What secret?" Mei said.

He turned toward Jenny. Mei's eyes followed, curious.

"Mother, this is my twin. Her adopted name is Jen Hae Chu. They call her Jenny." He looked at Jenny, who had a pleading look on her face. Pleading that her mother would accept her. "Jenny, this is our mom."

The two women eyed each other for a few minutes. Not saying a word. Then Mei broke into tears while smiling and held out her arms.

Jenny's heart felt like a balloon about to burst. She had secretly longed for this moment since as far back as she found out about her biological mother and now that it was finally here, she wanted it to last a lifetime. She wished Dave was still alive so she could share this with him, but he was still in her heart and his baby was in her womb.

Her longing was over. Her family was now almost complete with the exception being the baby she carried. She latched onto Mei and held tight. Yìchén put his arms around both of them and didn't let go for about five or ten minutes. Their moods changed from intermittent laughter to tears streaming down their faces.

"Jenny has another surprise for you," Yìchén said.

"What is it?" Mei asked.

"You tell her, Jenny," Yìchén said.

"You're going to be a grandmother," Jenny said, smiling.

"What?" Mei said.

"Yes. My baby is due in February."

"Who's the father? Where is he?" Mei said.

"Dead, I'm afraid," Jenny said. "He was a decent man. Funny and kind. You would've liked him."

"It's my fault," Yìchén said. "We have a lot to talk about, Mother."

"You can talk later," Jenny said. "Don't spoil this moment. I want to remember it forever."

AUTHOR'S NOTE

It is interesting to note that in 2023, during a segment on the television show *60 Minutes*, the Five Eyes—which includes top intelligence representatives from the U.S., United Kingdom, Australia, Canada and New Zealand—agreed, "There is no country that presents a greater threat than China, alarmed by the greatest espionage threat democracy has ever faced."

When asked if all countries spy," Mike Burgess of Australia replied, "The behavior we're talking about goes beyond traditional espionage, the scale of this theft is unprecedented in human history."

FBI director Christopher Wray, said: "We have seen efforts by the Chinese government, directly or indirectly, trying to steal intellectual property, trade secrets, and personal data, all across the country—everything from Fortune 100 companies to smaller startups. We're talking about agriculture, biotech, health care, robotics, aviation, and academic research. We probably have about 2,000 active investigations that are just related to the Chinese government's effort to steal information. ... We welcome business from China, visitors from China and academic exchanges. What we don't welcome is cheating, theft and repression."

That said, *The Spy from Beijing* is a work of fiction and a product of the author's imagination and should be read as such. The character names, except where indicated, in the Acknowledgements or Author's

Note, as well as the incidents portrayed in the story are fictitious. Any resemblance to people, living or dead, as well as incidents or contacts with any Chinese, is coincidental.

The company LineageFinder does not exist. It's headquarters' address in the novel, northeast Bellevue on 110th Avenue, is the address of the King County Public Library in Bellevue which also houses the collection of the Eastside Genealogical Society. Ancestry.com once had an office in Bellevue, however, I chose the above location in Bellevue, rather than near Lehi, Utah, where Ancestry's headquarters are located, because it was easier for me to do research there.

The Charles and Elizabeth Liu case is fictional; however, Su Bin is a real person. He was a Chinese national who also went by the names Stephen Su and Stephen Subin. He was arrested in the summer of 2014 in the Richmond suburb of Vancouver and was extradited to the U.S. He pleaded guilty to conspiring to hack into the computer networks of Boeing and other major defense contractors to steal secrets about the C-17 military transport plane and F-22 and F-35 fighter jets. He sold them to aviation firms sponsored by the Chinese government. He was charged with one count of conspiring to gain unauthorized access to a protected computer and to violate the Arms Export Control Act. For that he got four years in prison and a $10,000 fine.

ACKNOWLEDGEMENTS

I'm thankful to the CIA for the employment opportunity they gave me back in the early 70s when I was just nineteen years old. It fed my love for adventure and I had the pleasure of meeting many intelligent unsung heroes who are keeping the world safe for democracy for which I'll always be grateful. Special thanks to the CIA's Publication Review Board for making sure my manuscript did not reveal any sources, methods or classified material.

Ginormous thanks to my friend, David Kamakaris, a geologist-turned-eighth-grade-science-teacher, who gave me permission to use his true name for one of my characters and for his humor, patience, love, input, understanding, and praise. He helped motivate me to write faster and do the best job I possibly could. It has been a fun ride with you, Dave, and, you might not agree, but the pleasure was mostly mine.

Huge thanks to my editor and writing coach, A.E. Schwartz, who gave me invaluable lessons about the writing craft. I remain blown away by her professionalism and incredible editing skill. Many thanks to Eric Miller, of 3ibooks, who never let me forget I had a great book and encouraged me to persevere. He also introduced me to an author friend of his, Pat Nohrden, an English teacher and China expert.

My critique groups read several chapters and were also very helpful. Many thanks to PNWA members—Rachelle Braido in Portland, Oregon, and Joan Cabreza in Seattle, Washington. Also, thanks to the

Geriatric Writers Group in Spokane, Washington: Diana Wickes, Kay Dixon, Carol Allen and Hyunki Ahn.

I am also indebted to Jerri Williams and Andy Caster; two retired FBI agents who helped catch what could have been errors early on in my plot. Jerri has authored several police procedural novels and hosts a podcast called "the FBI Retired Case File Review with Jerri Williams."

Many thanks to Joe Navarro, a Cuban-born, retired FBI Special Agent and internationally acclaimed expert on body language and non-verbal communication, who also gave me permission to use his true name and excerpts from his wonderful book, *Dangerous Personalities*. The book is a bonanza for any author who has a villain in their novel.

I am also indebted to Captain Jennifer Schneider at the King County Jail as well as Noah, a Civilian Public Information Officer at the Jail.

Big thanks to those involved in the virtual Thriller Fest XVI that I was able to attend in 2021, including Executive Director Kimberly Howe, Jeff Ayers, Samuel Octavius, Lisa Unger, Jenny Milchman and others. I especially liked the following interviews: Gayle Lynds & Katherine Neville, Robert Dugoni & Joel Rosenberg, J.T. Ellison & Robin Burcell, Jason Kaufman & Ben Sevier, Dean Koontz, J.D. Barker & Meryl Moss, and J.A. Jance & Catherine Coulter.

I read a variety of thrillers, including authors such as John Le Carre, Daniel Silva, David McCloskey, Gillian Flynn, Paula Hawkins, Stieg Larsson, Jason Matthews, Scott Spacek, Paul Vidich, Len Deighton, Harlan Coben, James Patterson, Robert Dugoni, Steven James, Gayle Lynds, Lee Child, David Ignatius, Frederick Forsyth, Robert Ludlum, Brad Thor, and Jenny Milchman. Although I liked many of these authors' books, I was particularly drawn to Daniel Silva's spy thrillers because of his excellent dialogue and ended up reading fifteen of his during the pandemic.

I would also like to thank a Facebook group called Spybrarians (Shane Whaley, Karl Gunner Oen, Martin Paul, Joe Modzelewski,

Jason King, Tim Shipman, and others) who introduced me to several British spy thrillers I might not have read otherwise, which made me wiser but poorer. Another Facebook group I'd like to thank is The Real Book Spy Thriller Book Club, especially Steven Hendricks and his Hendricks Book Reviews in Tampa, Florida, which helped me discover new books. Steven is legendary for accompanying his reviews with "books and booze" pairings.

I gleaned information from a variety of other sources and highly recommend reading these extraordinary books: *The Hundred-Year Marathon—China's Secret Strategy to Replace America as the Global Superpower* by Michael Pillsbury, *Spies and Lies – How China's Greatest Covert Operations Fooled the World* by Alex Joske, *Sapiens* and *21 Lessons for the 21st Century* by Yuval Noah Harari, *Codebreaker* by Walter Isaacson, *The Pretender—My Life Undercover for the FBI* by Marc Ruskin, *The Unexpected Spy* by Tracy Walder, *Breaking Cover* by Michele Rigby Assad, *Spy The Lie* by Philip Houston, Michael Floyd and Susan Carnicero, *Truth to Power* by Al Gore, *A Promised Land* by Barack Obama, *The Fourth Man* by Robert Baer, *Exercise of Power* by Robert M. Gates, *The Room Where it Happened* by John Bolton, *Deep Under Cover* by Jack Barsky (written with Cindy Coloma), *Fair Play – The Moral Dilemmas of Spying* by James M. Olson, and *Into the Kill Zone—A Cop's Eye View of Deadly Force* by David Klinger.

Other groups I would like to thank which have aided my quest to become a better writer include: the Pacific Northwest Writers Association, Writer's Digest, the Author Learning Center, the Inland Northwest Writer's Guild and Spokane Authors.

Big thanks to Tara Mayberry at Teaberry Creative for her artistic eye and hard work on the book: the cover, the interior and the e-book format. It has always been a pleasure to work with you. Also, thanks to my publishing coach, Stacey Smekofske, for her advice and guidance in publishing and marketing. You rock!

It takes a village to produce a book and part of my tribe who has supported me and to whom I'm eternally grateful include Dave Reed, Betty Deuber, Bobbi Ajax (now deceased), Brian & Jessica Kopczynski, Kyra & Brad Hughes, Lee & Jamie Kroeger, Jim Reed, Mike & Libby Moore, Duane Wessels, Karen O'Shaughnessy, Don Kopczynski, Karen Stubbs, Larry & Darce Kopczynski, Maureen Gaeke, Connie Esser, Allan & Lisa Kopczynski, Marilyn & Dan Kuhlmann, Judy Reed, Peggy Dorf, Miriam Hansen, Shelley Powell, Theresa Wessels, Maxine Kopczynski, Sue Jostrom and Chris Kopczynski. Love you all!

My biggest supporter, who made an immense difference in my life and my heart, is Bill Holbrook. His generosity, kindness, humor, infectious enthusiasm for my small achievements, as well as constant love and support were unparalleled. Love you to the sun, stars, moon and back, Bill. Thank you so much for all you've done for me.

Dear Reader

I hope you enjoyed my book. The best way you can thank me is to write an honest review of this book.

Also, check out my website: www.JoanMKop.com and sign up for my newsletter.

ABOUT THE AUTHOR

JOAN M KOP grew up in the Pacific Northwest. After attending school to become a legal secretary, she was recruited by the Central Intelligence Agency. She later graduated from Gonzaga University and is the author of *Spies, Lies & Psychosis*, and *The Freedom Chaser*, a 2020 finalist in the PNWA Pearl Book Award.